The Promise

DENISE
ROBERTSON

The Promise

Published in the United Kingdom in 2008 by Little Books Ltd,
48 Catherine Place, London SW1E 6HL

10 9 8 7 6 5 4 3 2

Text copyright © 2008 by Denise Robertson
Design and layout copyright © by Little Books Ltd

A CIP catalogue record for this book is available from the British Library.

ISBN 978 1 904435 97 6

Printed in the UK by CPI Bookmarque, Croydon, CR0 4TD

Chapter One

BEN KNEW BEFORE HE OPENED his eyes that it was going to be a difficult day. Beside him, Diana was sleeping soundly. He could smell her, touch her, feel the warmth of her body. For a moment he contemplated reaching out, gathering her to him... but only for a moment. Last night he had done just that and the memory of her tone, indulgent as to a naughty child, still had the power to sting. 'Not tonight, darling. Do you mind? I'm soooo sleepy...' He had turned obediently away then. Now he closed his eyes and contemplated. He was losing his wife, and soon, in all probability, he would lose his job – and not only his job, but control of Webcon, the mighty company his father and his grandfather before him had built. For a few seconds, he wallowed in misery. Then he told himself not to be a bloody fool, to get up and get going. He was about to throw back the covers when the phone's trill cut through the silence.

'I'm sorry to ring so early, Mr Ben, but your grandmother hasn't had a good night. She's agitated about something and says she must see you.'

Beside him Diana stirred, raising her head from the pillow, eyes still closed. 'Who in God's name is ringing in the middle of the night?'

'It's quarter to eight... It's Gran. Well, it's Sue. Go back to sleep.' But she was already curling down again, all interest gone. He shifted the phone to his other ear. 'Is she alright, Susan?' The nurse's tone was reassuring. 'Yes, no emergency... but she's fretting. She wants to see you. I suggested your sister, but she said no one else but you would do. I'm sorry to call so early but I thought if I caught you before you left for work, you might...'

'Okay.' He was already swinging his legs out of bed. 'I'll call in on my way to the office.'

In the shower he thought over what the nurse had said: 'She's fretting.' That wasn't like Gran. Imperturbable even at 87. He had been there two days ago – no, three – but now that he came to think about it, she had been more quiet than usual. He dressed swiftly, planted a kiss on his wife's unresponsive cheek, took the stairs two at a time, let Max, his black Labrador, into the garden, and bolted toast and coffee in a silent kitchen. Mrs Corey, the housekeeper, was having a rare day off – otherwise bacon, eggs and toast would have been pressed upon him. Today he must fend for himself. When he let the dog in, it pressed its great head against his knee, eyes imploring a walk. 'Not just now, old chap. Your mum will take you out later.' He gave the dog a treat from the jar in the kitchen and hurried out to the waiting car.

'Nice morning, Mr Ben.' English, his driver, was reaching for his briefcase, holding the door wide. 'Yes, it looks like a good day. I need to call at my grandmother's place as we go. I won't be long.'

A moment later the Bentley was purring through Bloomsbury, heading north past Regent's Park towards The Bishops Avenue beyond. His grandmother's house was set back from the road on a rise. His grandfather had bought it forty years ago from a film mogul and the house had an air of Hollywood about it, except that the producer had worked out of Pinewood and the construction was solidly British. Not for the first time Ben wondered why his grandfather, the owner of a construction company, had bought instead of building... but then the electronic gates were swinging open. He had arrived.

Maya, his grandmother's Filipina housekeeper, was waiting in the hall. 'Mr Ben, nice to see you. I bring you breakfast.' He bent down and planted a kiss on her smooth black head, greying only at the temples. Maya had been with his grandmother almost as long as he could remember.

'Just coffee, please, and one of your biscuits.' He turned on the half-landing to see her still smiling up at him before she headed for the kitchen.

In the bedroom his grandmother sat, propped on pillows in a wing chair. Her white hair was immaculate, the hands that rested on the arms of the chair were pink-tipped, and when he bent to kiss her cheek it smelled of roses. He smiled inwardly. If she was fretting it wasn't causing her to neglect her appearance – except that it was Susan, her nurse, who took care of that now. Susan had smiled gratefully as he entered and now was fussing with the pillows. To Ben's surprise his grandmother put a finger to her lips to signal silence. 'Thank you, Sue. Go and have some coffee. We'll be fine.' It was not a request, it was a command and Susan obeyed.

'Now,' he said when the nurse had gone, as he settled on a pouffe at her side. 'Tell me what's up.' She patted his hand and he saw that two spots of colour had come up on her cheeks, bright pink against the papery-white of her skin. 'Is Maya bringing you coffee?' He nodded. 'We'll leave it then, until she's been and gone. How's Diana? And your sister, Adele? I never see that girl. Is she as mad as ever?'

'Madder! But very happy with her hens and her geese and her kids... They are two terrific children. And Harry is writing...' They were both smiling now. Adele's husband had been, in turn, a musician, a sculptor, a farmer and now a would-be novelist. Adele farmed after a fashion and her Webcon dividends kept them in acceptable style. He did not mention Diana. There was nothing much to say.

The coffee arrived with a plate piled high with Maya's homemade biscuits. While she fussed over the tray and poured two cups, he moved to the window and looked out. There were other rooftops visible, each surrounded in their own trees and somehow remote. He tried to calculate how many millionaires lived within a square half-mile. Too many to count. He turned back as the clatter of cups ceased and called his thanks as Maya glided to the door. 'It's too early in the morning for biscuits, darling. Doesn't Diana make sure you have a good breakfast?' She didn't wait for an answer and he was glad. No need to discuss his marriage, not at this stage. 'Well,' he said, as he resumed his seat and topped up his cup. 'What's the mystery?' If he was expecting an immediate denial of any mystery he was disappointed. 'It's difficult,' his grandmother began. She was stirring her coffee and he felt a sudden irritation. There would be a thousand and one problems waiting at the office and more time for his enemies to plot in his absence. Why the urgent summons? Surely not something trivial like altering the garden or a need to redecorate the living room? These were the tasks she usually gave him, so why the umming and ahing? Love for the old lady made him hold his tongue, however, and eventually she began to speak.

'I'm not well, darling. You know that. It's only a matter of time now. No, don't shake your head. I've had a good run for my money, longer than I expected. Anyway, I don't get out now. I'm weary of four walls, even these four walls. Posh, aren't they?' She smiled suddenly and he saw a trace of the woman she had once been. 'Not bad for a girl from the Elephant and Castle. Still, I'm going to tell you something shameful. Something I did... we did, your grandfather and I... a long time ago. I don't want to die with it on my conscience, Ben. Without making amends of some sort. But I need you to help me. I can't do things for myself; I'm trapped here. I'm hoping you'll do them for me.'

'Do what?' Ben felt unease grow within him. What

could she have done that troubled her so? She was inca-pable of harming a fly. Thoughts of dementia and delusion fluttered through his mind, but her voice, when she spoke again was resolute. 'You've grown up with the business. Webster Construction, Webcon as it is now. Huge, mighty, profitable. It wasn't always like that. When I married your grandfather he was a bookkeeper. Oh, he was partner in the firm but in reality he was a bookkeeper. Brewis and Webster it was called. Jack Brewis was a joiner, aptly named because he was a jack-of-all-trades. But he was a good man. He did the work and your grandfather ran the office and looked after the money. And then the war came. Jack Brewis was in the Terriers... the Territorial Army... and they called him up in 1939. They were bringing in conscription but they needed people who were already trained to lick the con-scripts into shape. A lot of the TA were soldiers from the First World War but Jack Brewis was just a boy with a love of the military. I dare say he could've got out of it. He was 29 and had three children, but he still wanted to go. They said he'd get early release when the tide turned, but it was still a wrench for his wife. Mollie she was called. She was twenty-four. I was nineteen. Your grand-father and I had just been married. He'd had polio as a child so he walked with a limp. You remember?' Ben nodded, remembering his grandfather: small, limping but still dominant. 'The business should have folded when Jack went off but your grandfather wouldn't let it... and, of course, he thought Jack would be back before long. He took old men on, retired joiners or school-leavers he could train, and they did odd jobs. The raids began then, in 1940. Mollie took fright for the children and Jack wanted them out of London.' She paused for a moment to sip her coffee. Her eyes were hooded and he could see that she was remembering. When she began again she did not look at him but stared straight ahead.

'Some people fled London as soon as war was announced. A million and a half, they said. Mollie didn't go then. I think she was half-expecting Jack to walk back in and say it had all been a false alarm. And it felt like that for a while. A Phoney War, they called it. A lot of parents rued sending their children away and brought them back, but the raids began in the summer. Jack was overseas... Mollie didn't know where but she knew he wasn't in England any longer, so she decided to go. The first evacuations had already been organised. They lined up the children in the schoolyards and marched them onto coaches or trains, just tore them away from some mothers. Everyone was crying. What the kiddies made of it, I can't imagine. They were supposed to have a suitcase with their requirements in. That was a farce because most of them just had a paper bag with a change of underwear, if they were lucky. And they tied tags on them, poor kids, as though they were parcels. By the time Mollie went it was different. A lot of mothers went with their children and to someone they knew, family in the country or away from the cities. Mollie didn't have anyone, so they helped her get to Yorkshire. She told me a Billeting Officer took them from door to door, begging people to take them in.

And some people did it for money, of course. She went off in August. August 1940. The raids were heavy. They never stopped, day and night, up until November. Then they stopped bombing London and started on Coventry. I think that was what brought Mollie back that day. She thought it might be over.'

The clock on the bedside table showed 9.25am. Ben thought of his office, the e-mails, the calls needing answers, his in-tray. If they were only on 1940, how long would this take? 'She came back?' he said, to urge her on. She ignored his question. 'A telegram came. Your grandfather was round at Mollie's collecting her post when the boy came. He knew what it was. Jack Brewis had been killed in France, somewhere near the Belgian border, I think it was. I don't really remember. He had to get on a train and go and tell her. He said the colour drained from her face but she never said a word. And the three children hanging round her knees.'

Ben cleared his throat. 'How old were the children?' The old lady pursed her lips in thought. 'Margaret was the eldest. She was eight or nine, I think. Mollie and Jack had had a shotgun wedding when they were both hardly more than children. Then there was Dorothy. She was the bonny one. She was five, I think, or perhaps it was four, and Billy was the baby. Just a toddler, one or two.'

'What happened to them?' His coffee had grown cold and he pushed away the cup.

'That's the whole point,' she said. 'That's what I need you to find out.' He would have spoken but she stilled him with an upraised hand. 'They were there in

Yorkshire and your grandfather sent money when he could. Mollie was due to half of what the business made... but she didn't seem interested in the business or anything else for that matter.'

'Didn't she have family?' Ben was wondering about a funeral, but if Jack had died on active service there couldn't have been one.

'Brothers or sisters?' His grandmother was shaking her head. 'No. It might have turned out differently if there had been someone but there was no one. And then she came to London. I don't know why, but the Germans had just switched the bombing to Coventry and I think she was lonely in Yorkshire. She wanted to see what it would be like if she brought the children home. She left them where they were billeted and she came here. It must have been spur of the moment because it was late afternoon when she got here. I remember it quite clearly because I'd just found out I was expecting your father. It was a lovely day for November and I was excited. I was only 20 and I was going to have a baby. She arrived and I made her some tea and then she said she was going to their old house. We lived in the East End then. Well, the yard was there. We had a flat a street away and they lived near the docks. She was going to talk to Grandpa when he was finished at the yard, but she wanted to go home for an hour or so. And that was when it happened. When she made me promise.' She fell silent and Ben leaned towards her. 'Promise what?' She looked at him and her face was anguished. 'She said: "Promise you will take care of my kids, Gwen, if the worst comes to the worst. Promise me that." And then she gathered up her things and went. She'd been gone about an hour when I heard the German planes. 300 of them coming over in waves. They were after the docks, I think. 400 people were killed in that raid and Mollie was one of them.'

For a moment neither of them spoke and the sound of the ticking clock seemed to grow louder in the silent room. 'So the children were orphaned,' Ben said at last. His grandmother nodded. 'Yes. They were orphans.' Ben couldn't resist another question. 'Did you promise to look after them?'

Her pale blue eyes filled with tears. 'I said "You leave them to me, Mollie." And we both laughed because it didn't seem possible that anything could happen to her. I let her down, Ben. Worse than that, we robbed her.' Around them the room seemed shadowed suddenly, as though the sun had gone in. Ben shifted in his seat. 'What do you mean?' Anxiety was overcoming him. Was she thinking straight? His grandparents had had little or nothing. Where was the opportunity to rob?

'Jack owned half the business, Ben. By rights that came to Mollie and after her, the children.'

'And they didn't get it?' His grandmother shook her head. 'We went up together to tell them their mother had died. But your grandfather saw to everything. He never mentioned any inheritance. He told the authorities there was no family and they accepted it. They took the children into care and when they suggested adoption he agreed. We couldn't have taken them, and the business wasn't worth much. That's how Grandpa put it to me.

"They'll be better off, Gwen." That's how he put it. "They'll get good homes, they'll want for nothing." I thought of my own baby coming and how we would manage if we had to sell the business to give them their share. So I said nothing. I did nothing. And then the business took off. There was war damage and after the war, when the men came home, there was house building. London had lost thousands of houses and there were men coming home clamouring for a roof over their heads. Your Grandpa was clever. More than that, he was a wheeler and dealer. He got contracts, he made the business grow.'

'And now it's worth the best part of 500 million,' Ben thought, and then tried not to think of orphaned children cast off without their heritage. 'I want you to find them, Ben. I have money. Neither you nor Adele need it. I hope to put things right, darling. Before I die I have to make good that promise. I had an excuse back then. I have no excuse now. I can't sleep for thinking of it. Find them for me, Ben. Because if you don't I can't rest.'

Chapter Two

A S BEN WAS DRIVEN AWAY from The Bishops Avenue, thoughts were racing around in his head. What his grandmother wanted was resolution but what did resolution mean? Were the Brewis children entitled to half the present business? Or half its worth at the time of their parents' death? No, that was shabby. If he found them he must be fair. But how would he find them? He did rapid mental sums as the car passed Lord's and moved towards the city centre. Margaret had been eight or nine in 1940. That would make her 75 or 76 now. She might be dead. They might all be dead, might not have survived the war. There had been bombing in rural areas too. The ignoble thought that their deaths would solve his problem came and went. Some of the three would have survived. Would be parents and grandparents now, perhaps with ravening descendants who would demand their pound of flesh. He would have to get legal advice. What a mess! If only his father were still alive, but Simon Webster had been dead for twenty years, perished with his wife in a car crash as they came back from Ascot. Memories of his mother's Ascot finery, torn and bloodied as she was ferried to hospital, came and had to be firmly subdued. He had to think of the living now, or the almost living. 'I don't think she has too long to go,' Sue had said as she saw him to the door. 'She may see Christmas. Perhaps not.' It was September now. Three months to unravel a near seventy-year-old riddle. It couldn't be done.

He had been 14 when his parents died. Mike Astor, his father's chief lieutenant and his godfather, and Edgar Webster, his father's cousin and a board member, had taken over. But Mike had retired after eleven years and Edgar had died some time previously from the cigars he had constantly smoked. Ben knew he had been far too young to head a big corporation after Mike's retirement, but he had been elected nevertheless. Keep it a family company, everyone had said, even Adele. Webcon had grown in the intervening years, but the present board had none of the old allegiances and vultures were circling. The company was a good prospect for a bigger firm, which would swallow up its lucrative contracts and expertise, but there would be no room for a chairman with no other qualification than a good degree and a family name. He had worked for Webcon since he had come down from Cambridge about thirteen years ago and had been chairman for nine of these, but that would count for nothing. They would want him out.

He ordered the car to come back at 1pm and went in through the doors of the Farringdon Road building that now housed Webcon in a splendour of glass and chrome. His own office had conventional walls and a solid oak door. The other offices were open-plan. He could see Peter Hammond at his desk. He was tilted back in his chair, talking on his mobile phone. When he had come to the company nine years ago Ben had been delighted to get him. Hammond had asked for a free hand and Ben had given it gladly. Now he wondered if the move had been a mistake. Hammond treated him with a deference which, Ben felt, really masked contempt. And he had brought in Neil Pyke as Chief Accountant. Pyke was someone Ben had never warmed to. Neither had Adele. 'Sly as a box of monkeys,' she had said when first she met him. Ben could probably count on James Purnell and Nigel Gatsby, the other executive directors. And Diana's brother, Neville, if he ever made a board meeting. Which was why he was meeting Neville Carteret for lunch today. It wasn't a meeting he anticipated with pleasure – but with predators circling, it would pay to martial his forces.

He sat down at his desk and pressed a button for his PA. Madge should really have retired by now, but she was devoted to the firm she had served from her first day at work. She had been a typist under his grandfather's regime and then secretary to his father. Now she was his personal assistant – and much, much more. She had sat him on her desk when he was in knee socks and kept Chinese Figs in a drawer when he developed a passion for the sickly sweet confections. Now he trusted her with his life and all his secrets.

'I need a private detective,' he said bluntly when she

appeared. Her eyes flared wide for a second and then she recovered her composure. 'Business or private?'

Ben suppressed a grin. Madge didn't care for Diana; that much had been plain for some time. She was hoping he was going to check up on his wife. 'Neither,' he said. 'Well, both. I need to find someone... some people... vaguely connected with the firm sixty-odd years ago. Only vaguely connected with the firm.' It wouldn't do to tell anyone too much. Not yet. Madge thought for a moment. 'You have to be careful. Some firms run you up a big bill and then say there's nothing to be found. I do know someone. Ex-CID. I don't know what he's like on tracing but he's honest.' He looked up at her, seeing that her cheeks had grown quite pink. 'Madge? Do I detect a liaison?'

'None of your business, Mr Ben. Now, do I ring him or not?'

They agreed a meeting for 3.30pm. 'I should be back from L'Etoile by then. See if you can get him here.'

By the time he had signed his letters, opened his post and checked his e-mails, it was time to leave for his lunch meeting. He was almost ready when Peter Hammond knocked and came in. 'Headey's are about to bid for us. I just heard from a contact. One new share for two of our ordinary shares. They're eight per cent up on their quoted price. They'll need to issue 19 million if they succeed.'

'Why are they so keen?' Hammond shrugged. 'They're our chief competitor for most contracts. Combining the two companies would be lucrative, given the appropriate streamlining and rationalisation.' Euphemisms for closure and redundancy, Ben thought, and always in the taken-over company, never the devourer. 'We'll fight it, of course,' Ben said, moving round his desk. There was a pause before Hammond replied. 'Of course it'll have to be a board decision, but I expect they'll be hostile.'

Ben was getting ready to leave but Hammond lingered. 'Look,' he said at last, but didn't continue. Ben pondered the pause. Hammond was weighing his words. Or about to tell an outright lie. If Headey's kept his place open, gave him a seat on their board... Hammond had roughly one per cent of Webcon shares. If there was a takeover he could make a killing. 'Look,' Hammond said again. 'You and I have never really gelled... No, don't deny it. I thought you were here only by virtue of birth. Well, I was wrong. Now that I know you better, I respect you and your place here. If it comes to a fight you can count on me.' Ben tried not to display his astonishment, much less the guilt he felt at his doubts. 'Thank you,' he said. 'That's good to know.'

As he settled into the soft bustle of L'Etoile, Ben felt himself relax. Elena had given him a secluded table, as she always did. She looked wonderful today, neat in grey, her every movement belying her age. She was well over 80 and ran her restaurant with élan. She asked how he was, presented him with his usual Kir Royal and left him to study the menu, even though they both knew it would be his usual choice: smoked salmon blinis followed by scallops with green beans and celeriac purée. He ordered a bottle of dry white and settled back to wait for Neville Carteret. He was younger than Diana and less imperious, but Ben did not find him easy company. Never mind. Neville was one of his few allies and must be cultivated. On an impulse he got out his phone and dialled Diana's number. All he got was the answer phone. He rang the house. 'She's out, Mr Ben.' The housekeeper's voice was apologetic. 'I don't know where she's gone but she said it was dinner for one, so I expect she'll be late back.'

'Of course,' Ben said, automatically. 'I knew she was out tonight, I hoped to catch her before she went.' And then Neville was coming towards the table and he rose to greet him.

Over lunch he outlined the situation. 'So you see why you must come to meetings, Neville. If I'm to fight off any bids I need your vote.'

'It's yours, dear boy. Goes without saying. Now what is my sister up to?'

'Goes without saying' was the best he was going to get, Ben thought, and gave himself up to gossip.

When he got back to the office, Madge was waiting.

'He can't see you until tomorrow. He'll be here at four o'clock. You're free now till home-time.' Ben felt disappointed that the detective wasn't available today. He needed to talk to someone, someone he could trust. On an impulse he telephoned his sister. 'I'm coming over, Adele. If that's okay with you and Harry?'

'Of course... It'll be lovely to see you, but what's up? You don't often honour me with your presence. We haven't gone bust, have we?' That brought a smile to his face. 'No, Adele. We haven't gone bust.' Time enough to worry her when he got there.

He sent English home and took the wheel of the Bentley himself. As he drove into Hampshire, he thought about Adele. If there was a takeover she would get a lump sum for her shares but her income as a major shareholder would cease. If they used the money sensibly it would see out their days and launch their children into careers, but what if they invested it in one of Harry's schemes? He put that worry out of his mind. Telling her about her grandmother's revelation would be worry enough.

'You're kidding,' Adele said when he did tell her. They were sitting out on the verandah that ran along the back of the farmhouse. The sun was low in the west but still giving warmth, and he had a glass of good red in his hand. He would have to make it the one though, now that he was driving himself.

'I wish I was, but it's all too true, apparently.' Adele was six years older than him. Could she know more than he did? 'Did Dad ever say anything? Or mum?' Adele shrugged.

'Would he have known? I expect it was all buried with the war, but it's a bit of a poser now. I mean, are they legally entitled?'

'I don't know, to be truthful. I suppose it would go to court if they wanted to make a fight of it, and then the lawyers would make a killing. They'd get something but not, I think, a half-share.'

'They're entitled to something though.' Adele uncrossed her jeaned legs and pushed off her boots, one foot after the other. 'We could give them a pay-off. They must be pensioners by now. We could make them rich in their old age.'

She clearly liked that idea and refilled her glass, offering the bottle to him but not arguing when he shook his head. In the distance he could hear a dog barking and children shouting and laughing. That was what he disliked about his own home when Diana wasn't there: the silence. He asked about his brother-in-law. 'Harry okay?'

'Happy as a pig in muck. He's halfway through a novel. He says this is it. He's at the library now, reading up on something. He'll be back before you go, I expect. If you stay to dinner you'll definitely see him.'

She was smiling and he felt a pang of envy. She was completely and totally happy with her lot and if the money went tomorrow she would still be happy. Now, though, she became thoughtful. 'Fancy Gran keeping it to herself all these years. Poor old girl. She had several miscarriages, you know. Mum told me. That's why Dad going was such a loss. And Mum too. They got on…. Which is more than can be said for most mothers and daughters-in-law.' Just then, Harry arrived home, to the obvious delight of his wife and children. As he watched the welcome, Ben felt another pang of envy, but it was short-lived. Harry was a good sort and Adele was lucky to have him. I'm glad they're happy, he thought, and put thoughts of his own marriage out of the way for the time being.

Over dinner they talked about the farm, writing as an occupation and the world in general, and for a little while Ben's troubles receded. When he got up to go, Adele put her arms around him. 'Bear up, my son. And come here more often. As for your problems with the firm, I hope it is bought out. I'd like to see you free of it.

I'd like to see you free of a lot of things.' They both knew she meant his marriage, so there was no need to respond.

It was midnight when he got back home. The house was in darkness but when he checked the garage he saw that Diana's car was there, its bonnet still slightly warm, which meant she had not been in long. He mounted the stairs in the dark and pushed open the bedroom door. At first he thought his bed was empty, but when he switched on the bedside lamp he saw that Diana was there, asleep, her hand curled in front of her face like a baby's. When he slipped in beside her and switched off the lamp, he lay on his back, staring down the dark. She was his wife. He needed to talk to her, to tell her his life was shit and he needed comfort. But it wouldn't do to wake her so he lay still. It was five or ten minutes before he realised that Diana was awake. She whispered his name but, for reasons he couldn't explain, he didn't reply. The next moment she slid carefully out of bed. He heard her fumble on the bedside table and knew she was reaching for her phone. There was enough moonlight for him to see her move across to the en-suite bathroom and carefully shut the door behind her, before light appeared in the crack beneath. She had gone in there to phone him. Whoever the current him was. And she had been feigning sleep so that he would not trouble her. He turned onto his side, his eyes welling with tears of shame, that he wanted someone who didn't want him.

Chapter Three

THE BUSINESS PAGES WERE FLATTERING. 'Further expansion by Webcon.' 'Webcon still prospering.' 'Webcon buoyant in spite of market tremors.' Ben always felt relief when he saw headlines like that, even though they could change overnight. The headline he dreaded was 'Writing on the wall for yet another family company.'

Not for the first time he contemplated an unpleasant truth: he had never envisaged being at the helm of Webcon, did not feel he was particularly suited to the role, and wasn't sure he wanted to be there for the rest of his life. And yet he felt responsible. He had seen what had happened to other family companies: the owner died and a son took over, and before long the economic writing was on the wall. If his father had lived, if he had had a chance to make his own way in the world, it might have been different. He might have been better equipped to deal with a crisis. But that kind of thinking was a waste of time. For better or worse he did occupy the hot seat and had better get on with it. He spent the rest of the day dealing with paperwork, sending out for a sandwich lunch and working as he ate. He had promised to play squash with a former colleague at five but he telephoned an apology and promised another game as soon as possible.

He was clearing his desk for the visit of the private detective when Hammond stuck his head in the door. 'Share prices up one and a quarter. That's fourteen pence since Friday. The market smells a deal.' Ben nodded. 'Looks like it. We'll just have to sit it out.' But when Hammond had gone he reviewed the situation. Webcon could fight off a bid if the shareholders stood firm. But the institutions would jump whichever way the profit beckoned. If the board turned the bid down, someone, anyone, could call an emergency shareholders' meeting and overturn it – but at least an initial refusal would give him time to persuade the major shareholders. It was vital that he got a 'no' vote at the board. He knew now that he could count on Hammond and Neville Carteret but the other directors were less certain. The executive directors had probably all been got at by Headey's and at least some of them would succumb to persuasion. It was a relief when Madge put a business card in front of him. 'James Sparrow, Private Investigator. Discretion guaranteed.' 'That's him. You can trust him,' she said. Ben wondered fleetingly how Madge could be sure about a private eye's discretion and then a tall, burly man in a checked sports jacket was ushered into the room. They shook hands and Ben struggled for a way to begin conversation. It was Sparrow who eased the tension. 'No dirty raincoat, I'm afraid. Amazing how many people expect us to look like Columbo.' Ben smiled and relaxed, motioning Sparrow towards a seat. 'Can I get you something? Coffee? Tea?' But Madge was already bringing in a tray. 'That's yours, Jim. Black no sugar.'

Ben noted the Christian name, uttered thanks for his own – white, no sugar – and settled back in his chair.

Sparrow listened carefully, sometimes making a note, as Ben recounted his grandmother's tale. 'And this was 1940?' he said at last. Ben nodded and Sparrow puffed out his lips. 'Umm...' He shook a wary head. 'Wartime records... not always reliable. Do you know for a fact the children were adopted?'

'No. That was the intention. My grandfather may have followed it up but if so there's no note of it and he never discussed it with my grandmother.'

'The children were nine, four, and two?' Ben shrugged to indicate uncertainty. The other man's lips pursed again. 'Two and four... easily adoptable. A nine-year-old less so. My guess is she'd stay in the system.'

Ben thought of his niece, Adele's oldest daughter, nine years old and sassy with it. Impossible to think of her in a 'system'.

'Cottage Homes,' Sparrow continued. 'Workhouses, really, but they went off that word in the Thirties. So it was Cottage Homes or something similar. They trained the boys for manual labour, the girls for domestic work.'

So the son of Jack Brewis might be a navvy somewhere while he, grandson of the other partner, had gone to Sedbergh and Cambridge and lived now in a fair degree of comfort. Ben felt uncomfortable until he realised that the son of toil might have less on his mind than he had. 'I'll see what I can do,' Sparrow said, as he got up to go. 'Don't expect miracles but I'll do my best.' As if by magic, Madge appeared in the doorway, ushering Sparrow out with a hand on his arm. Ben had never thought of Madge in connection with a man, but now that he did, he realised she was still an attractive woman. 'Good on her,' he thought and gathered up his briefcase and car keys. He was almost at the lift when he realised he should have telephoned his grandmother after Sparrow's visit.

She was anxious; news that something was being done would calm her. He shifted from one foot to the other, wondering whether to call on her in person or ring when he got home. In the end he retraced his steps to his office and sat down at his desk. But not before he had noticed, through the glass wall of Neil Pyke's office, that the other executive directors were congregated there. They had obviously waited until he had left to have a powwow. Something was going on and he was not part of it. He had never cared for Neil Pyke. The man was clever, good at his job, but arrogant and, to Ben's mind, too much of a dandy. Today, however, he found it hard to care. 'Gran?' Her voice, when she was handed the phone by an attentive Sue, was tremulous and he realised with a pang that she was, indeed, a very old lady. He told her about the detective's visit. 'You'll like Sparrow, Gran. He'll be in touch soon, I'm sure. If anyone can find them, I think he can.'

'Thank you, darling. I promised, you see. I promised

I'd make sure they were alright.' There was a pause and he was just about to speak, when she continued. 'You don't think they died, do you? We should have brought them back with us... I told Ben... I said...' Her voice trailed off and he stepped into the pause. 'You couldn't have brought them back. It was the Blitz, remember? It would have been dangerous to bring them back to London.' She had cheered up by the time the call finished and he promised to call in soon. He left his office once more, smiling to himself over the fact that the coterie in Pyke's office had melted away.

Diana was in the kitchen when he reached the house. 'In here, darling. You're early. That's lovely because I've cooked. I gave Mrs Corey the rest of the day off and I've slaved over a hot stove. Haah... burns.' She held out two small white hands, one of them with a scorch mark on the index finger. Impulsively he took that hand in his and lifted it to his lips. 'There, it's kissed better. Now what are we eating?'

It was coq au vin and he sniffed appreciatively when she lifted the lid off the casserole. Max was shut in the utility room and Ben let him out in response to frantic whimpering from behind the closed door. 'He can't stay here while I'm busy,' Diana said firmly. 'He can come with me,' Ben said, stooping to fondle Max's silky square head. 'I'll change and be down in two ticks. I'm looking forward to this evening.' He went upstairs, half of him looking forward to an evening alone with his wife, the other half wondering just what that wife was up to.

They ate well: smoked salmon with avocado, the

chicken with green beans and duchesse potatoes, and then the pièce de résistance, summer pudding, which she had been taught to make during the Cordon Bleu course which had completed her formal education. She often expressed a strong antipathy for everything culinary, so tonight was special, but when he asked why she just blew him a kiss across the table and said it was no more than he deserved. He tried to enjoy the food, which was good, and not dwell on the fact that the cooking session smacked strongly of a guilty conscience.

Afterwards, they carried coffee and Benedictine through to the morning room and settled in facing armchairs. 'What have you done today?' she demanded. She was 29 but she looked seventeen, a little heated and dishevelled from her efforts in the kitchen, her white cotton shirt open at the neck, a red satin mule swinging from one foot, the jean-clad legs curled beneath her as she sat.

'Work,' he said. 'And I talked with a private detective.' Just for a second she was disconcerted, and then she laughed. 'How lovely. A gumshoe. Who are you checking up on, darling? Not your wife, I hope.'

He shook his head. 'It's a long story.' She listened as he went over his grandmother's call, his visit to her and the interview with Sparrow.

'It's ridiculous.' She had recovered her composure now. 'You're not going to pander to an old lady's whim, I hope. I mean, it's priceless. It was a lifetime ago. Two lifetimes. And the business was just a handcart then, if what you said your father used to say is true. You told me he always said it took off with the post-war boom.'

'But it was there in 1940. It existed.'

'Yes, and so did he, this Brewis man. But he died. She died. End of story. They're not entitled to a penny – and that's if they're alive. They're probably dead. People didn't live long in those days.'

'Gran did.'

'But she's an exception. I've always said she is made of steel. Don't let that fragile look deceive you. Anyway, let's not talk about it. You'll probably not be able to find them and it will all just fade away. Let me tell you my news. I want to go to Prague.'

So that was the purpose of this evening; she was planning a trip.

'Prague? What's in Prague?'

'Architecture.' The ridiculousness of the idea that she was interested in architecture struck them simultaneously and for a moment the laughter was genuine.

'Well,' she said, ruefully, 'you have to say that, don't you. But Flicky is going... Something she wants to see there... and she can't go alone, and apparently the hotels and the food there are first-class. So she'll do the culture thing and I'll just laze and enjoy the fleshpots.'

He emptied his mouth of the liqueur before he replied. 'Sounds good.' Flicky was Felicity Vosburgh, her friend from school days. It was entirely understandable that they should want a few days together. So he smiled and listened and made a suggestion here and there, and then she was crossing to sit on his knee and twine her arms around his neck and put her mouth on his, and all he could think of was the waste of time of carrying her to bed. In the end they saved time by sinking to the floor together, wriggling free of confining clothes until they were close, skin to skin, mouth to mouth, riding together to fulfilment with only a watchful Labrador as witness.

Chapter Four

DURING THE NEXT FEW DAYS he tried to put the Brewis affair out of his mind; there was no shortage of other things on which to concentrate. Now he could almost see his grandmother failing. Her face still lit up at the sight of him and she was hungry for news of Sparrow and his quest, but at times she seemed scarcely able to lift her arms. Her hands, still be-ringed, rested in her lap, occasionally plucking at the cashmere blanket that covered her legs. But the colour in her cheeks was garish now, rather than natural, and he wondered if Sue had resorted to rouge to make her patient look healthier.

He sometimes prolonged his visits, half out of concern for the woman who had virtually taken his parents' place and half out of a reluctance to go home to Diana. When he and Diana were together she prattled endlessly about Prague. It was 'Flicky says we must see the Kinsky Palace' or 'Flicky says not to pack too much. There are divine shops there... Strange when you think it was behind the iron curtain.' He had suggested they take Flicky and her husband, Paul, to dinner but Diana was firm. 'Definitely not, darling. He's such a bore and we'll only talk Prague all the while and bore you to death.'

Two days later, he picked up the phone and dialled Paul Vosburgh. He used a pretext – a query about Old Boy's Day at the school they had both attended – and then he broached the real subject of his call. 'Do you think those two will be safe in Prague? Perhaps one of us should ride shotgun?' He said it as lightly as he could, even injecting a chuckle, but the silence at the other end of the line was almost palpable.

''Fraid I don't know too much about it,' Paul said at last. 'You know my wife, a law unto herself.' And then, in a definite change of conversation, 'What do you think of Northern Rock? That's set some timbers shivering in the City.'

They discussed the rocky state of international banking long enough for it to seem a legitimate subject and then, with almost audible relief on both sides, made their goodbyes. 'He knows,' Ben thought. 'He knows his wife is providing an alibi, and he doesn't like it but he's going along with it.' Because it was the easiest thing to do, that was the truth of it. Which was why he, the cuckolded husband, was not seizing his wife by the throat and wringing the truth from her. It was easier to pretend it wasn't happening.

It was the same when he was forced to confront the

situation at the office. Somehow, since the emergence of the story of his grandfather's cheating, he had not had the same intense feelings of loyalty towards the family firm. His grandfather had cheated three orphans out of their rightful inheritance. Never mind that it had been a tin-pot little business which could easily have gone under before the war's end. The principle was the same. The Brewis children were entitled to something. When – and if –they were found, there would have to be some form of compensation. His grandmother had said they were around nine, four and two in 1940. So they were old now, providing they had survived. He started toying with sums in his head. Webcon was worth a projected £500 million, of which he and his family held shares amounting to 7.5 per cent. Peter Hammond had one per cent, Diana owned one per cent and the institutions owned the rest. If it was done legally the banks and big corporations would not part with a penny. It would be up to the Webster family to pay compensation. Adele would not jib, his grandmother was hell-bent on doing the right thing. So was he. Which left Diana, or rather Neville, her brother, who handled her financial affairs. He half-smiled to himself, remembering Diana's firm response to the news. 'Not a penny,' she had said. The one per cent she owned was the amount necessary to balance their tax affairs. Well, if push came to shove, he and his grandmother could arrange it between them.

He put aside thoughts of what would be fair reparation and gave in to Madge's repeated entreaties that he keep his eyes open. 'They're up to something, Ben.

Whispering, shuffling papers if I walk past. Putting me off if I ask for figures. I asked Neil Pyke three times for the cost analysis of the Liverpool job and you could feel the resentment. They're keeping you in the dark and I don't like it.'

Madge was always paranoid about treachery, but there was bound to be unease in the office. There had been rumours of a bid in the City for months now. Headey's, Webcon's Irish equivalent, or the German company, Hecht. Until a bid was put formally, there was little or nothing he could do except stay alert. The likelihood was that somebody within the organisation was briefing Headey's. He was contemplating the unwelcome prospect of having to defend his company from attack, within and without, when the phone rang. It was Sparrow. 'Put him through,' Ben said, wondering in the second it took for them to be linked whether he wanted to hear that contact had been made with the living or that details had emerged of children buried long ago.

'Okay,' Sparrow said. 'We've struck lucky. Nothing on the younger two. My guess is they were adopted, so that'll need some digging. But the older girl, Margaret, she didn't change her name. Well, not at first. She married in 1956. She's Riley now, Margaret Riley. Widowed. No kids as far as I can tell. She lives in County Durham. 37 Laburnum Terrace, Belgate. She's 76 now so she's cracking on. Do you want me to make an approach or shall I keep after the others?'

They agreed that Sparrow would make initial

contact. 'But tell her I'd like to meet her myself,' Ben added. 'Don't say anything about what happened in 1940. Just say my grandmother is in failing health and wants to contact old friends, that kind of thing. Actually...' He thought for a moment, caution overwhelming him. 'I wouldn't mention Webcon. She's unlikely to make a connection. Just say Gwen Webster wants to re-establish contact. We can fill in details later.'

But as he sat at his desk when the call was finished, he felt ashamed. Why be reluctant to tell the truth? What did it matter if Margaret Riley turned out to be militant and sued the pants off Webcon? As he left the office he saw Fitzsimmons, the Projects Manager, and Pyke in close conversation and chuckled to himself at the thought of what a claim against the company would do to prospects of a takeover. 'Serve the buggers right,' he thought and subsided into the back seat of the Bentley.

His grandmother's face lit up at news of the finding. 'County Durham? How on earth did she get there? Is she well? Does she know we've been searching for her? For all of them?' He did his best to answer her questions. 'But I don't really know anything at the moment and won't until I've talked to her.'

'She was the one I knew best. A bonny little thing she was. Very quiet. Freckles... yes... she had freckles right across the bridge of her nose. She was a daddy's girl... "My little Mags," he used to call her.'

'And now she is 76,' Ben thought, 'and God only

knows what might have happened to her in the time between.'

On the way home he thought about the evening ahead. It was not altogether a social occasion, although the host was an old friend of Diana's family. Hamish Cameron was a Scot and a laird, though you would never guess it from his Eton and Oxbridge accent. They had been at Cambridge together and Hamish's wife had been a bridesmaid at his wedding to Diana.

Now Webcon were building a marina on the West Coast, near to Fort William and the Cameron estate. The deal was worth £12 million and had been partially won through their old acquaintance. It was important that the job went through without a hitch, otherwise it would give his enemies on the board a weapon. So tonight was an opportunity to keep the client sweet as well as greet an old friend from university.

His dress shirt was laid out for him when he got home and Diana was on hand to fix his tie and thread links into his cuffs. 'I like doing the geisha bit,' she said when he was ready to her satisfaction. 'Now pour me a G & T. We've got time before we go.' As they drank he watched her. She was beautiful but, more than that, she was attractive. He had never quite believed his luck in getting her to marry him. In fact, she had had to do the actual proposing because he had lost his nerve at the last moment.

He had kept on the car and they went out onto the steps together as English sprang to open the door. He was beaming at Diana, admiration in his gaze. She did look fetching in a cream brocade skirt and plain black top. 'We look the perfect couple,' he thought, and then, as the car purred towards Eaton Square, he pondered the fact that he had spent the last few years of their marriage waiting for her to leave him.

In spite of everything, he enjoyed the evening. Conversation sparkled over dinner and afterwards he and Hamish carried brandy through to the study while the women went upstairs to gloat over some new purchase.

'I'm shooting next week,' Hamish said, as they settled either side of the fireplace. It was monumental, a true focal point, but like most London grates it contained nothing more warming than a piece of artwork constructed from wood washed by the sea and moulded into a weird but aesthetically pleasing shape. Hamish was looking at him. 'You look strained, old chap. Why not come up for the shoot next week? You'll know everyone... Well, almost. We could visit the site, see how it's going. And Penny tells me Diana will be in Prague, so there's nothing to keep you in London.' There was an odd note in his voice, sympathy perhaps, but also almost a note of disapproval.

'He knows,' Ben thought, and for a wild moment considered leaning forward to ask a question. 'Do you know who is fucking my wife at the moment, old chap? If so, I'd be awfully pleased to know.' To his horror, he heard himself chuckle at the thought, but Hamish took it as an acceptance. 'Good, I'm delighted. We'll expect you on Wednesday then. Penny will liaise with your

PA... Madge, isn't it? The redoubtable Madge...'

Panic subsided in Ben and he settled back in his chair. The matter had been settled for him. He had never been keen on shooting, but it would be good to get out of London, and on the way back from Scotland he would call in at Laburnum Terrace, Belgate, and confront at least one of his demons.

Chapter Five

THE NEXT FEW DAYS SAW a flurry of preparations at home and work. Diana talked less about Prague but went into agonies over what to pack and what to leave behind. Unless Mrs Corey was on duty, meals came out of the microwave or were non-existent. Once or twice he suggested eating out, but this was met with a pout. 'Not tonight, darling, if you don't mind. Too much to do... There's food galore in the freezer. I just have to sort out a few things I need to pack.' He felt like administering a sharp reminder that she was going off for six days with a female friend, so why were clothes so important? – but he never did. She was so much better with words than he was. It would only cause a pointless argument. Besides, what was the point? All the same, the fact that he was avoiding finding out what was really going on in his marriage bugged him. Why was he proving so inadequate? He answered his own question. Because if he pushed the point, she might leave him.

At the office, rumours of counter-bids still swirled. 'We can't hold off a meeting much longer,' Peter Hammond warned. 'It's not just the execs, the other directors are getting restive. They want to know what the proposed strategy is.'

'As soon as I get back,' Ben promised. 'Right now I need to mug up on the marina details so I will know what I'm talking about up there.' He studied plans and specifications until his eyes rebelled and drove him home. Increasingly he was looking forward to the Scottish trip, even though in the back of his mind he knew it was simply another escape from reality. When the time came for Diana to leave, he drove her to Heathrow and kissed her warmly at the entrance to the departure lounge. Paul was there, seeing off his wife. 'Be good,' he said indulgently, as the two women walked off, arm in arm. But he declined Ben's invitation to a drink. 'Got to go, old chap. The kids, you know. The dogs.' The Vosburghs had both nanny and housekeeper – no urgent need to get home. 'He doesn't want to meet my eye,' Ben thought.

On the way back to the office he wondered why he hadn't just come out with it. 'I don't know where they're going, Paul, but I'm damn sure they're not going together.' But it wouldn't have done. Had it been like this for that other cuckold, Parker Bowles, when friends of Charles and Camilla had conspired for them? Had he too kept his mouth shut and if he did, had he found it as shaming as he, Ben, was finding it now?

He was leaving for Scotland the following morning on the 7am from King's Cross. He did what he could during the rest of the day and delegated several urgent matters to Peter and Madge. His last task was to collect everything he would need if Hamish wanted a detailed discussion on the marina. 'Hopefully he won't because it sounds as though it's going well, but I'd better be prepared. Did you get me the latest cost analysis?'

'It's here,' Peter said, indicating a file. 'Neil Pyke did it before he left.' Ben looked up. 'Where's he gone?'

'Bermuda. Lucky sod. Some kind of international money conference. You know accountants. Always swanning off somewhere.' Somehow the mists of Scotland seemed much more inviting than the Bermudan heat. 'He's welcome to it,' Ben said, and began to gather up his papers.

That night he walked Max until they were both exhausted. 'Be good for Mrs Corey,' he said, as he fondled its great head. The dog looked at him for a moment and then lumbered to its basket. 'He knows I'm going and he doesn't like it,' Ben thought. 'If only Diana had cared as much.'

He enjoyed the train ride north, watching the landscape change as they crossed the border, imagining that it had grown colder, although that was ridiculous in an air-conditioned carriage. The train pulled into Glasgow at 12.45pm. He had half an hour before his connection to Oban and he downed a gin and tonic in the station bar. Madge had given him an itinerary, correct down to the tiniest detail. Inwardly, he gave thanks for her. What would he do if she retired? She was really past retiring age but soldiering on for his sake, and he would be lost without her. And what would happen if she went off with some man? She was suspiciously familiar with Sparrow. But somehow the thought of romance late in life cheered him. He would like Madge to be happy. It was no less than she deserved.

When the train pulled into Oban the light was already lessening, but there was still time for him to see the site and touch base with the site manager. A car was waiting for him as he came out into the station forecourt.

'Mr Webster?' The driver was red and bewhiskered and very Scottish. His bag was whisked from his hand and he sank into leather upholstery. The car did not so much drive as purr and for the next half hour he gave himself up to the beauty of the scenery.

The site, when they reached it, was impressive, set around a natural basin that would give a degree of shelter in bad weather. The foreman was a Scot with a distinct resemblance to Walter Matthau. His responses were laconic but he knew his stuff and was obviously bound up in the project. Henderson, the site manager, was a tried and trusted Webcon man. Together the three men surveyed every inch of the development. 'It's not a natural harbour,' Henderson said. 'There's a bay of sorts, but he needed a deeper draught. We've installed gates. They hold in the tide... Hold it in or out till the pressure equalises. Otherwise the keels would be sitting on the bottom.'

'Not a good idea,' Ben said. 'But why build here if there isn't a natural basin?' Henderson shrugged. 'It's his land. His money. He wanted it here.'

'It's as simple as that,' the foreman said in tones so

doleful that Ben had to suppress a chuckle.

'I'm leaving this in good hands,' Ben thought, as he stepped back into the car. They were nosing inland towards Hamish's place at Kinlochleven and he was drawn by the beauty of the wooded peaks, before the thought struck him that the marina might be the last job Webcon completed under his direction.

His reverie was interrupted by a call from Madge. 'It's all quiet here at the moment. Hammond's been missing all day. Pyke's gone off somewhere... A foreign trip, he said. I'm shedding no tears for that, but in a way it's too quiet.' He chuckled over the alarm in her voice and told her she had an over-active imagination. She changed the subject, telling him what she had arranged for his trip to Durham, and they said goodbye with mutual pleas to take it easy.

When he put away his phone, he smiled to himself, remembering how he had been in awe of Madge when his father brought him to the office as a child. And then they were on a road high above a loch and the gates of Cruag Ben were opening to admit him. There were to be eleven other guests, Hamish told him as he ushered him into the great hall. Penny ran through the list as she took him up the wide staircase. 'Not sure you know anyone after all, but they're good sorts. You'll like them.' His room looked out over the loch. 'Loch Leven,' Penny said, pushing the heavy curtains further back. There was a degree of pride in her voice as she said it, and looking out over the tranquil water Ben was not surprised.

When he had showered and changed, he sat for a

while in the window seat. Time enough to go down and join the throng. It was growing dark but the whole scene seemed luminous, as though some lighting genius had designed it. Mist wreathed around the tops of the peaks that encircled the loch. Far off he could see a minute white house seemingly clinging to the craggy face and down below sheep were tiny white-grey dots on the landscape. On his right, and beyond Loch Leven, lay Loch Linnhe with Fort William at its head. On his right, lost in darkness now, would be Glen Coe, menacing in sunlight, no doubt terrifying in the half-light of dusk.

A few days later, he would pick up the hire car Madge had arranged and head through that infamous glen and on to Rannoch Moor and civilisation. He knew that because it was all in Madge's brief. He smiled to himself, thinking of the crowd below, Eton and Oxford most of them, if he had guessed correctly; Scots aristocrats with not a Scottish accent between them. He drew the curtains together and then, on an impulse, pulled them apart again. Tonight he would sleep with the moon for company. Now it was time to go down to dinner.

The following day they were out by 8am, a good Scots breakfast inside them, dogs bounding at their feet. He had discussed the marina project with Hamish over breakfast so he could put work behind him and give himself up to the shoot. He was shooting with a borrowed gun and regretted he had not brought his own Purdey – but the heather was crisp under his feet and the grouse, always the trickiest target as they escalated up to 70 miles per hour in their efforts to escape, were plentiful. So plentiful that at times the sky seemed dark with them and the dogs ran feverishly back and forth, retrieving their treasure.

'Good day,' he told his host appreciatively, as they sipped bull shots at eleven. The tiny metal cups held a liquid that seared the throat and fired the limbs. Ben had tasted chilli-laced whisky before, but this was different. Hamish was grinning. 'Penny's concoction. Chicken bouillon laced with sherry, amply laced with chilli. Hits the spot, doesn't it?' He glanced around him. 'I love a day like this, every gun a friend. The commercial days are not such fun.' Ben raised quizzical eyebrows and Hamish continued. 'The moor has to pay its way. The upkeep is astronomical but if it wasn't done... if we left it to nature... the whole ecology of the place would be overrun. And, of course, it's good for the local economy. Shooting parties stay in local hotels, eat out, things like that. The average bag over the last ten years is five thousand brace. We're lucky up here: the birds come at you from all directions in a good wind and we average forty shooting days a season... I don't do them all but I need to show my face sometimes. Still, today's a day for my own pleasure, so better get on.'

Around them the women's tweeds of muted green or blue blended with the heathered landscape. They were well worn. New tweeds at a shoot were not *comme il faut*, according to Diana. But as they laughed and talked, their hands flashed bright with diamonds, rubies and emeralds. Only the mounting pile of dead birds, feathers ruffling in the breeze, showed this was not a social occasion. As the day wore on, Ben tried not to look at the funeral pile, concentrating instead on being clinical in his sightings, clean in his shots, breaking, reloading and firing in one fluid movement. The shoot was part of rural life and this was not a day for moralising about blood sports.

'I'm glad I came up. I thought they were making good progress at the site, so that's good to know. And today has been splendid,' Ben said, as they climbed back into the Land Rovers.

'I'm glad you came, too,' Hamish replied. 'Your man Henderson is reassuring, but it's good to have the boss cast his eye over things.' Ben smiled.

'I'm glad we got the job – but, tell me, why didn't you use a firm up here?'

'Couldn't find one, old chap. Business is booming, construction everywhere... Scotland is feeling its oats since devolution. But there'll be tears before bedtime, mark my words.'

At dinner Ben found himself seated next to a woman who had been competitive and voluble during the day's shoot. 'I've met your wife several times. She's not with you? Doesn't she shoot?'

It was a direct question and he had seen enough of her behaviour that day to know she wanted a direct answer. 'She's an accomplished shot, as a matter of fact. But she's in Prague at the moment. With a friend.'

'Prague?' She managed to make the Czech capital sound like the other side of the moon and he felt his cheeks burn. 'An old school friend persuaded her. She's into architecture.'

'Architecture? How intellectual.' She laughed in a way that suggested she had heard it called many things, but architecture was a new one.

'She knows,' he thought. 'She's playing with me.' Her teeth were small and white and even her lips were thin. He heard a voice say 'Bitch' but mercifully it was only in his head, and before she could pursue her questioning, Hamish intervened with a remark about David Cameron versus Gordon Brown that sent the table into a hubbub of argument.

Ben sank gratefully back into his seat. He was becoming paranoid. The woman had asked a perfectly normal question. She couldn't have known who Diana was in Prague with. If she was in Prague. He could have demanded the name of her hotel. Instead, he had hinted he would like it but she had shaken her head. 'No need, darling. I'll ring you every hour on the hour. We'll be moving around anyway. You know Flick.'

As glass and silver tinkled around him, he thought about the situation. Diana behaved as she did because his silence gave her permission. And if he did ever take her to task she would either silence him with a sharp retort or wind her arms around him and rebellion would be over in seconds.

Suddenly and unexpectedly he remembered his mother's arms. One dress had had sleeves cuffed at the wrist but slit to the shoulders, so that when she held him close he had felt her flesh against his cheek. 'Good night, darling,' she had said before she left that night. 'Don't stay up too late. I'll tell you all about it in the morning.'

45

But the morning brought only his grandmother, ashen-faced, arriving in his bedroom to tell him his mother and father were dead. Perhaps that was why he could not deal with his wife. He was afraid of losing her as he had lost that other woman years before.

There was a message on his phone when he at last reached his bedroom.

'Prague amazing. Lost in the splendour but missing you and Max. Talk soon. Much, much love. Di.'

Chapter Six

HE DIALLED DIANA'S MOBILE WHEN he received the message, but all he got was the answering service. 'Missing you, darling,' he said. 'Have fun. I love you. Hurry home.' After that there was nothing to do but go to bed.

He slept fitfully, once waking from a dream in which he had been trying to crawl through a space between two rocks. But the space grew narrower, his body enlarged with each movement. He woke in a sweat, although the bedroom was chilly. He turned onto his side, trying not to read too much into what the rocks might symbolise. It was the fault of the game at dinner, that was all. That or the haggis with which it had been stuffed. In the end he drifted off to sleep and woke to sunlight streaming in through the mullioned windows.

Again the day was productive and spirits high among the group. 'I like them,' Ben thought. 'But I have nothing in common with them.' They were more Diana's people than his, landed gentry with pedigrees back to the flood. 'And I am third generation rich, grandson of a man with a limp and a facility for figures. A man who filched the birthright of three orphans.' His pondering was interrupted by Hamish's hand on his shoulder.

'You should do this more often.' He was smiling but his eyes were wary and Ben wished he knew what lay behind them. He nodded. 'Yes, it's good to get away.' Hamish looked down at his feet for a moment and then met Ben's gaze.

'I know you have some problems... One hears rumours.'

'In the City?' Ben countered.

'Yes, the City. And over the dinner table...'

He means Diana, Ben thought, but before he could speak Hamish was picking up his gun and calling his Labrador to heel. 'Let it go,' he said, as he moved away. 'That's what I do when it all gets too much. I let it go.'

The day continued with the same rounds of slaughter interspersed with refreshments and bright chatter. The scent of the moors was heady, the scenery superb, 'but this is not for me,' Ben thought. He was still glad he had come, but he would have preferred to have been tramping the moors rather than littering them with feathered corpses.

Dinner in the evening was even jollier than the night before. Most of the party were leaving the following day and were determined to make the most of their last night. It was two in the morning when they flowed into the hall and made their farewells. 'We'll talk tomorrow,'

Hamish said, as he bade goodnight to Ben. He turned to look at the chattering crew behind him and pulled a wry face. 'It'll be quieter then.'

As he mounted the wide stairs, Ben reflected that, although Hamish was not a close acquaintance, he really liked the man. Tomorrow looked to be a good day.

It was a good day. They shared a leisurely breakfast. 'Penny won't be down till later,' Hamish apologised.

'Too much company?' Ben suggested. 'Too much St Emilion,' Hamish said wryly and helped himself to kedgeree.

After breakfast they walked the dogs and then climbed aboard a four-wheel drive. 'I'll take you to a favourite place of mine,' Hamish said and pointed the vehicle in the direction of Fort William. It wasn't long, however, before they turned left and drove down to the shore of a loch. 'Loch Linnhe,' Hamish said. 'We'll take the Corran Ferry across to Ardnamurchan, the western-most point of the British Isles. But we'll go north towards Moidart first. You'll appreciate the views.' They followed a narrow road skirting the loch and then turned sharply left. For a while they ran between mountains, and then the sea was before them, studded with islands, and in the far distance a range of mountain peaks.

Ben would have liked to have parked and walked down to the shore but Hamish turned off the road and drove down to a smokery. 'You must try the smoked cheese. You can't get anything like it in London.' They bought cheese and smoked salmon and packed it into the boot. 'Now we find lunch.' It was miles before they came to a hotel, tucked away in a small village. The menu was good but Ben was not hungry. They settled for gravadlax followed by griddled kidneys and green beans, washed down with a good wine. For a while they talked about the marina but eventually the conversation turned to other things.

'Did you choose to head your company,' Hamish asked. 'Or was it expected of you?'

Ben considered for a moment. 'A bit of both, I expect. I could have said no. There've been times when I've wished that my father hadn't died as he did.' Hamish was raising enquiring eyebrows. 'He was killed in a motor accident when I was a kid. I was the only child – well, the only boy... So was he. My godfather headed the firm after my father died. I went into it when I came down from Cambridge, then he retired a few years later and I was in the hot seat.'

'Headey's is interested, isn't it?'

Ben nodded. 'We're waiting for a formal bid. And they may not be the only one.' Hamish was twiddling his spoon. 'Well, as I said the other day, watch your back. Unpleasant things, takeovers.'

Ben decided to be direct. 'I get the feeling you're telling me something.'

'Oh, not really... but there's usually a villain or two around in these situations.' Ben nodded. Whatever it was, the other man was not going to say outright. They drove to Ardnamurchan Point, where the vista was just as magnificent, and then took the Corran Ferry back to the Fort William road.

Dinner that evening was less formal, just Hamish and

Penny and himself. They served themselves from the huge sideboard, as the servants had a well-earned rest. 'Shooting parties are wonderful but a hell of a lot of work,' Penny admitted. The conversation flowed over the meal but no one mentioned Diana and that was significant. Usually one's wife, if absent, was well discussed.

Ben made his goodbyes after dinner. 'I'll be leaving at the crack of dawn,' he said apologetically. 'But I've enjoyed the last few days immensely. Let me know when you're next in town. Diana would love to give you dinner. Perhaps we could get some tickets for...'

'Not opera,' Penny said, patting his arm. 'I can't bear it. But dinner would be lovely. Tell Diana we missed her.' Hamish accompanied him to his room. 'I'll see you in the morning before you go.' Ben shook his head. 'No, please. If they leave something out I'll gobble it and be away. I don't want to wake the household.' The car was already waiting in the courtyard, a sleek black Audi that looked as though it could eat the Highland roads and come back for more. 'We'll see,' Hamish said. 'McGregor will be up for you, of that you can be sure.'

But when Ben came down, his host was already at the breakfast table and the morning room was redolent with the smell of hot food. 'You've got a good day for the drive down,' Hamish said, between mouthfuls of kedgeree. 'What made you decide against the train?'

Ben gave a garbled story of looking up an old acquaintance of his grandmother and Hamish appeared to accept it. Breakfast over, they went out into the courtyard together.

'I've thoroughly enjoyed these few days,' Ben said. 'Thank you.' Hamish cleared his throat. 'You know where I am, Ben. If you ever want to talk, that is. About the project... or anything really.' Inside Ben, embarrassment grew at the sympathy in the other man's voice. He half-wondered what it would be like to blub like a baby and feel the strong arms of a man around him, but it wouldn't do. 'You bet,' he said cheerfully. 'Hopefully the marina will all go according to plan. Henderson knows his stuff. But don't hesitate to call me if the need arises.' They looked at one another for a moment and then the other man clapped Ben's arm and stood back from the car. A few moments later, the Audi was wheeling out of the courtyard and onto the road that skirted the loch.

He joined the main road just south of the bridge at Ballachulish and turned for Crianlarich. Ahead, Glen Coe loomed, a legendary place of death but surprisingly benign in the early morning sunlight, and then he was out on Rannoch Moor. The landscape was identical on both sides of the road, barren and rocky, broken here and there by the gleam of water. It took him twenty minutes to reach the Bridge Of Orchy and ten minutes more to Tyndrum. He was back in civilisation, and the border and England lay ahead. The roads were increasingly tree-lined now, mostly firs, huge trees that made him think of Christmas. They would be laden with snow in winter and the road would quite possibly be impassable. Where would he be then? Safe at home with Diana or cast adrift, the cuckold, to eat his Christmas dinner from a tray on his knee? But the sun was shining and the

Audi responding to his commands, and he put such gloomy thoughts aside and concentrated on the road. Stirling passed, then Jedburgh, Otterburn... He was in England again. And after that he drove through Northumberland and into Durham.

Belgate was a small village and Laburnum Terrace a row of what looked like pensioners' cottages. Number 37 had a pocket-hanky garden in front and a white-painted door so clean it was almost blinding. He had formed a picture in his mind of the nine-year-old Margaret, but the woman who answered the door was old. That was his first impression. Later, as she bustled around making the tea she had pressed upon him, he saw that she was not so much old as careworn. Life had not treated her kindly, if the lines around her eyes were any indication, and once again he felt a pricking of conscience. His life had not been a bed of roses but he had never had to worry over the simple business of existence.

'I believe you've talked with Mr Sparrow,' he began. She nodded, pushing a plate of fruitcake towards him. 'I still bake. Don't take the crust, there's a nice soft bit. He said my dad was something to do with your dad?'

'My grandfather, actually. Your father went to war...'

'And never came back,' she finished for him. He nodded encouragingly but there was no need. She seemed anxious to talk.

'We were in the country, away from the bombs. My mum was with us. The three of us. Me and my sister Dorothy and Billy. He was the baby. "An imp of Satan," Mam used to say, but he was good really. They were both good bairns.' She was silent for a while and then went on, speaking more quickly, as though she wanted to get it over. 'Well, I expect you know. Mam went up to London for something... I never knew what. "I'll be back directly," she had said. And then a man came and told me she was blown up...'

'My grandfather?' Ben suggested.

'Yes, he said he was from Dad's work. They said we weren't to worry. We'd be taken care of. He had a woman with him. She was his wife, I think. She said she'd come back for us, but she didn't. And they wouldn't keep us where we were.'

'So where did you go? Were you kept together?'

'No... It wasn't five minutes before Dorothy went. She was pretty, our Dolly. A little picture. The billeting woman took her – and there was a man as well. He drove the car but he had to carry Dolly out. She didn't want to go. I said I could look after her and Billy but they wouldn't listen. She went off in the car. Screaming, she was, "Maggie, Maggie."' She looked down at her hands for a moment before she continued. 'And then, about ten days later, a vicar came, a vicar and his wife. She had a navy hat on with a white band and a fur coat. I can see her now, clear as day. He was nice. "What's happening to the little girl?" he said. I felt like saying I wasn't a little girl, I was nine, but they wouldn't have listened. His wife only had eyes for our Billy. Well, he was a lovely bairn. And then they went off with him.'

'How did you know he was a vicar?'

Her eyes twinkled. 'He wore a dog-collar.' Then she

put up a hand and fingered the neck of her own blouse and he could see her lips were trembling. How that moment must have seared her memory for her to remember it so clearly nearly seventy years later. 'Mrs Clegg, the woman whose house it was, said I should be thankful they would be cared for. "I'll care for them," I said, but she said not to be silly I was just a little girl.' She paused again. 'Thankful? I wasn't thankful.' She shook her head as though trying to dispense painful memories. 'Anyroad, it's a long time ago. Your granddad, is he still alive?'

'No. But my grandmother is. She's never forgotten you. That's why I'm here.' No need to mention money yet but he must give her something to hold on to. 'Do you have family?' Around him the little house sparkled, every flat surface full of china cats or cupids or bright pink and blue teacups with the months of the year on them. There were artificial roses in a glass vase and a photograph of a white-haired man, smiling as he squinted into the sun.

'No family,' she said. 'That's Jim, my husband. He died a long time ago. His heart just gave out. It was sudden.' And then, musingly. 'I remember your grandma. She had yellow hair.'

'It's white now. Perhaps we could arrange a visit. She's very frail but I know she'd like to see you again.'

'Will you be looking for the others, our Billy and Dorothy?' There was a hopeful note in her voice and he tried not to sound too positive. 'I'd like to, but it might be difficult if they were adopted. The change of name, you see. And details were kept very secret years ago.'

She looked crestfallen and he hurried on. 'But we'll try. Mr Sparrow is very good at his job. He's an ex-policeman. If anyone can find them, he can.'

There was silence for a moment, except for the loud ticking of the clock that hung on the wall above the fireplace. 'It must cost money,' she said at last. 'Why would you want to spend money looking for people you never knew?' So she was shrewder than he had given her credit for. The answer, when it came, was not far from the truth. 'I love my grandmother,' he said. 'She brought me up after my parents died. She's not well and, frankly, I'd do anything which would make her happy.' She seemed content with that and he was glad. Too early yet to talk of old wrongs.

He wondered if he should embrace her as he left. She was old enough to be his grandmother so it would not be out of place. Instead, he shook her hand, which was small and rough but surprisingly firm. 'I'll be in touch,' he said and waved at the gate.

He felt a sense of relief as he climbed into the Audi and headed south. He might not have felt so sanguine if he had known he was leaving behind a woman equally relieved that she had managed not to tell him too much. As she went back into the house to put the kettle on again, she reflected that it would never have done to have told him everything.

Chapter Seven

Maggie's Story
November 1940

IT WAS STRANGE TO WAKE in the dark and not hear
mother already moving quietly about the bedroom so
as not to wake the baby. Once Billy was awake he would
chew on to be carried everywhere, so the longer he slept
the better. This morning, though, he wasn't sleeping in
Mam's bed. He was in her bed, the bed she shared with
Dolly. She knew that because of the warm wetness and
leaking around her bum. His nappy must be soaked and
it would be up to her to change it and rinse the old one
and peg it out. 'I don't do nappies no more,' Mrs Clegg
had said firmly when Mam said she was going to
London. 'Only two days,' she had pleaded. 'A day and a
half really, I'll be back on Sunday night. And Maggie'll
see to the other two.' Mam had looked at her and smiled,
and Maggie had nodded her head and felt proud she was
trusted. 'Alright,' Mrs Clegg had said, grudgingly. 'But
she'll need to see to him and his potty. I don't do nappies
no more. Not since my own grew up.'

Maggie turned gingerly in the bed, anxious to get a few minutes peace before they started. Dolly lay on her back, one arm up on the pillow, the other hidden by the sheet. Her golden hair curled round her face, black eyelashes lay on her cheeks – pink cheeks, but paler than her pink lips. 'A Cupid's bow,' Mam always said. 'Our Dolly's got a Cupid's bow.'

In the darkness Maggie pulled a face. 'Our Dolly's got all the looks,' she thought. Her own hair was brown, her lashes stubby and her cheeks rosy rather than pink. Still, she was a little treasure. Mam always said that – and she was in charge now, would be till Mam got back at five o'clock. 'I have to see to things, pet. Since your Dad...' Her voice had wobbled a bit but then she had carried on. 'Since your Dad died no one's seen to things. I need to talk to Mr Webster. And Mrs Webster says I can stop there Saturday night. The beds won't be aired at our place. I'll pick up a few things... I'm going to give back the rent-book, Maggie. It looks like we'll be here for a bit and... Well, the war pension won't stretch to everything.'

Dad had died in the war. If he'd got to the beach he'd have been alright, Mam said, but the Germans got him first. Mam had cried after Mr Webster had told her and left, and then the other two started, and Mrs Clegg had said, 'God Almighty, I'll put the kettle on.' She closed her eyes hard so that tears wouldn't come. She still thought of Dad sometimes, coming home on Friday nights with Maltesers for them, a packet each. He had always been in a good mood on Friday nights and he and Mam had gone to the Lamb and Flag and come home merry. Dad had waved to them when he left. 'You lot should get out of London,' he'd said, smiling a smile that was different to usual. It had fooled Dolly but not her. It wasn't the way he smiled usually. His mouth was open, his teeth were together and his lips looked thin. 'I'll sort Hitler out,' he'd said. 'Leave it to the Terriers.'

Mr Webster couldn't go to sort Hitler because he wore a funny boot on his leg, but Dad was fit. 'As a lop,' he'd say, and show her how the muscles in his arm would wiggle up and down when he clenched his fist. Mam said they would go to Europe when the war was over and find his grave. Mrs Clegg had humphed at that. She humphed at a lot of things and talked about 'getting her home to herself'. She also talked nice to the WVS woman, when she came to check they were okay, and then called her a nosey bitch as soon as she was down the path.

'I don't like Mrs Clegg,' Dolly had said once, and Mam had shushed her and said they should all be grateful they'd been able to get out of London. Except that nothing had happened in London for ages and ages. There were reports of bombings on the BBC but Mam said they were happening somewhere else.

'I'll be alright,' she'd said yesterday. 'I'll be in and out of there and Mrs Webster says it's really quiet. It's the airfields outside of London they're bombing, just the odd one in London. In the posh parts. I'll be alright in the East End and back on the train before you can say Jack Robinson.'

Maggie turned gently to look at the alarm clock. She could have five minutes more and then she'd have to get started if she wanted to get everything done.

Dolly stirred and her eyelids fluttered but then a thumb went to her mouth and she settled again. Mam would put bitter aloes on her thumb if she kept on sucking it. 'It ruins your teeth,' she'd said when she did it to her. 'And you've got lovely teeth, our Mags.' Her teeth were good, she'd looked at them in the mirror and they were quite nice. She ground them together now, testing them for strength. She didn't have a Cupid's bow but she had good teeth. She eased herself up on the pillow and began to extricate herself from the bed. Light was coming through the thin curtains. Time to begin the day.

She had changed Billy, given him his breakfast and put him in his highchair by half-past eight. Mrs Clegg was getting ready for church, but she cut a slice of bread each for Dolly and Margaret and let them toast it at the fire. 'Don't burn it. I don't want nasty black scrapings in the sink. And one knob of marge. That's got to last till Wednesday.' Mam thought Mrs Clegg did the dirty with their rations but it didn't do to say anything. 'We won't be here forever,' she would say. 'When we get back to London we'll pig it out as much as we like. Bananas... What I'd give for a banana... and best butter...' They had thought they would get butter in the country. 'It's right in the country,' Mam had said when the billeting officer told them where they were going. But butter never appeared on Mrs Clegg's table. Only Stork margarine. And they didn't have joints like they'd had at home.

'Mince and lucky to get it' was the most meat they

saw at Mrs Clegg's, so that's what they called it. 'Mince and lucky to get it.' She chuckled as she pulled the crisp toast from the fork and spread it for Dolly's breakfast.

Mrs Clegg looked funny when she came back from church. She spent a long time unpinning her hat and plugging the pins back in it, folding her scarf into half then quarters then eighths. 'There's been a big raid,' she said, as she hung up her coat. 'A bad one.' They listened to the radio and peeled the potatoes for dinner. The voice was droning on about raids on the docks and the City. 'At five o'clock teatime yesterday,' Mrs Clegg said, shocked. 'Broad daylight.'

There was a lot about British fighter planes. 'They always say that,' Mrs Clegg said. 'They can't tell you the truth. Hitler's got thousands of aeroplanes. We weren't ready, but they can't say that, so they say we were.' She looked at Margaret's face and her own softened somewhat.

'Your Mam'll have been in a shelter. They've dug them all over London. And there are the tubes. She'll be back at teatime, you'll see.'

The afternoon was funny. Billy was missing his mother and chewed on, crying for nothing and fighting with Dolly. He even pushed her in the chest when she tried to soothe him, which wasn't like him because he was a good bairn usually. It made her chest feel funny when he pushed her. She had noticed it swelling. So had Mam. 'You're developing, our Maggie,' she'd said. 'But don't grow up too quick. I love my little girl... big girl. What would I do without you?' She had given her a cuddle then, a good long one like she gave Billy. It had been nice. 'When she comes home I might get another one,' Maggie thought. 'Once she's seen to the bairns.' At three o'clock there was a proper to-do. Dolly fell down on the cinder path and got bits of cinder embedded in her bloodied knee. 'That noise'll be heard out at sea,' Mrs Clegg said, but she sat Dolly on the kitchen table and picked out the cinders bit by bit. Dolly's sobs subsided until the iodine went on and then she let out a roar of anguish. 'Alright, Nellie Melba,' Mrs Clegg said. 'That's enough opera for now.'

It was half-past four when the car drew up at the door. 'It's bad,' Maggie thought when she saw it was Mr and Mrs Webster. Mr Webster always walked quickly, as though, if he went fast enough, no one would notice his limp. Today, though, he took ages to open the gate and come up the path. Mrs Webster was young and pretty. 'Only a bairn,' Mam had said once, in tones that suggested she was the wrong wife for Mr Webster. Or he was the wrong husband for her. One or the other. Today she looked as though she'd been crying.

'Not now, Margaret,' Mrs Clegg said when Maggie made for the door. 'See to your brother and sister.' She was ushering the Websters into the parlour, which was never ever used and smelled mouldy. 'Take Billy into the garden,' Maggie said when the door closed, pushing Dolly towards the back door.

'Why should I?' Dolly had her awkward face on but Margaret wasn't having it. 'Because I'll smack your bum if you don't.' She lifted her hand in the way Mam did when you defied her and it worked.

'It's not fair,' Dolly wailed, but she grabbed Billy's jumper and manhandled him over the step.

At first Maggie couldn't hear anything, just the murmur of voices, but then she felt the door give slightly and knew it wasn't snecked.

'The sky was black with them. Black.' That was Mr Webster. 'They went for Docklands and then gas and power. Woolwich Arsenal caught it. They knew what they were after.' Maggie heard Mr Webster's tongue tut tut against his teeth. 'And broad daylight. The cheek of it.' Mr Webster cleared this throat. 'They came back again and again... Right up to 4am... but we think Mollie was caught in the first or second raid because she never got to us.' Margaret felt a sudden pain in her stomach and then a wet trickle between her legs. 'We think Mollie was caught.' Did that mean no one knew where Mollie was? 'Mam,' she said out loud, but it must have been soft because they never heard.

Mrs Webster was speaking now, in a funny, choking way. 'She must have collected the post from her place because that's how they got back to us. They found her bag and the letters were in it. Her place has gone... flattened. They found her body... dug it out... under a gable end. Ben had to identify it.' She was crying now and he took it up. 'It was her rings. There wasn't much else. I've got them here.' There was obviously a handing over because Mrs Clegg said, 'They'll be safe with me.' And then, 'Who's going to tell them?'

Maggie ran out into the sunlit garden. The sun was going down but it was still strong enough to dazzle the laurel bush with light, making it oddly beautiful. Mam had never liked that bush. 'Laurel is a cemetery plant, our Maggie. Laurel and ivy give me the shudders.' And they had all laughed when she jiggled her shoulders up and down and made a face.

'My Mam laughs a lot,' Maggie thought. 'She does, she does. Even after Dad died, she was still funny.' She shook her head. Laughing people didn't die. Dying was for sad people. Mam said, 'Mince and lucky to get it' just like Mrs Clegg, and sometimes put her finger under her nose to make Hitler's moustache when the landlady wasn't looking.

She was still laughing at that memory when they came out into the garden. As they advanced along the cinder path, she tried to retreat. If they never reached her she would never need to hear it. A long way off, Billy started to cry and she knew she should go to him, but her legs wouldn't carry her. 'I'm sorry,' Mr Webster was saying. He was wearing a blue silk tie with a pattern like peacocks' tails. And then she heard her mother's voice quite clear: 'You're my big girl, our Maggie. What would I do without you?' And suddenly she knew what she had to do. 'I've got to see to the bairn,' she said and pushed past their startled faces.

She was still holding Billy in one arm and Dolly by the other hand when they went off in the car. Mrs Webster kissed them all and her face was wet. Margaret licked in a tear and found it salty. It was Mrs Webster's tear not hers. Her eyes were dry. 'She's a funny girl,' Mrs Clegg said. 'Hard as the hobs of hell, that one.' But Mrs

Webster was leaning out of the car. 'I'll come back for you, Maggie. You and the others. When we get things sorted, I'll be back. I promise.'

Mrs Clegg made them bread and dripping for tea and even offered them afters of caraway seed cake out of the tin that was never opened. Mam had made Victoria sponge in London with raspberry jam put on while the cake was still warm, so that the jam would soak in. No more Victoria sponge. Just like no more Maltesers.

They went to bed early. 'Where's Mam?' Dolly asked. Margaret struggled for an answer but then she said, 'Tell you tomorrow.' Billy went in the middle this time and she managed to stretch her arm across till it took in half of Dolly too. 'I'll take care of you,' she said. It was the least she could do for Mam and Dad.

Chapter Eight

S HE DIDN'T GO TO SCHOOL on Monday. 'You can stay off and watch the bairns,' Mrs Clegg said. She was trying to be kind and seemed uneasy about it. Once or twice Maggie caught the woman looking at her strangely and once she sighed and shook her head. 'She doesn't know what to do with us,' Maggie thought, and redoubled her efforts to keep the other two quiet. If they were quiet she might let them stay, even without Mam. If she wouldn't and they had to leave, where would they go? She knew how to get to London on the train and once there, she could ask a policeman for directions. Except that she had no money for train fares and even if they hid from the ticket collector there was no house now. What had Mr Webster said? 'Flattened.' That was what he'd said. She tried to imagine what home would look like flattened. Perhaps it would be like the magic Japanese flowers Mam had bought sometimes as a treat. Little squares of coloured paper, thin as windowpanes, until you dropped them into water, when they swelled into amazing and unusual shapes. But a flattened house was no good for a baby like Billy. The best bet was still to stay here, at least till she was old enough to sort something better. She began to do jobs, whatever came to hand, cleaning, tidying. 'Keep her sweet,' Mam had warned them all. Now it was doubly important.

Dolly was quieter than usual, but Billy whinged and sometimes said 'Mama' and worried his head from side to side to show he was cross. Two days later the green WVS woman came, taking off her gloves and loosening her coat at the neck. She gave each of them a mint and then went into the front room with Mrs Clegg. Again Maggie put her ear to the door. 'Tragic,' she heard and then the door was pushed shut.

It seemed like a lifetime before it opened again. She was holding Billy but she put him down on the floor and moved nearer. 'Don't worry about the arrangements.' That was the green WVS woman. 'It'll go through like clockwork. They're lovely children.' Mrs Clegg said something but the words were indistinct. The WVS woman spoke again. 'Only problem is the eldest... She's a plain little thing. And her age is against her. Not much chance there, I'm afraid.' And then they were coming out, gloves were pulled over fat white hands and the WVS woman was bending towards her. There was a sweet, flowery smell and another... mothballs. 'Now you are not to worry about anything, Margaret. It's all being taken care of, so be a good girl for Mrs Clegg and it'll all be alright.' Mrs Clegg ushered the woman towards the front door. 'I would help, you know that, but one way and another...' The green hat nodded. 'I know, I know.'

Mrs Clegg was quiet the rest of the day and at teatime she gave them jam tarts, warning them not to burn their lip on the jam because they were fresh out of the oven. That night in bed Maggie lay, listening to the sounds of her brother and sister sleeping and trying to piece it all together. Why was she a problem? She was more use than the other two, that was a plain fact. She went on puzzling till she felt the warm sensation of Billy's sodden nappy seeping through her nightdress, but sleep overcame her before she could do anything about it.

She went back to school on Tuesday, in spite of her protests that she was needed at home. 'It's the best thing,' Mrs Clegg said. 'Life has to go on. You'll learn that. And you're going to need your schooling if you're going to make your way in this world.' Her tone suggested Maggie's chances of succeeding were wafer thin. Maggie cried a bit on the way to school but before she reached the playground she dried her tears. It didn't do to let anyone see your guard was down.

It was obvious word had gone round at school. Girls looked at her strangely in the schoolyard and for once no boys pushed her over or tried to pull the hair Mrs Clegg had put into ribboned bunches. But she was aware she was an object of curiosity rather than pity. Even the teachers eyed her strangely and were gentler than usual in their manner. She got an eight out of ten for mental arithmetic and was allowed to be flower monitor two days running, an unheard of honour. As the days went by, school life returned to normal. This was something of a relief: she didn't want to be marked out as someone special.

Each day when she got home, Dolly was waiting in the garden, swinging on the gate that shut off the way to the hen cree. She would gabble out details of how badly she had been treated or, once, how the woman next door had given her a jam tart so fresh out of the oven the jam had stuck to her lip and burned it. 'Well, you should have had more sense,' Maggie said unsympathetically, and then, regretting her harshness, she pulled the ribbons from her bunches and tied them into Dolly's curls to her sister's infinite pleasure. On Friday Dolly was not there at the gate and a car stood outside on the road. Maggie broke into a run when she saw it. She came in at the back door and went through to the sitting room. She saw the case first, Mam's case. And then Mrs Clegg appeared, holding Billy in her arms. There was a man behind her, holding Dolly by the hand, and the WVS woman bringing up the rear. At the sight of her sister, Dolly tried to wriggle free and Maggie darted forward. The WVS woman looked upset and put a hand up to her cheek but the man didn't let go of Dolly. 'Now, now,' he said. 'Let's be sensible.' 'I want Maggie!' Dolly was shouting and struggling but Maggie's legs had turned to lead. She had known it would come ever since she had heard the word 'arrangements'. Dolly was going and Billy would follow and she would be left alone in the wide bed.

'Get it over,' the man said, picking Dolly up and arching his body to avoid her flailing legs. 'You explain,' he said to the green WVS woman, but she had tears in her eyes and was looking at Mrs Clegg. Billy squirmed in her arms and started to cry.

'Here,' the landlady said, and put Billy into Maggie's arms. Dolly was screaming, 'Please, Maggie, please.' And then 'I want my mammy' in a sad little wail.

'She can't go.' Maggie could hear her own voice, clear and calm. 'I can look after her. And Mrs Webster is coming for us directly. You can't take Dolly away.' But Dolly had gone into the car and Billy had stopped crying and was quietly hiccupping distress.

'It's for the best, pet.' The endearment slipped out from Mrs Clegg's lips when the door had closed. For a few moments she barred it with her body, afraid that Maggie might tear it open and run down the path. But inside Maggie, resistance had died. There was nothing you could do against a man and a car when there was no one in the wide world to help you. Mrs Clegg put the kettle on and they sat at the kitchen table. Billy had fallen asleep in Maggie's arms and together they had laid him on the settee and covered him with his 'silky', the cot quilt he always needed at bedtime, pinching it between finger and thumb as his eyelids drooped.

'Here, have this tea,' Mrs Clegg said when they returned to their seats. She pushed the cup forward. Her face was flushed and hairs had escaped from the pins at her temples and wisped at her cheeks. 'She'll have a good home, Maggie. They've promised that. People who adopt do it because they want someone to love, and they say they're a lovely couple with a nice home. She'll have every advantage, you can depend on it. Yes, Dolly will be alright… You have to look after yourself now. You're a big girl.' It didn't sound the same coming from Mrs Clegg as it had done when Mam said it. 'You're my big girl,' Mam had said, and she had felt big. She didn't feel big now. She felt small and frightened and there was a sick feeling inside her, as though she was coming down with something. It was better when Billy woke up and they put him in the bath in front of the fire. Mrs Clegg carried it in and put in the hot water but she let Maggie wash him and lift him out to dry. 'Get the creases,' was all she said, as Maggie dried the fat white limbs with little bracelets at the wrists and ankles and dimples at the knees and elbows.

'Dolly?' he asked at bedtime, but she shushed him and climbed in beside him. Normally she had a little while after he and Dolly went to bed, but he would never go to bed on his own. Besides, they had limited time together now. She knew that as sure as God made little apples. She felt her eyes prick at the memory of something her mother had said whenever she was sure of something, but she didn't let herself cry. She didn't want to waste a minute. She had always liked the smell of him after a bath and now she drank it in as if to store it in memory. His hair was still damp and dark on his neck, going into little c-shaped curls. 'I love you Billy,' she whispered against the soft folds of his neck where it peeped from the top of his sleep suit. She would never see him grow up now, go to school, get long trousers. She had meant to read *Milly-Molly-Mandy* to him when he was old enough to sit still for books. She had done that for Dolly, done it for a long time. Now there would be no more bedtime reading. No more laughter and tears and kissing better after falls. Because they would be coming for Billy next, that much was for sure. She wondered if she should let herself cry but no tears would come. Her eyes felt hot and sore but that was all. She was looking forward to going to sleep and not having to think any more, but sleep was slow in coming. Her last waking thought was who she would read *Milly-Molly-Mandy* to when Billy was gone. Maybe they would find her a place with a baby and another little girl. But they wouldn't be the same.

It was a week and a half before they came for Billy. 'It's a vicar,' Mrs Clegg said in tones of wonder. 'A good Christian home, that's what they said.' She dressed Billy in his very best suit: a white top with a blue collar and blue trousers that buttoned onto the top. He had white socks and his red bar shoes and she brushed his hair and put a left hand parting in it. 'There now,' Mrs Clegg said. 'He looks a picture.' There was a man and a woman in the front room, and the man who had taken Dolly. The green WVS woman had obviously stayed away, anticipating another scene. The woman had a navy hat and a coat with a fur collar and they both looked rich. The man looked kind but a bit sad, and the white collar at his neck looked odd. 'What will happen to the little girl?' he said, but the woman didn't say anything. She held out her arms and Billy went into them quite naturally. 'Oh,' the woman said, and buried her face in his neck. 'He's a charmer, isn't he?' She held him away from her, looking into his face. Billy smiled and the woman cuddled him again.

The vicar spotted Maggie who was watching and holding the *Milly-Molly-Mandy* book. 'You must be Margaret,' he was saying. Maggie didn't answer. She just kept looking at Billy because there wasn't much time left. 'Yes,' Mrs Clegg said, pushing Maggie forward. 'This is Margaret and she's a good girl.' The man bent down and his eyes were kind. 'We'll take very good care of him,' he said. She could feel tears coming and she tried to keep them back because if she cried she would lose precious minutes of sight. 'Perhaps...' the vicar started. He looked at his wife, but she had eyes only for the baby in her arms. Maggie proffered the book. The vicar moved to take it, but the woman shook her head. Then he straightened up and picked up his black hat from the chair. 'Well...' He was holding out a hand to Mrs Clegg, who wiped her hand on her apron before she took it. Then the other man was ushering them towards the door and Billy was still staring curiously into the woman's face. 'Remember me, Billy,' Maggie pleaded inside her head. 'I'll remember you.' They halted on the path and the vicar spoke to the woman for what seemed like a long time, but she shook her head a lot and eventually they moved towards the car.

Maggie didn't go out to the step with Mrs Clegg. Instead she went to the window and moved the lace curtain – but just a little because she didn't want them to see. The man looked back once and his brow wrinkled as though he wasn't sure, and then they were in the car and Mrs Clegg was coming back into the house. 'There now,' she said, sounding relieved. 'All for the best. Cling on to that.'

Two days later, the man Margaret didn't like came to collect her. The night before Mrs Clegg had packed her case, putting in those things of her mother's she had chosen. 'The rest'll go to refugees,' Mrs Clegg said. 'They've got nothing so they'll be appreciated.' Maggie was going to a place where they sent girls, a place called Northfield. Mrs Clegg had sat down on the bed when the case was closed and pulled Margaret to her. 'I'm not given to sentiment but I'm sorry for you, Margaret. You're a casualty of war, like the rest of them. If you'd had a family... but Mr Webster said there was no one either side. So it's up to the council to take care of you and one day you'll make a family of your own. So will Dorothy and Billy and they'll have advantages. It's up to you to make your own advantages. They'll help you. There's many a one came out of Northfield and made good. So mind your Ps and Qs and say your prayers. You can make your Mam and Dad proud of you. They'll be watching over you. Now, close that case and I'll make some nice black pudding sandwiches for supper.'

They listened to the radio while they ate. There was a lot about Japan signing a pact with Germany and something about someone called Greta Garbo making a film about a Russian. 'Ninotchka,' Mrs Clegg said twice, as though she liked the word. 'You'll likely go to the pictures when you're at Northfield. The older girls do, I've seen them in the Regent. Someone goes with them but they go in the one and nines, not the cheap seats.'

It was eight o'clock when Maggie went upstairs. She sat for a long time looking at the single bed where she used to be. Before Mam died. Before she had to take Mam's place and be there in the big bed for the other two. Mam had trusted her to look after the family and she had let her down.

'I'll find them again,' she resolved when at last she lay down. 'I'll get a job and I'll save every penny and I'll find them.' She lay on her back, seeing the moonlight through the thin curtains, wondering if Dolly was seeing the same moon and how many miles away she was. Billy would be asleep in the vicar's house. 'The holy of holies,' Mam had called the vicarage in London. It had been grey and grim with high walls. She didn't want Billy in a grim house. She squeezed her eyes shut and imagined a white-painted vicarage with a garden like they put on calendars. She was nine years old. In five years she would be earning. If she lived on thin air she could save up quite quickly and find them. Dolly first. She would be nine then, as old as she herself was now, and sensible. Together they would get to Billy and get him back too. He would be seven. Some day she would do it. They wouldn't be too old for *Milly-Molly-Mandy* even then. And they would both be able to take turns reading. She must take care of that book and keep it safe until it was needed again.

Chapter Nine

Maggie's first sight of Northfield was intimidating. A tall house in a garden full of cemetery plants, it looked like something from a ghost story, but she was welcomed by the warden, Miss Eccles, who smiled at her in a kindly way and told her she was welcome. 'You'll soon settle in, Margaret, and learn our little ways. We hope you'll be happy here.' After that she was handed over to an older girl who showed her where she would sleep and told her to put her possessions in her locker. Amazingly, she slept well that first night, her bed in the middle of a long dormitory lined with similar beds, each with a red blanket to cover them and a bedside water jug. The following morning she went down to breakfast less apprehensive than when she had arrived.

Life in Northfield followed a strict pattern. 6.30am get up and put your bed to air. Get washed, dressed and be down for breakfast at 7am – woe betide you if Miss Eccles had embarked on grace before you reached your table. At 8am you went back upstairs and made your bed, tidied away any stray possessions, and went downstairs to join the crocodile that wound its way to Gunner St School, first making sure that you had your gasmask in its case and your pen and pencil set.

The Northfield girls were something of a curiosity in the town and for once Maggie was glad that she didn't stand out. There was a girl called Maisie, who had blonde hair that defied every effort Miss Eccles and her assistant, Miss Micklewhite, made to tame it and it bubbled around her face. Maisie was fourteen and had breasts, an object of wonder to the younger girls. But her face, which Maggie thought was nearly but not quite as pretty as Dolly's, reminded Maggie too much of her sister and she tried to avoid looking at her as much as possible.

At night in the six-bedded room, she lay listening to the breathing of the other girls and wondered about Billy and Dolly. Most of the girls slept soundly but occasionally one would let out a troubled sound as though in a bad dream. And one, a girl called Freda who wore wire-rimmed spectacles, would occasionally sob herself to sleep. The first time this happened Maggie crept across to her bed, the lino cold beneath her bare feet, and kneeled down. 'Are you alright?' If Freda had said something welcoming she would have crept in beside her and put out an arm. That had always fixed it for the bairns. But all Freda said was 'Yes' and after a little while Maggie crept back to her own bed.

She felt strange, as though in some kind of suspended state. Inside her, there was a pain she couldn't explain, a raw feeling. And yet she was perfectly able to function, getting praise for good work at school, and at Northfield hardly ever getting one of Miss Eccles' glares. At times she wondered if home still existed somewhere, Daddy coming home on Fridays with Maltesers and kissing the back of Mam's neck till she threatened to hit him with her knitting needle. And Billy in the tin bath and Dolly rocking one of her dolls and the war never happening at all.

But the war was happening. Occasionally a siren would sound and they would all be roused from their beds and taken to the Anderson shelters. There were four of these in the garden and they smelled of damp. Freda said there were rats in there, and during night raids they sat more terrified of the sound of scratching than of any German bomb. Rats' eyes gleamed in the dark, Freda told them, so there was no possibility of closing your eyes and dozing.

But the dreaded raids never came. 'They're not interested in rural areas,' Miss Eccles said, meaning to reassure. 'You're lucky not to live in London.' London, she implied, was being bombed to bits. 'They don't bury them in coffins anymore,' Freda said one night, as they were getting ready for bed. 'They just chuck them in the ground and cover them up.'

That night Maggie woke from a nightmare and lay in bed trying to work out how long Mam had been dead. Would they still have had coffins then or was Mam lying there with dirt filling her nose and mouth? She must have let out a moan at some stage because Maisie appeared at her bed with a torch. Its beam was half obliterated by a circle of gummed brown paper, but there was enough light for Maggie to see her face and the halo of blonde hair looking for all the world like a Bible picture. There was a strange smell about Maisie's breath when she leaned forward, a smell which somehow made Maggie think of Dad and Friday nights. 'What's up?' Maisie said. And then again: 'What's up? Bad dream?' Her tone was so sympathetic that Maggie found herself explaining about the lack of coffins and the worms and her worries over Mam's nose and mouth.

Even in the half-light she could see Maisie's face harden. 'She's a bloody little liar, that Freda. 'Course they've got coffins and your ma would get a satin-lined one, I've seen them. Luscious they are. All padded and ribbons and everything. Now go to sleep and I'll see to Freda and her shit in the morning.' Oddly comforted, Maggie turned on her side and slept. She had a friend, someone who would deal with Freda's shit. She wasn't quite sure what that meant but she knew it was good.

Maisie's presence gave her comfort and kept Freda off her back, but only for the next few weeks. One day she wasn't there. Maggie was too scared to ask anyone where she was, but hung on every word uttered, hoping for news of Maisie's imminent return. It was Freda who enlightened her. 'She's in trouble. One of the blokes from the army camp.' The army camp was in a field in a road near to the school and sometimes soldiers whistled as the girls filed past.

'Did they whistle at her?' Maggie asked, hungry for more information. She couldn't understand why that made Freda laugh but Freda was at pains to explain. 'He did more than whistle. He poked her with his thing and now she has a baby growing inside her and they'll have to cut it out.'

It would be two more years before Miss Eccles would summon Maggie to the office and give her the facts of life, along with dire warnings of what happened to girls who put this grown-up knowledge to use, but even then she could never quite escape from Freda's lip-licking as she talked about Maisie and a baby growing inside her and it being cut out. If that was a fact of life it was too horrible to contemplate.

After her tenth birthday in 1941 Maggie was allowed to stay up an hour later and listen to the news on Miss Eccles' radio after tea on Sundays. There was a lot of talk about Russia and details of the Royal Air Force bombing Germany, but Miss Eccles' furrowed brow had signalled that things weren't going well. And then, one Sunday, the radio was alive with talk of a place called Pearl Harbor. It was being bombed and Maggie was confused as to why that was making Miss Eccles and the other staff members smile. 'It'll be alright now,' Miss Eccles explained. 'America's entered the war.' Within weeks the army camp had been taken over by GIs and words like 'bubblegum' and 'jive' had entered their language. The entry of the Yanks into the war did indeed make a difference. Everyone was more cheerful now, and sometimes you could catch a glimpse of GIs in town, always in twos and threes and wearing lovely uniforms that made British servicemen look somehow lumpy and not quite finished off. She had never seen her dad in uniform. He had gone off in his best suit and had never come back, even though he had promised. People always said things they didn't mean. Mrs Webster had promised to come back for them all and she hadn't kept her word. Unless she had come back and found them gone. If that had happened she might have looked for Dolly and Billy and taken them home with her. As Maggie got into bed, that thought caused a little knot of comfort to form inside, but only for a moment. Dolly had gone off with a man in a car and Billy with a vicar in the other direction. 'To good Christian homes,' someone had said. Perhaps Dolly had gone to a vicar too, which would be good and a lot safer than some places.

That December the government announced that unmarried women between twenty and thirty would be called up to join anti-aircraft batteries and free fit men from behind desks. A million and a half women would be affected, but mercifully Miss Eccles was too old and Miss Micklewhite too short-sighted for conscription. Boys and girls aged sixteen to eighteen must also register, and this caused Maggie some anxiety. What if the war lasted until her 16th birthday and she was prevented from getting a job and a wage? But all was not doom and gloom. Sometimes Miss Eccles let the older girls listen to *ITMA* with its cheerful catchphrases. 'Can I do you now, sir?' and 'I don't mind if I do' were on everyone's lips. Best of all, though, was listening to Vera Lynn. She sang lovely songs, but Maggie preferred 'We'll Meet Again'. Some of the girls cried when they heard it but she never did. To her it was an anthem of hope. And America's participation seemed to turn a tide. The RAF began to get their own back on Germany, and Churchill had the previously forbidden church bells rung to celebrate the victory at El Alamein in 1942.

When Maggie was thirteen in 1944, Miss Eccles took her to the pictures for a treat. 'It's Leslie Howard,' she told Maggie. 'Poor Leslie Howard. What a loss.' Seeing Maggie's incomprehension, she explained. Leslie Howard was just the most famous film star in the world and too handsome for words. 'Such pictures,' Miss Eccles said, raising her eyes to heaven. '*Pimpernel Smith* was the best.... or maybe *First of the Few*. And now the Germans have shot him down. They'll answer for that one day.' She gave one of her glares. The film they were going to see was *Intermezzo* with Ingrid Bergman. It was a joint treat and birthday present, and apparently a reward for being a good girl. 'You'll go far, Maggie, if you persevere. You haven't the looks of some girls but that can only be a blessing.' Maggie knew what that meant. There had been other girls who had vanished since Maisie, doubtless to have babies cut out of them, and it was obvious that it was the pretty ones who went. 'You have a lot going for you,' Miss Eccles continued. 'You're sensible and good with your hands, and your marks for domestic science are top-whole. I think we can get you a good place when you leave here, with a nice family, even titled. And if you prove yourself you could wind up a head cook, even a housekeeper with staff under you.'

In the cinema, Miss Eccles sobbing quietly beside her in the dark as Leslie spoke words of love to Ingrid, Maggie thought about leaving Northfield. She could go at fourteen, if she had a place. Some girls stayed on until they were old enough for war work, but if she had things going for her she could get out at fourteen. Not that she had been unhappy in the institution. Once she had got used to the fact that girls like Freda liked to frighten the life out of you, she had managed very well, even liked the routine of it all. But it had really been marking time until she could carry out her purpose: to find Dolly and Billy and make a family again. Dolly would be nearly nine now. Only five years to save her from a fate like Maisie's. If she, Maggie, got a good place and saved every penny of her wages... She wondered if she dare ask Miss Eccles how much she would earn, but another girl had asked that on departing for service and Miss Eccles had called her 'mercenary', which was obviously not a compliment. Besides, there were other ways of making money if you were good with your hands. She was learning smocking in needlework, liking the honeycomb pattern she could make with the coloured silks. And smocking on baby clothes was all the rage and earned fortunes, Miss Micklewhite said. If she put all her wages into cotton and silks and smocked in her time off, she could be rich in no time.

On the way home from the cinema, Miss Eccles hummed the music from the film and enthused about Leslie Howard. His only mistake had been to be in an American film called *Gone with the Wind* when he hadn't even played the lead, although he had acted Clark Gable, the leading man, off the screen. And going back to America had been the death of him. 'Keep away from Americans,

Maggie,' she warned, as they reached the gates of Northfield. 'Not that you'll have much trouble, but they're dangerous with their nylons and their tinned fruit. Bribery and corruption, Maggie, and silly girls fall for it. I know it's made a difference them coming into the war and we should be grateful. Well, I am in a way, but their morals...' At this she bit off her words and contented herself with a theatrical shudder, remembering her companion was only just thirteen, and put her key into the lock.

There were three more trips to the cinema before she left Northfield. Twice with Miss Eccles and once with Miss Micklewhite, who took Maggie's arm on the way home and bought her fish and chips. 'Don't tell Eccles,' Miss Micklewhite said, licking in a stray bit of batter. 'She's a good soul but a stickler for rules. Never had a life, you see. Men? She wouldn't know what to do with one. Not romantic like me. I can't wait for some man to come back and get me out of...' She remembered that Maggie was an inmate, not a staff member, and tempered her criticism of the institution they both inhabited. 'Well, you know what I mean.' Maggie wondered if she should mention Miss Eccles' undying love for Leslie Howard but decided against it. Everyone was entitled to their private life.

Things cheered up as 1944 proceeded. Instead of the radio listing defeats, it was mostly triumphs. Occasionally, though, Miss Eccles would get upset. News that prisoners of war were being tortured by the Japanese brought tearful indignation. According to Anthony Eden, 1,800 prisoners aboard a Japanese ship had been left to drown when it was torpedoed. 'Plain murder,' Miss

Eccles said, and Miss Micklewhite reminded her of the thousands dead building the railways with which the Japanese seemed obsessed. Mostly, though, it was a tale of success: in Burma, in Russia, in Italy and other far-flung places. Miss Micklewhite took to musing about the day the men would return from war and weddings would be an everyday occurrence. Obviously she thought one of them would be hers, causing Miss Eccles to sniff and opine that daydreaming was the cause of half the trouble in the world. When D-Day came and the Allied invasion of Europe began, Miss Eccles asked them to pray for the troops going ashore in the face of enemy gunfire. Obviously the end of the war was only a matter of time, she said, but Maggie had another goal in mind. In less than a year she would enter the world of work and, more importantly, the world of the wage earner. Then she could begin her quest.

The day after her 14th birthday, she left school. 'You've been a good pupil, Margaret,' the headmistress told her, and gave her a brand-new book called *Essays in Wisdom*. 'Read this when you come up against a problem. Although, from what I hear, you're a lucky girl.'

It was Miss Eccles who outlined the full extent of her luck. The authorities had obtained a place for her with a titled family, the De Vere Wentworths. 'Three houses, Margaret, and all of them grand. You'll start as a scullery maid, but there's no limit to how high you can go if you work hard. A housekeeper in one of these places won't have to lift a finger. They have their own staff. Yes, you may well look astonished. Staff having people to wait on them… But it happens. Well, it did before the war. You can't get good people now… but by the time you've moved up the war'll be over and things will be back to normal.'

Maggie packed her few possessions in a pressed cardboard case, brand-new and a gift from the authorities, making sure the *Milly-Molly-Mandy* book went in first, wrapped in the lisle petticoat she had worn when she came to Northfield. Mam had bought it in the market and then faggot-stitched the hem. Suddenly, Maggie realised she was smiling. That was where her good hands came from: her mother. She had been good at handiwork too. It was an amazing and very comforting thought.

Miss Eccles came with her to the station and saw her into a carriage. It was early morning but the train was still crowded. 'Don't talk to anyone till you're met at the other end, particularly not to soldiers,' Miss Eccles said. There were soldiers all over the place and women from the ATS too, all laughing and joking, which was fair enough considering the war was almost over. 'It'll be peace soon,' Maggie thought, as she settled into her seat. She waved to Miss Eccles, who looked oddly sad considering this was the start of everything. After the train pulled out of the station, Maggie fixed her eyes on the suitcase above her on the opposite rack and tried to quell the fears that fizzed around inside and sometimes threatened to obscure her mounting excitement.

Chapter Ten

MISS ECCLES HAD TOLD HER she would be met at Elmfield station, but not exactly where Elmfield station was. There was only one thing for it: each time the train slowed down she took down her case and got ready to dismount.

The carriage was crowded and everyone watched this pantomime for a while, until at last a man spoke. 'Are you getting ready to jump, love, or are you watching out for somewhere?' There was a general titter and Maggie felt her cheeks redden. 'I'm getting off at Elmfield.' The man smiled encouragement. 'Well, sit down, lass. It's fifty miles or more yet.'

Her advisor got off before her but briefed her carefully: 'It's not the next one, it's the one after that.' She felt comforted by his solicitude and began to feel slightly more optimistic. She had new clothes and shoes on. 'To make a good impression,' Miss Eccles had said, and there were more in her case.

She wouldn't need to buy anything for herself and could save every penny. She had not dared to ask about wages but she would surely get something above board. Even ten shillings would mount up in time. She spent the last half-hour making calculations. At a pound a week she would have £14 by Christmas. £40 by the end of 1946 and £64 by 1947. With £64 you could achieve anything.

If she had expected something grand at the station, she was not disappointed. The car that waited was huge and black, with running boards so high she had to strain to reach them. But the man driving it was dressed in work-soiled clothes and had dirt-rimmed fingernails. 'Name of Brewis?' he said, looking at her and reaching for her bag. 'Up you get.' He hefted her bag into the back seat and held open the front passenger door. 'You came from the orphanage,' he said, as the car groaned into action. It was a statement rather than a question. She had never thought of Northfield as an orphanage. It was an institution. But she was an orphan, so he must be right.

'Thought so,' he said gloomily. On the way to the house he moaned about the war and what it had done to life at Wentworth Hall. 'It's ruined women. Running around in headscarves, going with Yanks, earning more than their dads; lost sight of themselves, that's what it is. Four undermaids we had, good village girls. Went upstairs eventually and then became housekeepers if they didn't marry. Now we have married women from the village, an hour here and an hour there, and some of them's even gone to munitions. How can his lordship compete with those wages? It's been hard on me and the wife. Dogsbodies, jacks of all trades. "Couldn't manage without you, William," his lordship said last week. Too right he couldn't. Not that I wouldn't do it for him. Thorough gentleman. You keep your nose clean and you won't go far wrong at the Hall... Unless you go mad like the rest of them and go off to factory work.' Maggie would have liked to have asked how much factory work paid, but didn't dare. 'When in doubt, say nowt' was a good maxim. So she folded her hands in her lap and gazed out as field after field rolled by.

Wentworth Hall was so big that she had to turn her head from one side to the other to take it all in. The car rolled up a long drive and past a colonnaded front door and came to a halt at the back of the house. A woman, who Maggie thought must be 'Mrs William', was waiting there. She wore a grey dress that looked a bit like a prison warden's but her face was kind. She held out a hand. 'Welcome, Margaret. Am I glad to see you!' There was tea and angel cakes waiting in the kitchen. 'Only mock-cream,' Mrs William – who, as it turned out, was actually called Mrs Jeyes – apologised. 'We do quite well here compared with city folk but you can't get everything all the time.' After she had drunk her tea, Mrs Jeyes ushered Maggie out of the kitchen and up three flights of stairs. 'This is your room,' she said. 'Get yourself settled and then come down. Her ladyship'll see you before dinner.'

The room had a tall window with flowery curtains and a bed with a patchwork quilt. Maggie sat down on the bed and looked around her. A room of her own. She had never thought about where she would live, but never in her wildest dreams had she imagined a whole room to herself. There was a dressing table with a little three-sided mirror on it. She hung her new clothes in the wardrobe and then checked her appearance in the mirror. She was bright-eyed and had roses in her cheeks. All in all she didn't look too bad. There was a jug and basin on a side-table but no water. She wished she could wash her hands, grubby from the train, and she needed a wee. She peered out of the door, hoping to see a door marked 'WC' like at Northfield, but there was nothing. She moved onto the landing. There were five doors besides her own. She turned the handle of the first one but it was a cupboard as big as a room, with wooden shelves stacked with linen. Enough for a hospital. She let out a low whistle and closed the door. It took two more peeps before she found a bathroom. It was an enormous relief to empty her bladder. She washed her hands under a tap that groaned and shuddered when she turned it on, but it gave out plenty of warm water. Then she made her way downstairs and prepared to meet her employer.

Mrs Jeyes took her up one flight to a big room full of chairs and little tables filled with photo frames and pieces of china. 'You'll be responsible for this room, Margaret. Be careful with the china. It's priceless. You don't need to curtsey to madam but be respectful.' Maggie nodded and wondered what a ladyship would look like. The reality was different to anything she had imagined. Lady Wentworth was tall and thin, with hair that escaped in wisps from its kerby grips, and spectacles that hung from a chain around her neck. Mrs Jeyes stood respectfully in the background, as her ladyship motioned Maggie to a chair. 'Do sit down.' Her appearance may have been a disappointment but the voice was thrilling. Better than anything Maggie had heard on the wireless. She listened in a dream as Lady Wentworth outlined her future.

'You'll earn eighteen shillings a week with an increment each birthday. You'll have one day off a week, more if Mrs Jeyes can spare you, and you'll have two weeks' holiday. All your needs will be catered for and we'll try to make your time with us happy. You lost your parents in the war, I believe.' Maggie nodded. 'I'm so sorry.' The eyes behind the spectacles were kind. 'And do give me a smile before you go... That's better. You have had tea, I hope.' At this she looked at Mrs Jeyes and they both nodded. 'Well, off you go. And do feel free to tell Mrs Jeyes – or indeed myself – if anything bothers you. We're a little disorganised at the moment, thanks to Herr Hitler, but we'll cope better with your help. I've had such good reports of you.'

Maggie floated back to the kitchen in a cloud of euphoria. 'All needs catered for and eighteen shillings a week.' She wished she knew what increments were and hoped they didn't mean less money, but when a supper of sausage and fried potatoes was put in front of her she thought she had died and gone to Heaven.

The Jeyeses did not eat with her. Instead they hurried back and forth, carrying big dishes containing very little food to and from the dining room. Tomorrow she would have to help with this but tonight she was excused. She offered to help with the washing up but there was a rosy-cheeked woman hanging her hat and coat behind the door who had come in specifically for that task. 'Get to bed,' Mrs Jeyes said. 'It's a six-thirty start.'

She luxuriated in the space of her own room, putting out the light to look out on the quiet countryside with hardly a light visible. She was going to be very, very happy here. Her euphoria lasted until she climbed into the cold bed and realised, as the silence deepened, that for the first time in her life, she was sleeping alone.

Over the next few weeks she gave more than value for her eighteen shillings. In the mornings she cleaned out the grates in the sitting room, morning room and master bedroom. 'You're lucky,' Mrs Jeyes told her. 'When I started here there were 17 grates. They can't get the coal now, more's the pity.' As she humped coal up the stairs, Maggie occasionally gave thanks for a war that had made her workload manageable. And then the Wentworth children, a boy and a girl, came home on leave and there were five grates in action. Not that the young people always lit their fires or were much in the house. Master Michael wore Air Force uniform and Miss Vanessa was in khaki, although not the rough khaki of the ATS. 'I'm a Fany,' she told Maggie, laughing when Maggie's eyes widened at a word she knew to be rude. 'First Aid Nursing Yeomanry, to give us our proper name. We're a back-up corps, drivers and coders mostly. I'm a driver to a general, Margaret. Dodging doodlebugs in London. What do you think of that?' Maggie had heard about doodlebugs, pilot-less planes that dropped out of the sky and blew you up. Thereafter she looked at Miss Vanessa with a new respect.

On the last day of their leave there was a shooting party. 'There'll be no game tonight,' Mr Jeyes said. 'Wrong season, not that it matters. In the old days it would be hung for a decent interval. Now they'll eat it while it's still warm. Bloody war.' Maggie wasn't sure what was meant by 'game' or 'wrong season', but she peeled vegetables till her fingers were sore, so that there was soup for the moors and vegetables to pad out the dinner. 'Rabbit pie,' Mrs Jeyes said. 'Rabbit pie. What have we come down to?' All morning cars rolled up and people were ushered in, some to the rooms they would occupy that night, others just there for the shoot. They all wore tweed, men and women alike, and cravats at their necks, and they talked ninety to the dozen. That was what came with being rich, Maggie thought. Confidence in your voice and plenty to say for yourself. She might have that one day, with three pounds sixteen in the back of her drawer. To Maggie, as she ran backwards and forwards to the dinner table that night, the meal looked a feast and the wine certainly flowed. 'We had a good cellar in '39,' Jeyes told her. 'Half-empty now but it'll see us to victory, I dare say.' Before Maggie went to bed, feet and ankles aching and eyes drooping, he gave her some wine in a glass. 'Careful, William,' Mrs Jeyes said, but she didn't stop him. The remains of one of the rabbit pies was warm in Maggie's stomach and the wine, although unpleasant, made her feel somehow clever and grown up. It also made her hiccup. 'Get up to bed,' Mrs

Jeyes said, but it was more of a kindness than a command, and gave Maggie a glow that was warmer than pie and wine combined.

The following day newspapers contained pictures taken in a concentration camp called Buchenwald. '20,000 they say,' Mrs Jeyes said, the paper trembling in her hands. '20,000 close to death, women and children.' Suddenly she was crying and Mr Jeyes was saying, 'Come on, there now', and putting clumsy arms round her. 'He didn't die for nothing, Bill. I can see that now,' Mrs Jeyes said, and clutched at the neck of her grey dress.

It was Lady Wentworth, brought to the kitchen by Maggie at Mr Jeyes' behest, who sorted it all out, comforting Mrs Jeyes with tea laced with brandy and winking at Maggie to show that nothing should be said. When Mr Jeyes had taken his wife off to their quarters, Lady Wentworth looked around the kitchen. 'Well, we shall just have to fall-to over breakfast, Margaret. Thank heaven Mrs Hey will be in when she's seen the children to school.'

As they prepared toast and marmalade and tea, Lady Wentworth explained. 'Their boy was lost at El Alamein. They took it hard, losing an only child, but naturally it's worse for a mother. She felt it was a waste, you see. She was all for appeasement.' Maggie nodded because she felt it was expected, but Lady Wentworth continued. 'Appeasement was something some people believed in. Don't fight Herr Hitler, try to placate him. It would never have worked, but it was a temptation to people with children of military age. Now they see what Nazism means, they can see more clearly.'

His Lordship was deep in the papers when breakfast reached him. He greeted Maggie with a grunted 'Good morning' and looked questioningly at his wife. 'Mrs Jeyes is upset by the photographs in the newspapers,' Lady Wentworth said. 'It's all in hand, darling. Eat your toast.'

'Toast!' His tone was scornful. 'Bloody Hun.'

Two weeks later, Germany surrendered. The news came at teatime, flowing out of the kitchen radio and the radiogram in the sitting room upstairs. 'This calls for champagne, I think,' Lady Wentworth said. They gathered in the living room, Maggie and the Jeyeses, the two women up from the village and the De Vere Wentworths. 'Victory!' His Lordship said, when the fizzing liquid had been poured and everyone had a glass. The bubbles went straight up Maggie's nose. She spluttered but drank again when Mr Jeyes said 'Churchill'. By night time there was a bonfire in the paddock and the whole village had assembled. There was beer and cider and the village grocer made cheese sandwiches for lucky first-comers. The party from the big house drank wine, although Mrs Jeyes limited Maggie to a sip or two. 'You look quite giddy,' she said, and tucked a stray hair behind Maggie's ear in a kindly way. Suddenly Maggie remembered Mam doing the same thing. 'There's a bonny girl. Mammy's little treasure.' Briefly she thought of Freda and the coffin shortage, but that was shit after all and tonight was about victory.

Someone let off a firework and it spiralled up into the sky. One of the boys from the village had sidled up to Maggie and now reached for her hand. Someone started singing 'There'll Always Be An England' and it seemed churlish to snatch her hand away, but when he tried to plant a kiss on her cheek she pushed him away. He would be wanting to do things to her next, and she would be in trouble like Maisie. She couldn't let that happen, not when she had plans.

Chapter Eleven

CELEBRATION OF THE VICTORY IN Europe lasted for days. 'We've still got Japan to deal with,' Mr Jeyes warned, but no one listened. 'Pay no attention,' Mrs Jeyes would say when he prophesised that every last Japanese would die fighting. 'Leave it to Churchill.' To Mrs Jeyes, Winston Churchill was God. When the Labour/Conservative coalition, which had run the country during the war, resigned, she was confident that Churchill would be returned as Prime Minister. 'We owe him everything,' she said firmly. 'They'll need to weigh his votes, not count them.' Churchill's defeat in a land-slide victory for Labour saw her take to her chair by the kitchen range. 'The ingratitude,' she said, over and over. 'The damned ingratitude.' Not even a drop of the cooking brandy could console her. She had to be revived by a visit from her Ladyship who agreed it was disgrace-ful, but pointed out that there would be other chances. 'They won't find it so easy to govern in peacetime, Mrs

J. Not everyone pulls together then.' Mr Jeyes doubted the ability of a Labour administration to deal with the Japanese. 'They'll be over here before long,' he prophesised. 'Yellow peril? We'll see them marching up that drive, you mark my words.'

To Maggie, grappling with Mrs Jeyes' duties as well as her own, the Japanese marching up the drive was less of a threat than His Lordship finding an uncleared grate or an absence of hot water. It was a relief when atomic explosions at Hiroshima and Nagasaki brought Japan to its knees and the war was well and truly over. Mrs Jeyes took back the reins and staff began to trickle back from the factories and work on the land.

In October 1945, Maggie received a promotion to upstairs maid, which meant she was released from kitchen duties and would receive an extra one shilling and sixpence a week. 'They'll be opening up the London house now,' Mrs Jeyes said. 'You'll likely go there. Miss Vanessa and Master Michael will want to be there when they're demobbed. They'll come here most weekends but it'll be all dancing and dining. Cheated, they've been. Miss Vanessa's never even come out.' 'Coming out', Maggie learnt, meant being presented to the King and Queen and was reserved for the crème de la crème. 'Quality folk,' Mrs Jeyes explained, when the French phrase failed to register with her new upstairs maid. 'Grand times we used to have up London. Still, it'll take time to sort it all out, what with half of London flattened and worse shortages than in 1940.' There it was again, that word 'flattened'. It brought back painful memories but this time Maggie had too much to do to dwell on it.

Plans were underway to open the London house in early December. 'It will be so nice to get to the shops,' Lady Wentworth said when she announced it. Maggie was to go there with Mrs Jeyes. New staff would be recruited on the spot, and when everything was running smoothly, Mrs Jeyes would return to Wentworth for Christmas.

Almost as soon as they arrived, there would be a party – a small affair. 'Not a proper meal, a buffet,' Mrs Jeyes said gloomily. 'They'll have to wait till I find a cook for that. Though how they'll manage a buffet on rations, I don't know.' Maggie felt excited at the prospect of a party and even more excited at the prospect of travelling to London. Four hours in a train and a taxi at the other end. She knew she was an object of envy to the two recently recruited maids – both scullery – and tried very hard not to be uppish, which wouldn't have been fair, considering she was younger than them and only their senior because they had been engaged on war work. Mrs Jeyes considered them 'no better than they should be' because they both smoked and talked incessantly about men they had met the night before. Maggie wasn't too sure what the phrase meant but could easily see that whatever it was, it wasn't good.

The day before she and Mrs Jeyes were to take the train, disaster struck. 'It's her innards,' Mr Jeyes said, filling a hot water bottle for his prostrate wife. 'Do you think you can manage the journey alone?' Lady Wentworth inquired anxiously. 'If there was anyone else to go with you...' She looked anxiously at her husband but he just flexed his moustache once or twice and didn't speak. 'I can manage,' Maggie said.

In truth, she was relishing the prospect of a train ride and getting to grips with a mothballed house. She had already discussed it with Mrs Jeyes. Dustsheets off, polishing, sweeping. Getting out dishes for the caterers. Seeing to the grates, laying out linen and towels... It was a challenge and she was up to it. 'Miss Vanessa will be there and there's a char. And, of course, there's Charlie,' she had said. Charlie was the former butler and had guarded the London house since its closure. 'Keep your wits about you and do the best you can. Thank God it's not a big do. You can manage, Maggie. You're a good girl.'

Lady Wentworth was less sure. 'Are you sure you'll be alright? Vanessa will be there when you arrive and I'll come with Mrs Jeyes. Don't speak to anyone on the train unless it's the guard, and if you get off at the wrong station ask a policeman. I wish I could feel more certain about this... Still, you're a sensible girl and you should be there by nightfall.'

So it was that Maggie climbed into the middle carriage – if there was a crash it would be safer there – of the 12.15 to King's Cross and put her case and a basket of produce from the Home Farm on the opposite rack. She had her ration book too, the first time it had been in her possession, and for a while she sat and examined the coupons without being able to make any sense of them. Mrs Jeyes had given her a list of tradespeople who could be trusted, but she, Mrs Jeyes, would attend to all that when she finally made it to Eaton Square. 'Get this week over, there's a good girl, and then it'll fall into place. You're young but you've got a good head on your shoulders and Charlie'll keep you right. His bark's worse than his bite. You mind on about that.' She had sighed then and looked at Maggie. 'What a situation. Wet behind the ears and carrying it all on her shoulders. By gum, Hitler's got a lot to answer for.'

But Hitler was dead, his body burned, and she, Maggie, was alive with a valid train ticket and ten and six in her purse for a taxi. Things were on the up and up. She pondered those words as the train chugged into Doncaster. 'Up and up.' That's what Mam had said whenever Dad got a new job in. 'The up and up.' For a while, as the train filled up and people were standing in the corridors outside, she let herself remember what life had been like before the war. Would Dolly remember? Would Billy? Or was she the keeper of the family history? At Newark her eyelids drooped and she slept, to dream of days at Southend, Dad with his trousers rolled up to the knee and Mam picking sand out of the sandwiches and making them dry between their toes.

At Peterborough they were held in the station for what felt like hours, but it was actually thirty minutes. It was getting dark, and the mood in the train darkened with the skies. There were lots of soldiers aboard, going into London, and some of them seemed drunk, whether with beer or peacetime Maggie couldn't be sure. 'Demob happy' the woman across the way said. Maggie was not sure what that meant and dared not ask. Besides, she was becoming uncomfortably aware that she needed to pass water. Miss Eccles had explained train lavatories to her before she left Northfield and Mrs Jeyes had repeated the advice. But a solid wall of human flesh stood between her and the WC, wherever it was located. She wondered if she could jump out and find relief in Peterborough station, but what if the train started up without her and, anyway, she would never get her seat back if she vacated it. She was deliberating what to do when the train coughed and spluttered and then, falteringly, began to move. For a while they went along, the lights of Peterborough falling behind and black countryside enveloping them. Lights in the carriage flickered and then went out as the train shuddered slightly and came to a halt. At that moment Maggie felt a sudden wetness between her legs. If she didn't get up now she would wet herself. The horror of that prospect got her to her feet and out into the corridor in a second. She was in a forest of bodies, grumbling, sweating bodies, most of them unwilling to give way. Was the lavatory left or right? She allowed herself to be pushed on, sometimes by hands that dug into her, as though to pay her back for her cheek in wanting to pass. And then suddenly the bodies were khaki-clad. She could tell this from the rough feel of their clothes, and in the dim moonlight that penetrated the corridor she could see male faces looming about her. 'Let the lass pass,' one of them said, but another was less kind. 'A lass? What's one of them? I haven't had a lass for a long time. Give us a feel, love.' And the hands that clutched at her were not gentle. She heard someone say

'Wait on… You can't…' but that voice was swallowed up in other voices which clamoured for action. Someone was pulling at her coat, her blouse, she felt buttons rip and winced at the thought of how she would explain that to Mrs Jeyes.

Other hands were bearing her down and pulling at her drawers now and she could smell beer in the mouth that bore down on hers. Friday night. Dad had smelled like that on Friday nights. But someone was forcing her legs apart and something warm and hard was prodding at her. She heard someone cry out. Was it her? And then pain came, searing at first and then dull as the body above her rose and fell and went on pounding. She thought of Freda, eyes bright behind spectacles. 'She had to have a baby cut out of her.' And Mrs Eccles in the office. 'A husband passes a seed, Margaret. And the seed grows into a baby.' Except that this heaving thing above her was not her husband. 'I can't see his face,' she thought, and gave up struggling as the train started to move again. Perhaps it was all a dream. But dreams did not go on and on like this one did. At last there was a fresh gust of beer-laden breath as the man groaned, and then he was rolling off her and she heard herself whimpering as the train slowed down and stopped. There was a sudden shaft of cold air. Someone had opened a door and there was a stampede that left her alone in the corridor with the door swinging open and the night air like ice.

She lay for a while, not moving. There was wetness around and she realised her bladder had emptied. At last she struggled onto her elbows and leaned against the wall of the corridor. Any moment the lights might come on and she would be revealed there in her shame. She climbed to her feet at last. There was a door behind her and she bent the handle down. Porcelain gleamed in the darkness. She had been within reach of the lavatory all the time. For no reason she could understand she began to laugh. Then she sat down on the lavatory seat and closed the door. She stayed there for a long time, occasionally tugging at her clothes and adjusting them here and there. By the time the lights came on again and the train got under way, she had sluiced her face at the sink. In the mirror she looked ghastly, but composed enough to make her way back to the crowded carriage. Her legs felt wobbly under her and, as she had feared, her seat had been taken. Nothing for it but to lean against the wall in the corridor until the train came at last into Stevenage and a seat in the carriage which held her precious case became vacant.

Chapter Twelve

AFTERWARDS SHE COULD SCARCELY REMEMBER how she arrived at Eaton Square. She thought that perhaps she had been like an actress playing a part, stepping into the taxi, tendering the fare, thanking Mr Charles for admitting her and relieving her of her case. He had looked at her a little strangely but she had looked him straight in the eye and smiled. Like Ingrid Bergman. He made her tea in the great, silent kitchen, not as big as the basement at Wentworth but big enough for a dance troupe. She drank the tea he poured into a china cup, loving the thinness of the rim between her lips, lips which somehow seemed to have a life of their own and moved in funny ways, even when she wanted them to remain composed. Her hands were shaking, so she clasped them round the cup, loving the warmth that seeped through to her cold fingers. It would be alright in a moment. He gave her bread and cheese too, which made her want to gag, but she forced it down anyway.

Anything to hasten the moment when she could get away and take off the clothes which by now must reek of urine and fear. What if his nose wrinkled in distaste at the smell? Worse still, what if he asked her what was wrong? But Mr Charles talked on and never once wrinkled his nose. He asked about life at Wentworth and whether or not it had been austere in the war years compared with life in London. She answered as best she could, not from her own brief experience but from the tales of the Jeyeses, so often told over the kitchen table. Halfway through, a telephone shrilled somewhere and he lumbered off to answer. 'That was Betty Jeyes,' he said when he returned. 'I told her you'd got here alright. Three times she's rung. She's got gallstones apparently. Doctor told her today. We won't see her this side of Christmas.'

At last he led her up two flights to a room half the size of her room at Wentworth, but with a window that gave onto the rooftops of London. There was a WC on the landing and water on the washstand. He bade her good-night and lumbered off, humming softly under his breath.

For some reason Maggie switched off the light. There was enough light from the window for what she needed to do. She shed her clothes piece by piece until it came to her drawers. She had made them in needlework and Miss Micklewhite had held them up to the class and remarked on the excellence of her French seams. They were still intact but she could smell them at arms length and, even by moonlight, she could see the bloodstain. Perhaps she was still bleeding. Perhaps she would bleed to death as

Freda had said girls sometimes did, and then she need never think of tonight again.

When she had disposed of the soiled clothes in the brown paper bag which had held her sandwiches, she washed head to foot in cold water and then padded to the lavatory, the lino cold against her bare feet. It hurt to pass water and she sat shivering on the pedestal, trying to let it out drop by drop to ease the pain. After a while it was over and she could go back and climb into the narrow bed. She felt stiff from head to foot, but the most surprising thing of all was that she had not cried. She tried to make a tear come then but there was nothing. Perhaps some things were just too bad for tears. At first the bed was cold and unwelcoming and she was seized with terror that she would lie awake all night and be forced to think about what had happened on the train. Gradually, though, the bed warmed and her eyes, burning though they were, closed and let her sleep.

In the morning she got up, washed and dressed and began her chores. That was the best thing to do in a crisis, Miss Eccles had always said. Get on with your work. Everything in the house was sheeted and the sheets, when removed, revealed a degree of splendour that put Wentworth to shame. The chairs and sofas were brocade, a lovely silky stuff that felt bumpy under your fingers. And there were pictures and silver everywhere you looked. Just like Versailles, she thought, remembering Marie Antoinette and history lessons. Not that Lady De Vere Wentworth resembled the sad and beautiful queen, but the setting was surely as magnificent. When everything looked shipshape, they got out the silverware and glasses and sat either side of the kitchen table to polish. She was glad of the chance to sit down because sometimes her legs threatened to fold. The rest of her body felt tense, as though it was made of metal, and she had to keep flexing and unflexing her hands because they felt like they had seized up.

Miss Vanessa arrived the next day, rushing upstairs to cast off her uniform and coming downstairs looking for all the world like a film star.

'Brave you,' she said admiringly, when Mr Charles told her Maggie had come down on her own. 'Trains are terrible now. There was discipline in wartime. Now we're all demob happy.' There it was again, that phrase. 'Demobilisation,' Vanessa explained, seeing Maggie's puzzled face. 'We're all coming home.' For the first time Maggie thought about her attacker. He had been young but not a boy. The stubble that had ground into her face had been hard. Was he going back to a family, children, a wife? She couldn't imagine that. If he had been a man who had loved he could never have done... Her mind refused to finish the thought. Instead she polished a fork so fiercely that Mr Charles, laughing, removed it from her hand with a 'Steady on, you'll wear it away'.

The party was a great success. They had extra hands to help, London women with children at home and past experience of waiting on. She was happy to let them order her here and there, glad that the night was a great success and the Wentworths were happy. 'Well done, Maggie,' Lady Wentworth said when the last guests had retrieved wraps and overcoats and had gone out into the night. 'Not as good as our pre-war efforts but a triumph nevertheless. Off to bed, you look like a little ghost. I shall have Mrs Jeyes after me if we wear you out.' That night, for the first time in a long time, she slept a dreamless sleep – but in the morning she woke nauseous, regretting the several titbits she had relished from the party food the night before.

The sickness continued over the next two weeks, sometimes persisting well into the morning. She tried not eating breakfast, but that made it worse, and when she tried to eat, the sight of the food revolted her. Her monthlies had stopped too. She knew what that meant, thanks to Freda, but Freda had also said your breasts and belly swelled up like balloons – and as yet this had not happened. She couldn't be having a baby. A baby could never come out of an event like that night on the train, when she had twisted and turned and pulled away all the time. Or had she? She tried to relive it in her mind. Had there been time for a seed to be planted? She kept on thinking it couldn't have been possible until the day when her uniform dress could hardly button up over her breasts. She had dark roses around her nipples, which were more erect than they had ever been before.

She was contemplating where she could turn to, if eventually she ran away, when Miss Vanessa cornered her. 'Maggie, you're looking peaky and Charles says you don't eat enough to keep a bird alive. Are you okay?' She was about to lie and smile her way out of it, when the tears came and then the words tumbling out, in spite of how hard she tried to stop them.

'My God,' Vanessa said, when she was done. 'The utter bloody pig. But you mustn't cry, Maggie. It's not your fault. And Ma will look after you. And I will, and Michael...' Even through her tears, Maggie thought that Master Michael had never noticed her existence so was unlikely to be distraught that she had fallen wrong.

'I blame myself,' Lady Wentworth said when she arrived, summoned by her daughter's urgent phone call. 'It was so very wrong to send you off alone. It would never have happened before the war. We should have got one of the Home Farm men to go with you... or kept you safe at Wentworth. But girls seem so capable nowadays. All for a party. I will never forgive myself.' Suddenly Maggie felt herself clasped to her ladyship's bosom, the edge of her dangling spectacles biting into Maggie's cheek. 'But you're not to worry. We'll take care of you and the baby will go to a good home. You poor girl.'

Mrs Jeyes arrived three days later. 'I know, Margaret, and I blame myself. But it's all arranged. It would be different if you had a family to go back to, but in the circumstances it's best you go back to Wentworth for a few weeks and then you're going to St Clare's. You'll like it there. The nuns are kind.'

Nuns! Maggie had always been afraid of nuns, looking like crows as they did in their black habits. The nuns of St Clare, however, wore white and seemed to glide on castors. They managed to make her feel a sinful creature while telling her all the while that she was a child of God and loved beyond measure. But the food was wholesome and the bed clean and the chores they gave her hardly back breaking. All in all, Maggie decided, it could have been worse as wages of sin, for that was what she was earning now. The unfair thing was that the sins had been someone else's and she was paying for them.

The other girls were mostly country girls. At home they had boys who loved them and hopes of marriage. But the nuns disapproved of a girl taking her baby home. Even the baby-faced Sister Dymphna, whose dimples could have held cream, would sigh and say a baby needed a clean start, as though to stay with a mother who had known carnality was a disease. At night there would be muffled sobs from one bed or another, but mercifully there were no Fredas with frightening tales of what was to come. One or other of the girls would drag herself out of bed and go to give comfort, although climbing into someone else's bed was a cardinal sin. Quite why, Maggie couldn't make out, but the grim expressions on the faces of whichever nun found two in a bed left nothing to doubt. Some of the girls believed Sister Dymphna and Sister Mary Joseph were at it. 'At it?' Maggie asked, but all anyone would say was 'You know', and when she persisted, Elvira, one hand on her swollen belly and the other on her hip, told the entire company that Maggie Brewis was green as grass and her bairn an immaculate conception. 'She never got it the proper way,' Elvira said and everyone laughed. Maggie, who was inclined to agree with them, said nothing.

When a girl's time came, she disappeared. There were

tales of a soundproof room so that the screams of labour did not disturb the whole house. But when each girl came back, she was strangely silent and never brought a baby with her. Some would mutter 'a girl' or 'a boy' but on the whole they were silent, and a few days later they were gone. Sometimes, if a girl had made a particular friend, there would be a tearful farewell, but for the most part they went silently, as though glad to escape. Visitors were few and far between. 'They don't like people nosing around,' Maggie was told. But Lady Wentworth was an unstoppable force. She arrived with a flustered sister in tow, carrying fruit from the greenhouse and a jar of calf's-foot jelly 'to build her up'.

'We're looking forward to you coming back to Wentworth,' she told Maggie. 'Then we can put this whole unhappy episode behind us. You'll find life much easier at Wentworth. Some of the old staff have returned and there are new girls. Miss Vanessa is to be engaged soon and there's lots to get ready.' Maggie smiled and nodded, wondering all the while if it would do any good to ask if she could bring the baby back with her. But the words never came.

Two weeks later Maggie went into labour. The pains were nothing at first, little stirrings of discomfort. The other girls had warned her not to say anything until she could bear it no longer. 'It's better to stay here as long as you can,' they would say, and sometimes roll an eye towards the door that led to the other wing.

But at last the pain forced its way past her teeth in a wail of anguish and she was whisked away. 'It'll soon be over,' Sister Dymphna said. When the pain grew worse she was given a damp facecloth – not to wipe her face, which streamed with sweat, but to bite on. For twelve hours she laboured, alternating silence with crying for a dead mother, and then, to exhortations from the aproned sisters, she heaved her son into the world.

He was beautiful. A little old man with a wise expression and eyes that seemed not to look at her at all, while at the same time seeing into her soul. 'You can hold him for a moment,' Dymphna said, and for once her face was sad. 'There, there,' she said when another sister whisked the baby away.

They gave her pills 'to take away the milk' and had her out of bed in no time. She was allowed to see the baby once a day. 'It's best not to keep him by you,' Sister Mary Joseph told her. 'Otherwise it's hard to let go. And yours is a lucky baby. A lovely home. He'll have a sister and he'll be very, very happy and grow into a great man. Give thanks for that, Margaret. God has made good come out of evil.'

Maggie tried hard to see the good, but when she held the baby it felt right. She wanted to unbutton her blouse and put him to her breast. She had seen her mother do that with Billy and she had hummed while she did it. But the sisters were adamant. No breast-feeding. 'It couldn't be continued, you see, when he goes to his new mother. Best to get him used to the bottle from the start.' Maggie began to wonder if she could steal the baby away; she was its mother after all. But where would she go? She could survive in a hedge, under a tree, but the baby deserved better.

When they told her it was the last day she could see him, she did not cry. Instead, she asked if she could be alone with him – 'Just for a little while.' The sisters conferred wordlessly and then glided away. 'But only for a few moments,' Mary Joseph warned.

A few moments would be enough. When they were alone, she kissed his wrinkled forehead and tucked him more closely into the crook of her arm. Then she took out the *Milly-Molly-Mandy* book from inside her cardigan and began to read. She knew he could hear because occasionally his face creased with pleasure and his eyes looked unwaveringly up at her. She read him her favourite page, then she put him back in the crib. 'Are you ready, Margaret?'

'Yes, Sister. I'm ready.' As she walked away, she told herself that somewhere there was a mother waiting to read to him from the book she had tucked inside his blanket. It was the only gift she could give him.

Chapter Thirteen

SLOWLY BUT SURELY, MAGGIE'S LIFE returned to something resembling normal. Around her, Britain was still celebrating peace but wondering why so much wartime austerity remained. Food was still short, even shorter than ever, but with the need to be patriotic gone, the black market flourished outrageously. 'Disgraceful,' everyone said, but went on buying from it just the same.

Miss Vanessa came back to Wentworth in January. Her wedding would take place in May and there were, as her Ladyship had said, things to be done. 'Mrs Jeyes tells me you're good with your hands, Margaret. Miss Vanessa's trousseau is coming from Belgium, but if you could add a little embellishment to one or two things it would be wonderful. One can't have too much lingerie when one marries.'

So Margaret spent days in the sewing room, featherstitching and faggoting till the tips of her fingers stung. She knew it was a pretext to keep her from heavy work while she got over childbirth, and she was grateful for the gesture, but sewing gave her too much time to think. She longed to drag buckets of coal upstairs and riddle grates or toil over the tub with steam, shutting out everything except a desire to wring out the last garment. That way she might just escape from her memories. But she was no longer a scullery maid and with peacetime the old hierarchy had returned. She was a parlour maid and must behave as such.

Coal was a sore point in the household. 'They've nationalised the mines,' Mrs Jeyes told her. 'Or stolen them, more like. His Lordship's lost a fortune and all the fault of that Attlee.' In February snow fell day after day. 'Buckingham Palace is candlelit,' Miss Vanessa reported excitedly on her return from a trip to London. 'There are no lifts in the shops and I was lucky to get on a train.' By the middle of the month fuel supplies had petered out. 'Bloody socialists,' His Lordship would repeat, as hardship piled on hardship. Even fish dried up as fleets could not put to sea.

'What I'm expected to do with that between four, I do not know,' Mrs Jeyes said, contemplating a piece of beef. To Maggie's eye it looked gargantuan. They only had gravy in the kitchen most days, but it was delicious, glistening as it ran over their vegetables and congealing slightly on the edge of the plate.

The snow went and spring came and the fever of wedding preparations took over. There were more staff now; men and women come home from the war. 'Thoroughly unsettled,' Mr Jeyes decreed. The new people answered back occasionally and had political arguments at the meal-table.

Herries, an under-butler, was getting a divorce, which was apparently a disgraceful thing. 'Not that it's his fault,' Mrs Jeyes said. 'Came back to find she'd been no better than she should be. 50,000 divorces a year, it said in the *Daily Mail*. What things are coming to, I don't know.' But Herries caught Maggie in the pantry one night and seized her left breast between mean fingers. 'Come on now,' he said, when she tried to twist away. 'You're no shrinking violet, you with a bairn an' all. You know what it's for.' She was shutting down her mind when she heard Mrs Jeyes, angrier than she had ever heard her before.

'Get out, you mongrel. Get off out of it before I maim you.' He went muttering an explanation of meaning no harm. Margaret never saw him again, and although she would have liked to have known how he knew about her secret, she dared not ask.

The De Vere Wentworth-Huntley wedding took place at St Margaret's, Westminster. The entire staff went up for the big day. It was Margaret's first trip in a charabanc, and when they got to Eaton Square there was champagne all round and a place on the landing to see the bride depart. She looked strangely vulnerable as Mrs Jeyes and her mother fussed around her. She had always seemed so capable. Now she looked almost afraid. Perhaps she was thinking of the night and the ordeal ahead, Maggie thought, but when she confided this to one of the other maids on the journey home she was laughed to scorn. 'Her? First-night nerves? Wake up, Mags. She's had more men than you've had hot dinners.' It was a slight disappointment for Maggie, until she realised that if Vanessa had done it more than once she must have found it okay, so maybe there was a knack to it and you got to like it in the end. Not that she ever intended to find out. She tried not to think about the baby too much, but worries would seize hold of her suddenly, often at unexpected times. Was he feeding properly? Was his new family good to him? Would they read the *Milly-Molly-Mandy* to him when he was old enough? And did he know he had been loved and wanted? Above all, she wanted him to know that. In the few quiet moments she had to herself, usually before she fell asleep, she would ponder how something born out of so much pain and indignity could be so beautiful. She added her son to the album in her head, the pictures of Dolly and Billy. One day she would find them all. Convinced of that, she would fall asleep.

That summer, Maggie was almost happy, in spite of Mrs Jeyes' moans and grumbling over the lack of provisions. Food rations had been cut again: the tinned meat ration was cut to two-pence worth a week. 'Tuppence worth,' Mrs Jeyes said bitterly. 'We wouldn't have had tinned meat in the house before the war. My God, the Germans have a lot to answer for.'

'Bloody spam,' one of the footmen said. 'It wasn't what they promised us when we fought the fucking war for them.' 'Language, language,' Mrs Jeyes said, but she didn't sound as angry as she did when he criticised

Churchill. Even paper was in short supply, with newspapers reverting to their wartime four pages. 'It's so they can't print all the bad news,' Mrs Jeyes said. 'They'd have a revolution on their hands if they let us read all that.'

Winter came and went, but now Maggie was deemed fit again and her duties filled her days. In November, wedding fever descended upon them again – but this time it was Royal wedding fever. Princess Elizabeth, the future queen, was to marry a Greek prince, who was not only handsome but a war hero to boot. 'Such a good match,' her Ladyship said, beaming. 'A Mountbatten. She couldn't do better.' But by the time the bells rang out for the royal bride, Maggie had left Wentworth behind.

'I'm sending you to Belgate, Maggie. As a parlour maid and to help the housekeeper. You're still very young but Mrs Jeyes has the highest opinion of you.' To Maggie it sounded like exile, but Her Ladyship evidently saw it as a big promotion, so Maggie smiled appreciatively. Belgate was the Wentworth seat in Durham. 'Not as grand as Wentworth,' Mrs Jeyes told her, 'but you'll be in charge there to all intents and purposes. Mrs Botcherby's housekeeper but she's not well. I'll miss you, Maggie, but this is your chance. If she hangs on for a little while, you could be housekeeper and still not 25.'

She would travel to Belgate by car. No one mentioned trains, much to her relief. She sat in the back seat feeling like royalty, even though it was piled high with parcels, as was the passenger seat. Mr Jeyes drove the huge car, almost hidden by the height of the seats, which had thick padded headrests and were leather upholstered.

'Be a good girl and do as you're told,' he said before he set out on the homeward journey. 'Don't let the missus down. She thinks highly of you, Maggie. Like a daughter you are to her, although I don't think she'd thank me for telling you that.'

Alone in her new room, which was bigger than the last room and looked out on the kitchen garden, she pondered that news. 'Like a daughter.' And yet Mrs Jeyes had never hugged her or stroked her hair, or even, if the truth was known, smiled at her much. And that was what mothers did. She could remember that much.

Mrs Botcherby was not like Mrs Jeyes. She was, Maggie decided, bone-idle, but she raised no objection when Maggie took over the running of the house and ordered the scullery maids about, village girls all. It was a situation which suited everyone, and except for the rare occasions when the family came for brief visits, Maggie could consider the house her kingdom. She seldom went down to the village, but she treated herself to a wireless, a magnificent thing with the shape of a flower cut out on the front and filled in with hessian. She liked the music programmes best, particularly Mantovani and Henry Hall. One way and another life was good and her horde of money grew steadily. When she had enough, she would set out on her search. Once the stable lad persuaded her to put a shilling on a horse. 'Eight to one and a cert,' he told her. The horse came in fifth and she never bet again. Speculating to accumulate was one thing, money down the drain quite another.

Christmases at Belgate came and went. At Christmas

in 1948 she gave herself the gift of a trip to the cinema to see David Lean's *Oliver* and cried with relief when at last Oliver was safely restored to his grandfather. A few months later, clothes rationing ended and Miss Vanessa, or Lady Huntley as she now was, arrived at Belgate with a hamper full of clothes. 'I do hope you can make use of them, Margaret. I'm disgustingly fat since Fergie was born and won't ever get my waist back. And you've made such divine things for the new baby. I'm the envy of every Belgravia mother.' The hamper contained such wonders as she had never imagined. Velvet and silk, even a long-waisted coat with a Christian Dior label. 'Brand-new,' Maggie thought and was shocked at the extravagance, not that she would ever have the nerve to wear it outside the bedroom. But she loved its velvet collar and the way the skirt swirled when she turned on her heel. She hung it in the wardrobe covered with an old sheet and took it out occasionally to check for moths.

The following Christmas she treated herself to the cinema again, this time *The Red Shoes* with the ballerina, Moira Shearer, in the leading role. The music was haunting. There was a wind-up gramophone in the billiard room which was sometimes cleared and used for dances, according to Mrs Botcherby. Maggie deliberated for a long time before she spent precious money on a record of the *Red Shoes* music. Normally she spent only on necessities, but the music stirred her so much that she gave way to temptation and splurged. Alone in the billiard room when the household was asleep or out gallivanting in the village, she listened to the music, sometimes even venturing a few steps in imitation of the dance.

On New Year's Eve she drank a toast to the 1950s with Mrs Botcherby. 'They can't be worse than the 1940s,' the housekeeper said, but she didn't sound hopeful. 'I don't trust the Ruskies an inch,' she was fond of saying. When, in February, Dr Klaus Fuchs was charged with giving Russia the secret of the atom bomb, she was triumphant. 'Told you, didn't I? They'll do what Hitler couldn't, you mark my words.'

But Russia seemed a long way off to Maggie. She had a Post Office book with £257 in it now. The security it gave her far outweighed any threat from Russia. Not even the Korean War, when it came in the summer of 1950, could disconcert her, though some of the men from the estate were recalled to service and given tearful send-offs.

'I never thought I'd live to see another war,' Mrs Jeyes told her when the family arrived for the Glorious Twelfth and the start of grouse shooting. The war carried on till 1951 with no sign of abating, but in October of that year Churchill was returned to power, sending Wentworth into a rapture of celebrations. There was no celebration at Belgate. Mrs Botcherby cared little for politics and the surrounding area was staunch Labour. At Wentworth it was different. 'Fireworks,' Mrs Jeyes told Maggie over the telephone. 'And His Lordship's going round like a twenty-one-year-old. "The return of family," he calls it.' Maggie wondered if she ought to learn more about politics but she couldn't see how it had anything to do with her life. She had never voted, never felt the need or the desire.

She did care about royalty, however. The death of the King in February 1952 took her to the cinema to see the solemn funeral procession on the newsreel. It was a day of pageantry: the veiled queens, three of them; a princess, hollow-eyed at the loss of the father who had indulged her; the silent crowds lining the streets, many of them part of the 300,000 who had filed past the coffin as it lay in Westminster Hall; the muffled drums; the Household Cavalry walking in slow time… 'He was a good man,' Mrs Botcherby said. 'Stammer or not, he saw us through a war.'

The prospect of a new queen caused a flurry of excitement. 'The Elizabethan Age' everyone called it. For Maggie there was a special celebration. She was twenty-one and the fuss that was made took her by surprise. Miss Vanessa came, bringing Master Fergie and her new baby, Susie. Lord Wentworth sent best wishes and champagne all round, and her Ladyship presented her with a cheque for fifty pounds. 'You'll marry one day and need something to give you a start. Now, where are the glasses, Mrs B? We need to drink a toast.'

For Elizabeth's coronation in 1953 Lady Wentworth gave every member of staff a loving cup with the Queen's head on it. Maggie watched the coronation on the newsreel and marvelled at the young Queen's composure. 'Drugged,' Mrs Botcherby said. 'Most likely laudanum. They have doctors to see to that. Look at the easy end her father had. Died in his sleep? Seen off, more like. And why not? It's what anyone would want, to go in their sleep.'

Which is exactly what she did herself as 1953 slid into

1954. Maggie took over the reins of the house, reins she had held ever since she came to Belgate, and the only difference was an extra £1 a week in her pay-packet.

The following year, Churchill retired and his successor, Anthony Eden, called an election. Maggie came back to the house one day, arms laden with packages, to find a young man on the doorstep. He had come, he announced, to canvass on behalf of the Labour party. She listened as he extolled the virtues of a welfare state, but bridled a little when he suggested she was a lackey of the capitalist system. 'They've been good to me, Lord and Lady Wentworth.' Privately, she decided that her vote would go anywhere except to any party espoused by this cocky fellow. He had red hair in need of a cut and freckles on the bridge of his nose, but the hands clutching Labour pamphlets were clean and white, except for tiny blue flecks here and there. She told him politely that she never voted but if she did, how she did would be her own business and no one else's. As he walked off down the drive, she felt a twinge of regret. Had she been too abrupt? It was a relief when he came back two days later, red-faced but determined. 'There's a good film on at the Regent and I want you to come with me. My name is Jim Riley and I'm a deputy at the pit and not married or anything.' It came out in a rush – and so did her 'Alright, what time shall I meet you?'

Three months later, they were engaged to be married. Looking back, she could never understand how it had happened. She had feared men, even disliked them, but he had been different. His kisses on that first trip to the cinema were tentative and delivered with closed lips. He also kept his hands to himself, which was a great relief. Weeks later, when he would have touched her breast, she told him about the train and the baby. He said nothing, only held her close and kissed the top of her head repeatedly until she had to beg him to stop. But when she snuggled back into his arms it felt like coming home.

Chapter Fourteen

S HE WORE MISS VANESSA'S CHRISTIAN Dior coat to meet Jim's family – father, mother, two brothers and a kid sister called 'The Menace'. They were in awe of anyone who worked at the big house and hastily got out the eggshell china tea set, which had obviously not been in use since Jim was a boy and had dust in the handles. But they were warm and friendly and his mother embraced her when she was leaving. 'You'll be all right with our Jim,' she said.

At Maggie's insistence they slept together just once before the engagement was announced. 'I'm not sure I can, you see,' she said, but Jim just smiled and said 'Leave it to me'. She trusted him but her heart thudded uncomfortably when she came back into her bedroom and saw him sitting on the edge of the bed, naked except for his underpants. She had changed in the bathroom and now she spent a long time arranging her discarded clothes on a chair. 'Come on,' he said, coming up behind her. 'It's me, Jim.' And it was him and he smelled familiar and sweet and his flesh, when her hands touched it, was warm and dry and not frightening at all. He kissed her for a long time before he touched her gently, breast then stomach and then between her legs, until it seemed the most natural thing in the world to let her legs fall apart. He moved above her then but did not come down on her at once. 'All right?' he asked, and did not move until she whispered 'Yes'. He came into her easily. There was a second of pain and then he was moving slowly and gently and she felt herself move in rhythm. He kissed her then. 'Sweet,' he said, 'so sweet.' And then they were moving together, faster and faster and, as he let out a moan, she felt a curious sensation, as though all the pleasure in the world had just exploded inside her.

He moved off her and after a while she realised he was shaking with laughter. 'Here was me thinking you were clever,' he said when she raised herself up to question. 'You weren't sure you could do it? Well you certainly got that wrong.' And then they were both laughing and she knew it was going to be alright forever. He was loving her again when she remembered the quest for family. Dolly and Billy were out there somewhere. And her own little son. One day she must find them. It might have to be postponed but it would still happen. And now she had Jim to help her.

The Wentworths came to stay at Belgate in September. There was a flurry of shooting parties and preparing rooms for a flow of guests, so she kept her announcement for the day they left. She could have sworn Lady

Wentworth looked relieved at the news. 'I'm delighted, my dear. I had hoped, but one never knows. I felt such an obligation and now... Well, we must make plans. Vanessa will be delighted.' Mrs Jeyes was summoned to the telephone to hear the news. She said all the right things but Maggie could tell she was shedding tears. 'Jeyes and I will buy your dress.... No, let's have no argument, and I'll start the cake directly. I hope he's good enough for you. He'd better be or he'll have me and Jeyes to answer to.' Even his Lordship, when acquainted with the news by his wife, grunted his pleasure although, he informed her solemnly, the Riley family were socialists to the core and agitators to boot. This, Maggie knew, was tantamount to saying they were werewolves, but she knew how to cope with Jim. And His Lordship, come to that. She dared not allow herself to think about the ceremony. There should have been a bridesmaid there: Dolly. And Mam and Dad in a pew looking proud, except that Dad would have walked her down the aisle.

In the event, it was Mr Jeyes who took her to the altar and Mrs Jeyes who fussed over her and got the train of her satin dress just right. The Wentworths filled a whole pew and presented her with a Crown Derby tea and dinner service, complete down to different cups for coffee. 'Well, I never,' her mother-in-law-to-be exclaimed as they unpacked piece after piece in the deputy's house that came with Jim's job, now that he was to be a married man.

They married on October 31st 1955, the same day that a red-eyed Princess Margaret, the Queen's sister, declared that she would like it to be known that, mindful of the church's teaching against divorce, she had decided not to marry Group-Captain Peter Townsend. If Maggie had known of this she might have been sympathetic, but she was too lost in the wonder of her own day to think of anything but the wondrous ways of life. They honeymooned in Margate and every day was better than the one before. She had been alone and now she had Jim. And one day there would be children and, God willing, those other children, the ones she had left behind.

It was Jim's wish that she gave up her position at the Belgate. 'It wouldn't work,' he said. 'Me on shifts and you up there.' Secretly, she thought that it pained him to see her running after the so-called gentry but she never voiced this. He had his opinions, to which he was entitled, and she had hers. As far as gentry were concerned, it seemed to her that they were necessary. A necessary evil, perhaps, but necessary just the same. And although they could be thoughtless, at times they could also be kind. And they meant well. Above all else, they meant well. She saw the terrible discrepancies between life in the narrow streets of Belgate and life at the house, but there had been such gulfs in the Bible, rich and poor. It was the way of the world and no good kicking against it.

They came back from a week in Margate and settled down to married life in a two-up, two-down that seemed to Maggie like heaven on earth. She knew nothing of pit-life and she had to learn quickly. There were three shifts: day shift, tub-loading and back shift. Datal hands were the lower ranks, men with no specific job. Then came hewers, putters, pony-men, shot-firers, all experts in their particular art. Deputies were a cut above them all and Jim was the youngest ever deputy in Belgate's history. 'He'll be an under-manager one day,' his mother said proudly.

When he was on back shift, she lay awake, listening for his footfall in the street, the creak of the gate, the thud as his pit-boots hit the floor and then the splashing as he washed off the grime of the pit. When he came to their bed, she would reach for him and he would say 'You should be asleep', but as she began to love him his body would tell her that he was glad she was awake. On Sundays they redded the house. She had never heard that word. 'Because you're an ignorant townie,' he told her. It always tickled him that she was a Londoner. A cockney, he called her, and wouldn't listen when she tried to explain the intricacies of being born in or out of the sound of Bow Bells. The redding paid off. They had the smartest house in the row and certainly the only one with hand-embroidered cushions.

Outside, the world still seemed unsettled. Rows between leaders in Russia; unrest in Cyprus, where a bearded priest called Makarios was making trouble; the French coping with terrorism in Algeria; even a war in the Suez Canal. And finally a bloody uprising in Hungary, crushed by Soviet tanks. Jim pored endlessly over political pamphlets and tutted occasionally when he read the *Daily Express*, but Maggie felt safe inside the world they had made together. Nothing could hurt them there.

It was Christmas 1956 when she realised she was

pregnant. Morning sickness was an unpleasant reminder of that other pregnancy, but that feeling soon passed. She was giving Jim a son. Or a daughter. It didn't matter. He was like a dog with two tails over the thought of a baby. Its sex was immaterial.

She had just put the final touches to a nightie. Viyella, bought from the co-op for 8/6, embroidered now with roses in two shades of yellow, in case it was boy or girl, when she felt the pain. It rippled through her causing her mouth to open in shock. Not yet, she thought, putting a hand to her belly. She was only five months gone. It couldn't happen yet.

The baby was a boy. She miscarried it in the bedroom as a worried midwife gripped her hand and Jim sobbed quietly at the foot of the bed. The doctor came and took the baby away with him. 'It will go in a coffin with another burial,' the midwife told her. 'Don't worry, they'll treat it with respect.' There couldn't be a burial, a proper sending off, because the baby had never existed. She asked if she could know whose grave it had gone into but the midwife shook her head. 'Better not to know,' she said. 'Think about next time. You'll have a lovely baby then. This was just one of nature's mistakes.'

But it hadn't been a mistake. It had been a child of love, gone now to join those other children she had loved and would find one day. Except that this baby would not be found as Dolly and Billy and even her son would be found. This baby was gone for good.

Jim insisted they waited before they tried again. He cursed quietly as he learned the art of using a 'French letter' but he never wavered in his determination. 'I want a bairn as much as you but I won't rush you, Maggie. You're too important to me for that.'

It was the summer of 1958 before he relented and June 1959 before the doctor confirmed her suspicions. 'You're pregnant,' he told her, smiling, and she ran all the way home to tell Jim and write a letter to the Jeyeses at Wentworth, who would be as pleased as she was at the news. The delivery was due in February. At Christmas they made a stocking for the coming baby. 'No reason why he should miss out,' Jim said, patting her bump. 'He can have it as soon as he pops his head out.' '*She* can have it, you mean,' she said, though the sex didn't matter. She would give him twelve children if need be. Six of each.

She was reading about Princess Margaret's engagement to Antony Armstrong-Jones, thrilled that the sad princess had found happiness at last, when her waters broke. The birth was comparatively easy and not as painful as that first birth at St Clare's. She waited for them to wrap the baby and place it in her arms, but no one was moving. Nor was anyone telling her if it was boy or girl. It was the doctor who spoke at last. 'I'm sorry, my dear. Your daughter was stillborn. A beautiful little girl, but it couldn't be helped.'

Once again, she lay puzzled that no tears would come. She could hear Jim in the next room, angry at first and then grief-stricken. She did not cry then, nor when the doctor told her a week later that there were unlikely to be more children. 'He could be wrong,' Jim told her.

'Who's he to say? We'll find another doctor. Go to Newcastle. London even.' But Maggie knew in her heart that the doctor was right. Life was like that. Just when you thought you had got it right, perfect even, it swung gently in the wind and you saw the flaw.

When Jim at last accepted it, he kissed her more fiercely than ever. 'As long as I have you, Mags. That's all I need. I'm going to take you away as soon as you're on your feet. We'll see the world... Well, only Skegness to start with but there'll be other years. As long as I have you, Mags...' She did cry then but whether they were tears of grief or tears of joy at being loved, she couldn't be sure.

They were happy together in the years that followed, in spite of what Maggie considered to be her husband's obsession with the Labour Party. Once or twice she ventured to suggest the time had come to seek out her sister and brother. Jim didn't say no but his expression showed his disbelief that such a search would bear fruit. 'I'll do it next year,' Maggie thought. 'Next year there'll be more time.'

Each summer they went away for a fortnight. Blackpool and Southport at first, then the South Coast. In 1968, as Russian tanks rolled into Prague, they took their first trip abroad. Amsterdam seemed like the other side of the world. 'But they all speak English,' she exclaimed in wonder. 'Too right they do,' was her husband's reply. 'We've saved their necks in two world wars. They have a bloody good right to speak English.' The canals of Amsterdam gave them a taste for something more exotic. They went to Cyprus the following year, Yugoslavia the year after. 'But not Germany,' Jim said. 'It's too soon. Way too soon.' Sometimes they visited the Jeyeses, now retired in a village close to Wentworth Hall. When Mr Jeyes died in 1974, Maggie stayed with Mrs Jeyes for a fortnight. 'Least you can do,' Jim said, when she wondered if it was right to leave him. 'She's been like a mother to you.' Thereafter they stayed with the old lady once a year until her death in 1981. Jim took time off to accompany Maggie to the funeral, and afterwards a solicitor took them aside and told them that Maggie was to receive £3,000 under the terms of Mrs Jeyes' will. All the way home Maggie plotted how she would use the money to search for her sister and brother. Jim wouldn't object. He knew how much it meant to her. She was still making plans when Jim died, quite suddenly, sitting in his chair one Sunday morning. They had been married for 27 years.

There was insurance and some benefits that came from the union. 'You'll be alright, Mrs Riley,' the union official told her. Maggie nodded. She would be alright because you always were, in the end. Whether or not she would be happy was another matter. She gave Jim a good send-off and, when the ground settled, a handsome black marble stone. There would be room for her to lie above him when the time came, but before then there was something she must do.

She found a private detective agency by studying the small ads in the Sunday paper, and asked the owner how much it would cost to find her sister and brother. He asked for £500 on account and she wrote her first cheque. When six months had gone by and money was disappearing at an alarming rate without any result, she called off the search. Like her babies, the alive and the dead, Billy and Dolly were gone from her forever. She had a roof over her head, enough to live on and a card from Miss Vanessa, Lady Huntley, every Christmas. Jim's nephews and nieces sometimes called and she had friends at church. That was enough.

Sometimes months went by without her remembering, especially after she got a colour TV and could watch the snooker knowing which ball was which. And then a man knocked on her door and it had all come back, sharp as a knife wound, because someone else was searching. Someone with power and money. Hope sprang up again and would not be extinguished, however hard she tried.

Chapter Fifteen

PALE LIGHT WAS FILTERING THROUGH the curtains when Ben woke. He looked at the clock on the bedside table. 5.45am. Too early to get up, too late to settle to sleep again. Beside him, Diana lay on her face, one hand up to her cheek. She looked innocent in sleep. It was only when she was awake and her eyes were open that you sensed the depths beneath. Remembering her eyes, dark and mocking beneath her thick lashes, he realised that he no longer liked his wife. He desired her, craved her even, but he didn't like her. She was beautiful but she was betraying him. He had no proof, he just knew it. Perhaps it was his fault. There was a reason for most things. She had come back from Prague yesterday. They should have been mad for one another after more than a week apart, but last night she had pleaded fatigue and he had contented himself with a kiss she might have given a maiden aunt. Did that make him a gentleman or a fool? He slid away until he could put a foot down to the floor and lever himself quietly from the bed. It was better not to think about it. Not now with a complicated day ahead.

He was showered and had breakfasted when the call came. It was Sparrow. 'I got back late last night, so I decided to leave it till this morning.' The detective had been looking over notes of his conversation with Margaret Riley. 'Any good?' The reply came cautiously. 'I think so. She's certain the boy was taken off by a vicar. Adoptions were mostly local in those days. Transport being what it was, you could be pretty certain a child wouldn't meet up with a parent once it was outside a fifty-mile radius, so you could adopt with a degree of security. And, of course, in this case, there were no parents.'

'So you'll check the churches?'

'Initially. Get the names of previous incumbents. After that, *Crockford* should tell me what I need to know. That's the clerical *Who's Who*. I'll get details of the children of any clerics who might fit, see who has sons, check their ages... That'll narrow it to a handful. Most tracing can be done by computer nowadays.'

'And the girl? Dorothy.'

'Known as Dolly. She's a bigger problem. Straightforward adoption from the sound of it. I'll get it eventually, have no fear. It'll just take time.'

Diana was coming downstairs as Ben collected his car keys from the hall table. 'Are you off, darling? Don't be late tonight. It's the Haworths, remember.' Ben's heart sank at the thought of another dinner party. In the early days of their marriage, they had stayed at home, dinner from trays, listening to music until the desire for one another became too great. Sometimes they had made it to the bedroom, often they had come together on the rug in front of the fire. Now he kissed the cheek she proffered, promised to be home on time and escaped from the house. He was unlocking the car when he realised that it had been a relief to get out of his own home.

On an impulse, he pointed the car east instead of west towards the city. It was 8.00am. The office would not really spring to life until 9.30am, and if he was a little late today, so what.

Adele was ushering the children into her station wagon as he drew up at her door. 'Five minutes,' she said. 'Go in and put coffee on.' He had brewed coffee and was on to his second cup when she arrived back from the school run. 'This is early,' she said. 'Not that I'm not glad to see you at any time. There's nothing wrong with Granny, is there?'

He reassured her and poured her a coffee. 'I thought I'd bring you up to date. We found the eldest child: Margaret. Not that she's a child now. She must be 70... No, 76, about eleven years younger than Gran, but fit. Sprightly, I suppose you'd call her.'

'You've seen her? You liked her?' Adele asked. She sounded surprised.

'I did, I suppose. I called on her on my way down from Scotland, and yes, I did like her.'

'Which means you want to make up to her for... Well, I suppose, her dis-inheritance? If that's the word. Grandpa's skulduggery, if you like.'

'I don't know.' Ben rubbed his forehead. 'The business

can't have been worth much then... A cart and buggy affair. All the same...'

'Grandpa built it up.' Adele was refilling her cup, glancing around the yellow-walled kitchen as though in search of inspiration. 'He worked jolly hard. I can remember that much. Not at the beginning, of course, when he was still hands-on. By the time I was old enough to take notice, he was very grand, but he still kept an eye on business. He'd limp on that gammy leg of his... He could go at a rate of knots. Sometimes I'd go site-visiting with him. He'd buy me Fry's chocolate cream and let me ride on the JCBs.' They were both grinning.

'He couldn't do that now. Health and safety would throw a fit.'

'Exactly! But what I was meaning was that it was his energy that built Webcon. Dad told me once it was post-war reconstruction that did it. Thousands of Londoners needing houses. Grandpa didn't have to beg for work, they begged him.'

Ben was nodding. 'Seventy thousand homes went in London. But if there hadn't been an existing business, if he'd had to set up from scratch... And don't forget it was the other guy who had the initial expertise. Grandpa only got involved with that side when Brewis was called up.'

'Strange, isn't it?' Adele said. 'I bet that club foot of his was a cross when he was growing up, but it kept him out of a war.'

'While the other guy went off to fight and die.'

'Alright!' Adele was laughing now, holding up her

hands in mock-surrender. 'So you're going to give them half the firm. You won't get an argument from me.'

But it wouldn't be that easy, Ben thought, as he drove back to London. Webcon was no longer a family concern. Most of the stock was held by investors, a little by his family and a minuscule amount by Hammond. And big institutions wouldn't part with a red cent to settle a debt of honour.

Hammond was waiting for him when he arrived at the office. 'Where the hell have you been?' Before he could answer, Hammond spoke again. 'Sorry, I've been on edge. They say Headey's is about to make a fresh bid: four new ordinary shares of theirs plus 350 pence cash for every five of ours. It's not official yet, but I have it from a reliable source.' Ben's lips pursed in shock but no sound came out. Hammond continued. 'I knew they were building a stake but I thought it was well below a level where they'd come into the open.' He grimaced. 'They've been clever, and if this bid materialises it's come out of the blue.'

'Will they succeed? If they do bid, that is. We've been down this road before and nothing has come of it.' Ben could hear his own voice but the situation felt unreal. He had never lived for the business, had often resented it, if the truth were known. But that it should pass out of the family, that was unthinkable. Beside that, the question of what, if anything, should be given to Jack Brewis's children paled into insignificance. 'We'll fight it, of course.' He said it as matter-of-factly as he could, and Hammond nodded. 'I've got feelers out in the City. When I know anything...'

Ben watched as Hammond made his way across the open area and entered Neil Pyke's office. Pyke turned away almost at once but Ben could have sworn he was smiling. Nothing seemed to phase him, not even the prospect of unemployment.

He worked through the afternoon, eating a sandwich at his desk and trying to make sense of progress reports from the sites. The Scottish marina was ahead of schedule and he felt a sudden longing to go back there. But there could be no escape, not at the moment. At five he buzzed Hammond's office. 'Any news?'

'Not a whisper.' Hammond sounded happier. 'I'm wondering if it was just a rumour.' They agreed the immediate panic was over and Ben put down the phone. He decided to leave the office and told English he would drive himself. He headed towards Regent's Park. As he crossed Trafalgar Square it was thronged with tourists. A family party caught his eye. The father had lifted the little girl onto the plinth that supported a stone lion. She posed between its paws while he took a photograph and then he lifted her down. It must be pleasurable, Ben thought as he drove, to have a child, a son or a daughter, to lift aloft as that father had done. One day perhaps. Even Diana would get tired of lunching and dining eventually. Most of her friends had children already and she seemed fond enough of them.

'She's a little brighter today,' the nurse said when he reached The Bishops Avenue house. His grandmother sat in a Windsor chair. As usual, she was beautifully dressed: small pearls ornamented her ears, her white hair was waved about her head and arranged to cover the pink scalp where it showed through. When he bent to kiss her cheek, she smelled good. Not as old ladies should, as Margaret Riley had done, warm body smell and soap and something else that might have been butter. His grandmother smelled of roses and lavender. Smells like that did not come cheap.

He sat by her, sipping tea but refusing the chocolate bourbons, while he told of his trip to Belgate. 'Did you tell her?' she asked. 'Did she ask about the business?'

He smiled. 'She was nine, Gran. Nine when she lost her parents. She doesn't remember the business. She remembers you, though.' The moment he'd said it, he wished the words unsaid. Too late.

'I promised her.' His grandmother's voice was anguished. 'I said I'd come back for them. All this...' She gestured around the room. 'It's not right, Ben.'

'She's not in need, Gran. She has a nice home. She seemed very content.'

He painted an extra rosy picture of life in Belgate and then told her what he could about the others. 'We'll keep on trying but I wouldn't build up your hopes,' he finished. He hesitated. 'Do you want to meet her?' She didn't answer and then Sue bustled in. 'More tea? I could make a fresh pot.' After, they talked about anything and everything except his question. If that was the way she wanted it, so be it. Tea over, Ben made his excuses and stood up to go. He was halfway to the door when his grandmother spoke. 'I'd like to see her again, Ben. If she wants to see me, that is.'

The dinner party was in Kensington. He knew the Haworths but only slightly. One of the other guests was Neil Pyke and that surprised him. 'You know Neil. Of course you do.' Angela Haworth had been Diana's friend at school. Now she put out a hand to each man and drew him towards her. 'You and Neil work together in that vast organisation of yours, Ben – which is building half of London.'

'Half of Britain, Angela,' Neil Pyke said. He sounded proud, almost proprietorial. 'That's how I should sound,' Ben thought, and knew that he didn't. All the same, he was not letting go of Webcon without a fight. For the moment, at least, he must keep it in the family.

They dined well. Smoked salmon on sweetcorn blinis, rack of lamb with crisp vegetables, and chocolate torte, washed down with a variety of wines that tasted superb and had probably cost the earth. Diana was at her sparkling best, teasing the men, flattering the women, appearing to hang on his every word like the perfect wife. Perhaps he was wrong and his suspicions unworthy? He was content to sit there, becoming pleasantly drowsy, watching London at play.

The car returned for them at 11.30pm. 'There now,' Diana said when they were safe in the back seat. 'I knew you'd enjoy it.'

'Yes, it was pleasant. I didn't know Pyke knew the Haworths.'

'Didn't you, darling?'

'How did they meet?'

'How should I know, Ben? Now, tell me what you

thought of the meal.'

She went straight upstairs when they reached the house. He poured himself a brandy and drank it in his study. When he finally reached the bedroom, Diana was emerging from the shower. 'That's better,' she said. Her wet hair curled around her face. Her body, naked beneath the white towelling robe, was firm and peach-coloured. He had often wondered how that even, all-over colour was obtained and, once obtained, kept blemish-free. Now he moved to her and took her in his arms, bending to kiss her throat and the valley between her breasts. For once she didn't turn away. Instead, she put up her hand and held his head, letting his lips move first to the right nipple then the left. But when he began to travel down to her rounded belly and below, she stopped him. 'Let's go to bed, darling. I'm bushed.'

She let him take her, gently at first, and then so fiercely that the bed shuddered at his force. 'I want to have a child, Diana.' In his mind's eye, he saw the child between the lion's paws, squinting into the sunshine, smiling for its father. 'Did you hear? I want us to have a baby.' She didn't answer and he rolled off her. 'Don't you?' She put out a hand to turn out the lamp. 'Of course I do. One day. But not yet, darling. There's acres and acres of time.'

Chapter Sixteen

HE ROSE EARLY AND WENT to the gym, pounding a treadmill until his legs threatened to buckle. 'I'm letting myself go,' he thought. 'Too many business lunches, dinner parties, not enough sweat.' If the business went, he would have more time. Would that be a blessing or a curse?

Hammond was waiting when Ben arrived at the office. 'I've put out some feelers. Most people will take the offer when and if it comes. It's a good offer, Ben.'

'What will you do if that happens?' Ben asked. Hammond shrugged. 'Hard to say. What will they want, to run the two organisations separately? In which case I might survive in some capacity. Or merge, in which case I'd be out. I'm 51, Ben. Bad age for starting again. I'd do alright financially, as you will. But seven days of golf a week? Not for me. And Ann would go spare with me under her feet...'

Suddenly Hammond seemed vulnerable and Ben

warmed to him. Until their conversation the other day, he had always felt Hammond resented – even despised – him, seeing him as someone born with the proverbial silver spoon and coming to the head of a business about which he knew very little. In a way, that was true. His time with Webcon before he took over the helm had been brief in business terms. He had never blamed Hammond for resenting him but he had never thought of him as a friend. Now he was seeing a side of him which he had never suspected. He put out a hand and gave the other man's arm a reassuring pat.

'It hasn't happened yet. They may pull back. Why are they so keen? They've always specialised in government contracts, whereas we've always been private sector.'

'Diversification, I suppose. We really ought to call a meeting of the executive directors. They're in the same position as me, not knowing whether or not they'll be out on their ears.'

'We could make it a condition, retention of senior staff.'

Hammond raised an eyebrow. 'I'm glad you think they'll be willing to talk conditions. If they go ahead, they'll simply over-run us, taking no prisoners.'

It was true, Ben thought, when Hammond had gone back to his own office. If a takeover took place, it would take no prisoners. He looked at the clock. He ought to tell Adele about developments. She had a right to know, but should he take more time off? He picked up the phone. 'Del, any chance of your coming up here later today? No, it's not Gran. She's fine as far as I know. It's developments here I think you should be aware of. Harry too, if he's available.' They arranged to meet for lunch. 'Harry's not here and I must be back for school time,' Adele warned him. 'But a nice posh lunch would be heaven.'

They went to L'Etoile, spooned into his usual corner table by Elena. 'Now,' Adele said. 'Tell me why I've had to trek up here when I only saw you yesterday.' He told her about the takeover bid as she ate olives and sipped her Sauvignon. 'What does that mean exactly?'

'You'll acquire quite a lot of money, but you'll get nothing further from the firm. We won't have anything to do with it.'

'You'll lose your job?'

'Yes. I'll get a pay-off, I imagine, and cash in my shares, so I'll be far from destitute, but there won't be a role for me.'

'And the others? Hammond and Pyke and that lot?'

Ben shrugged. 'Some of them might be kept on, but remember Headey's has all its own people. They're bound to give them preference. It's possible that they'd keep Webcon autonomous – run it as a separate business – but I doubt it.'

She put out a hand and covered his hand. 'Would you mind?'

'For myself, no. I was drafted in, I didn't choose it. I'd mind about the firm going out of the family – quite a bit, actually. As though I'd let the family down, failed to carry on the torch.'

'That's silly, but I know what you mean. Have you told Gran?'

'No, that's the other problem. If I worry her and it fizzles out, I'll curse myself, but I don't want her to hear when it's a *fait accompli*.'

Adele nodded. 'It's difficult. And then there's this other thing.' But Ben was shaking his head. 'No, in a way, a takeover would make that easier. I'd have a lot of money, cash, not shares; I could give them a lump sum and call it quits.'

'Why should you pay? I'd go halves. I know Harry would agree. I suppose we'd need to invest the money if there were to be no more dividend cheques, but I could still pay my share.'

'Don't be so quick to part with your money,' he said. 'But I love you for the offer. Have you decided what you want to eat?'

He had been back in the office for half an hour when the phone rang. It was Diana. 'Darling? Could you possibly eat out tonight? I was going to make dinner because Mrs C has a day off, but I must pop out.' He tried not to sound annoyed. He had been looking forward to a quiet meal in his own home. 'Somewhere special?'

'No. Just a girl's thing. I won't be late.'

'Well, I'm not eating out. I'll get myself something from the freezer.'

There was a sound from the other end of the phone that signalled exasperation, but when she spoke she made an effort to be reasonable. 'I'll put you something out – M&S lasagne or something like that – and I won't be late.'

The phone rang again as soon as he replaced the receiver. It was Madge's detective. 'Got some news. I found the vicar. It was easier than I thought. That's the good news. The bad news is that if it's the right one – and I'm pretty sure it is, I just need to check a few more details – the boy is dead. He died in 1984, blown up in Northern Ireland. The vicar's retired and living in Twickenham. Nice chap. He's willing to talk to you, anxious even. The boy was obviously precious to him.'

Ben took down the details, although the thought of speaking to a grieving father didn't appeal. Perhaps he could leave it to Sparrow. Or put the vicar in touch with Margaret Riley. Now that was a thought. She was family, after all. He would have to tell his grandmother that the boy had died tragically. Would that be a fresh source of guilt?

Hammond came in at four o'clock, accompanied by Neil Pyke. Pyke seemed relatively unconcerned at the proposal of redundancy. 'He's young,' Ben thought. 'Young and sharp. He'll pocket the cash and be in a post somewhere else before you can say Jack Robinson.' He thought of Pyke as he had sat across the dinner table a few nights ago. He had been confident, almost cocky. 'Nothing phases him,' Ben thought and felt faintly envious. They discussed dates and times for a meeting with the executive directors and then Pyke stood up. 'I'm off, if no one minds. It's Friday after all and the weekend starts here.'

Ben leaned back in his chair when they had gone. Friday night. When first they married, he had looked forward to Friday nights, ceremonial candlelit dinners and lazy lie-ins on Saturday and Sunday. Tonight she was off God knows where and he would have a meal for one on a tray. The honeymoon was well and truly over. He reached for the phone and dialled the number the detective had given him. He arranged to meet the vicar in Twickenham at 9am the next day.

There was a note on the morning-room table when he got home. 'Sorry, no lasagne. Hope pasta will do. D.' He hated pasta, even when fresh with homemade sauce. Frozen pasta in goo was pretty disgusting but he shoved it in the microwave nevertheless. Later on, when Diana came home, he would open a bottle of something nice and then, perhaps, the weekend would look more promising.

It was quarter to twelve when she returned. Usually, when she was later than promised, she was apologetic. Tonight there was no apology.

'Where've I been? Oh it's the third degree, is it? I was going to tell you where I'd been but now you can sod off. Where I've been is my business.'

'You've obviously been somewhere where booze was available.'

'Yes.' She was struggling out of her coat and now she faced him. 'Yes, I have been drinking and smoking and I'm fucking late. I've probably been up to no good, too. I mean, leave no stone unturned. I am a bad wife... Well, that figures because you, my darling, are not quite the ideal husband.'

'I can't talk to you when you're like this.' He was

turning away when he felt her fist slam into his upper arm. 'Don't run away from me. Just because your fucking company is going down the tubes, don't think you can take it out on me.'

'How did you know about the takeover?'

'You told me.'

'I didn't.'

She looked a little nervous now, the defiance of a moment ago fled. 'You did. Anyway, does it matter? I know. And I'm going to bed. Don't wake me when you come up.'

Ben poured himself a large whisky and sat down in a wing chair. A moment later he felt Max's nose pushing at his hand, which was resting on the arm of the chair. 'Hey, old chap. You should be asleep by now.' There was no response except a muzzle laid gently across his knee and a large, warm head to fondle for their mutual comfort.

He spent the night in one of the guest rooms, Max lying beside his bed, but sleep was hard to come by. He felt as though a thousand hurdles faced him and he didn't feel capable of clearing any of them. His marriage, Webcon, his grandmother's health, the Brewis affair... What else could go wrong? Towards dawn he slept fitfully, only to dream that Diana had returned from a fancy-dress party wearing a Madame du Barry costume. When he woke he could still see her face under the powdered wig, almost touch the famous beauty spot. If dreams had significance, what did that mean? He had dreamed of his wife as a courtesan. In the mirror, as he shaved, his eyes gave him the answer. Last night his wife had had sex with another man. He knew it and she knew he knew it and she didn't care.

She had not appeared when he left the house and he did not feel inclined to check on whether or not she was awake. He turned right when he reached the bottom of the drive and took the road to Twickenham.

The vicar was frail, almost ghostly, but smiled a greeting. He lived on the second floor of a mansion block. 'Do come in. Your man did try to explain but I didn't quite get the connection. You weren't related to my son?'

'No, but my grandparents knew his parents. My grandmother is failing quite rapidly and she's anxious to know what happened to the children of her friends.' Ben followed the vicar through to the sitting room. They made slow progress, for the vicar was frail. He must be in his nineties, Ben thought, doing rapid sums in his head.

They settled in chairs in a round window that took up the corner of the building. Below them traffic flowed right and left, people going into the city to shop and city dwellers fleeing in search of open spaces. The vicar presided over a tea tray already set on a side-table. 'I'm glad you were on time. I didn't want to leave you for the kitchen as soon as you arrived. Do have some. It's Darjeeling. My favourite, although I sometimes indulge in a pot or two of Assam... Good.'

Then, suddenly, he was rising out of his chair, putting aside his cup and dabbing his mouth with a napkin. 'I must show you David's photograph.' 'David?' Ben felt suddenly shaken. Had there been a terrible mistake? The vicar was frail and elderly but he caught on quickly.

'We had him christened David William. There was some doubt as to whether or not he'd been baptised. My wife thought it best. She preferred David to William, so David he became.'

The man in the photograph was young and in uniform. 'He was commissioned,' Ben said, noting the pips. Pride suffused the vicar's whole body, causing him to brace his shoulders. 'A full colonel. He was a major at 25. An exceptional soldier, they said.' Ben studied the face. Like Margaret Riley, the boy had steady eyes and a mouth that would smile easily. 'You must have been proud of him.'

'I was.' For a moment the old man's voice trembled – but only for a moment. He picked up his cup. 'Now, where do I begin?'

Chapter Seventeen

Billy's Story

'MY WIFE AND I ALWAYS planned to have a large family. We were both only children, so we fancied quite a brood. They tell me that if you come from a large family, one or two is your ideal, but we were young. We thought they'd come easily, three boys, three girls, although quite how we'd have ensured the distribution of the sexes, I do not know. Well...' Again the voice trembled. 'It was not to be. We went on hoping for a year or two. Each time I performed a baptism I thought what it would be like to hold my own child in my arms. But we were very young. We married as soon as I was ordained, so I thought we had all the time in the world. My wife was more impatient – or more sensible. She asked for an investigation.' There was silence for a moment before the wavering voice continued. 'They were quite definite. There would be no children. Something to do with the fallopian tubes – and, of course, there were none of these modern miracles in those days. I don't regard it as interfering with God's will. The expertise is God-given, isn't it. Anyway, I mustn't sermonise. Jane took it badly. Nothing could console her. The war had just begun. I wasn't conscripted because of poor eyesight, though I'd've gone if I could. It was a just war. Anyway, as I said, my wife was inconsolable. And then there was something of a miracle. A colleague told me about three children, evacuees; the father had died in the early days of the war, the mother perished in an air raid. There was no family and they were destined for institutions. They were billeted in the next village and the woman who had them wanted them out. Too much responsibility, I suppose, and no end to it in sight. There were two girls and a boy. Jane had always hoped for a son. I was the one with the misgivings – she never had a doubt from the moment I mentioned it. And, for me, there was a feeling that we could be doing something for a man who had gone to war.

'We were told there was a little girl, pretty by all accounts and four years old, but by the time we got there she'd gone. The other girl was eight or nine. She looked dazed, but she wouldn't take her eyes off the other child, the little boy. It was quite touching. Jane took to the little fellow at once. He was a beautiful child. Quite chubby and friendly.' There was a pause and the old man seemed to be seeking for the right words. Ben was about to speak, when he continued.

'I don't mind telling you I wanted to take them both. It seemed barbaric to split them up. But Jane was adamant. She thought the girl too old, too set in her ways, probably. I argued but, as she pointed out, she would have to do most of the upbringing. I had to give way but I felt it.' He cleared his throat. 'I've felt guilty for sixty years. I should have put my foot down...'

'She's still alive, that child,' Ben said. 'And, I would say, very content. She's a widow but she seems to have had a happy life, so it didn't turn out badly.'

'I'm so glad.' Relief made the old man's voice stronger. 'It was distressing. She had this book, a reading book. She wanted Jane to take it, she said he liked to have it read to him at night, but... My wife worried about hygiene and the book was well-thumbed. I... Well, perhaps... Anyway... if, as you say, it turned out well...'

Ben was beginning to get the picture. Although the old man would never say it and probably had never acknowledged it, Jane had been a bit of a monster. He thought of Margaret Riley, nine years old, standing in the room, the reading book in her hand. The one thing she had left of her family, a family blown apart by war. Her baby brother being carried off and they wouldn't take a fucking book!

'He cried at first,' the vicar continued. 'He wanted his mama and Mags. The girl was called Margaret. And he kept asking about a dolly...'

'The other girl was called Dorothy, the four-year-old. She was Dolly for short. So, you took the boy?'

'Yes, we took him home. The woman who had them was anxious to be rid of the responsibility. The adoption papers took a while to come through because there was no next of kin or guardian.'

'Only my grandfather,' Ben thought wryly. 'And he was too busy obliterating all trace of the Brewis family.'

The vicar was well into his flow now. 'He was a very good little boy. We had a few sleepless nights in the beginning, but Jane was firm – I would have gone to him but she was firm with him.'

'I bet she was,' Ben thought.

'It doesn't take long for children to forget. After a while he didn't mention the others. I became Daddy. Jane was Mummy. Her mother was still alive and she was "Gangan". She was very good with him. I sometimes thought he preferred her – not that Jane wasn't good with him. Devoted really. I suggested we got another child, but no, she had her little boy. That was enough. He really was a good boy. Used to kneel down in his dressing gown and say his prayers. "God bless Daddy. God bless Gangan..." And mummy, of course. He'd bless his toys and the dog next door. We didn't have a dog of our own. Jane thought it risky. We sent him to the Montessori. Catholic, of course, but excellent tuition. He could read when he was five but he liked me to read to him at bedtimes. He had this quilt thing he called his silkies and he'd finger it between finger and thumb and his eyes would droop, but he'd blink himself awake so the story could continue. It had to stop, of course...'

'Jane thought it best?' Ben suggested.

'Yes. Of course, she was right. He could read for himself so it wasn't strictly necessary.' Ben saw that the old eyes had turned moist. 'But they're precious, these little routines, aren't they?'

'I don't have children but I should imagine they are.' If he had children and wanted to read to them, Diana wouldn't stop him, he could be sure of that – because she wouldn't give a damn either way. It was there again, that ambivalence in his feelings. 'I love her but do I like her?' He forced his attention back to the old man.

'I moved parishes in 1942. To Exeter. Jane thought it best not to come with me. There'd been a savage raid on Exeter in the April. Retaliation for the RAF's offensive against German arms factories, or so they said. She was afraid for the boy and, of course, she was right. So we were apart for most of the war really. I missed the little fellow but I went up to see them – they were in the Dales – as often as I could. I hated the war. Not just the separation; I had to go to homes where a son had been killed. The grief was terrible to behold, and what could I say? Not much use in pointing out the rightness of the cause. I had a child of my own then. I knew what he meant to me.' He was silent for a while, obviously reminiscing. 'Anyway, I moved to Slough at the end of the war. Jane came home. David was seven then, a little gentleman. Jane had done a good job.' The voice trembled but then recovered.

'He went to Prep School when he was nine. He was showing quite a flair for sport. Jane played tennis with him. I ran about a lot, ball games and that sort of thing. "Dad!" he used to say when I let a ball past me. I wasn't much use. He was…' Again the anguished clearing of his throat. 'He was quite a boy. Exceptionally bright, they said. He went to Wellingborough when he was eleven. He liked it there and he did well. Nine O levels and three

A levels. He was head of his house and played rugby for the school. The other boys looked up to him. I thought he would have made a good teacher. He was always good with other children. Jane thought the army was the right career path – her father had been a brigadier. But he was such a merry little boy...'

'And what Jane said, went,' Ben thought, but kept his thought to himself.

'He went to Oxford from Wellingborough. A squash blue, not a bad cricketer. Bit of an all-rounder.' The pride in the old man's voice was threatening to choke him. 'You must have been proud of him,' Ben said again. It was a trite thing to say, but he was trying to give the old man time to recover. The vicar nodded and went on. 'He read medieval and military history and then, in 1960, he entered Sandhurst. He did well there and was commissioned with the Grenadier Guards afterwards.'

There was silence for a few moments and the ticking of the two clocks in the room became almost mesmerising. Somewhere out there, someone was trying to take away his career, his wife was quite possibly lying in another man's bed, and yet the tracking down of three strangers had assumed enormous importance.

'He was posted after a year. Germany, Paderborn Barracks. He had two pips by then. "See?" Jane said. "I was right."' Again there was a silence. 'He didn't agree,' Ben thought, and wondered why. What had put doubts into the vicar's mind? 'Was he happy in the army?' The old man's shake of the head could have meant anything, but his words were positive.

'Oh yes, I'm sure he was. He still played active sport – tennis for his regiment. After that his career took off. They thought well of him. They told me that. Anyway, he went all over the world – after Germany, I mean. Hong Kong, Malta, all over the place. And then he was posted to Northern Ireland. Twice. He was on his second tour of duty there when he met Helen. Her father was his CO.'

'Helen?' As Ben spoke, the old man rose from his chair and moved to collect a photograph from the mantelpiece. 'This is their wedding day.' The bride was pretty. 'She's very pretty,' Ben said, but his eyes were on the uniformed groom standing beside her. Billy was about six-foot tall and looked every inch the major he had become.

'Yes, she was pretty.' The old man took back the photograph and replaced it carefully and precisely. 'But more important, she was kind. David was well into his thirties then, we'd almost given up hope and suddenly here was this lovely girl. They married in 1976. Do you remember that summer? No, of course not. You'd scarcely be born then. Well, it was a scorcher.' A memory stirred for Ben: his mother applying lotion to his back and grass tickling his bare feet. She had hugged him and said he mustn't burn. 'I think I do remember,' he said. 'There was a heat wave.'

'Record hours of sunshine. I said a prayer for rain at one stage and when rain stopped play at Lords, the crowd cheered. But the rain stopped after fifteen minutes!' They both laughed and the tension in the room was eased.

'So it was a happy marriage?' Ben prompted.

'Oh, very happy. She was a beautiful bride, quite radiant. He was... Well, happy is too small a word to describe it. They went to Corfu for their honeymoon and then she made them a home. She was such a good wife. I'd never seen him so happy. She drew us all together. She was good with Jane, drawing her in, that kind of thing.' He laughed suddenly. 'You know what they say about mothers-in-law, but Helen was... understanding.'

'Tolerant?' Ben suggested.

The priest was nodding. 'Tolerant, yes. Jane laid down the rules – even in the pregnancy. Well, this was going to be her first grandchild. David came home for the birth. My, what a day that was. A thousand christenings in my day but never there for those first few breaths in the outside world. And now this child was coming into the world and I was there.' He laughed again. 'David was quite calm. I was the one who paced the floor. "For goodness' sake, sit down, Dad," he said at one stage.'

'Wasn't he there at the delivery?' Ben asked.

'No, Jane didn't believe in it. I suppose she talked Helen round. Not that it mattered. We were there to all intents and purposes, in the waiting room. We went in when it was all over. It hadn't been an easy birth but they were both quite serene, tucked up together. Such a wise little face the baby had. And then we came back to the vicarage and drank champagne. Quite decadent at three in the morning but I'm sure the good Lord approved.' His lips were twitching slightly but not with amusement. 'I'm stirring memories,' Ben thought. Aloud, he said, 'I could come back if it helps. If this is upsetting you in any way. I know you must grieve for your son...'

'And my daughter-in-law. I loved Helen like a daughter.'

'Loved her?'

'She died. Cancer. In 1983. Barbara was four. "Where's mummy?" she used to ask. Once, we were driving past the infirmary where Helen died and she pointed. "Mummy lives there now," she said.' The rheumy eyes were watering.

'How did he cope after his wife died? A child, a young child, a girl, you said. It must have been difficult.'

'She came to us. Jane... Well, Jane was in her element. A baby in the house again.'

'David stayed in the army?'

'He came home when he could, but it was far from ideal. He even suggested having Barbara with him with a nanny...' Ben finished the sentence under his breath: 'But Jane didn't like the idea.'

'...but Jane put her foot down. It would have been difficult.' He frowned suddenly and looked over at the sideboard. 'I think perhaps we might have a small drink. Sherry?'

They sipped dry sherry from small glasses that quickly became sticky. The alcohol seemed to revive the old man and he continued. 'Barbara was a different child to her father. Even at that age. Not rebellious, you understand. Just determined. There were rows. David had been seconded to Army Intelligence. He couldn't tell us where he was part of the time. We were always in touch but it was.... remote. So he made a decision. He was going to surrender his commission and come home. I was relieved for the child's sake.' He drank again. 'Not that Jane wasn't a wonderful grandmother... but there was more than a generation between them. I feared for the child's spirit. David had a month left to serve, he was on a fourth tour of duty in Northern Ireland and the Provisionals were causing trouble. He was the liaison officer between the unit, the local Army brigade, and the Royal Ulster Constablulary. Jane said he was a fool. He could have gone on to great things, she said, but this time she couldn't stop him. He wanted to be with his daughter.'

The glass went to his lips again and returned empty. Without asking permission, Ben fetched the bottle and refilled it.

'He had a month to go. We were making plans... I knew when I saw them on the step. A brigadier and a half-colonel. "Is he gone?" I asked. Such a strange thing to say.' A tear collected in his eye and then wobbled slowly down the side of his nose. 'I'm sorry,' he said at last. 'Could we leave this for today?'

Chapter Eighteen

HE ARRANGED TO RETURN ON Monday morning and then drove to the office. It was deserted and for a while he relished the silence of the echoing offices. At lunchtime he bought a sandwich and coffee in a Starbucks and then went to the gym, but even exercise didn't calm him. Thoughts kept running through his head. Diana's face as she spat out her words last night, Hammond's words – 'The market's volatile, Ben. It responds instantly to rumour... In the shareholders' interests.' But where did the shareholders' interests lie, with him or with Headey's? When he had worn himself out on a rowing machine, he showered, got in the car and drove to his sister's home. There was sanctuary there.

He stayed till 9.30pm and then made his excuses. He felt a degree of trepidation at the prospect of Diana's reaction to his return, but when he let himself in and walked through to the kitchen, there was a note pinned to the kettle. 'I'm at Flicky's with the girls. Salad and pudding in fridge. Do go to bed, darling. I'll creep in and hug you when I get back.' He shook his head in wonder. It was as though she had completely forgotten the bitterness of the night before. She would creep in and hug him and everything would be alright. He left a light on for her in the hall and went upstairs to bed. When he woke in the morning, he was alone and Diana's side of the bed was undisturbed. He was emerging from the shower when he heard the phone and he sat, naked, on the side of the bed to answer it. 'Darling, hope you haven't set the police on me... I was sooo tired so Flicky said stay, and I couldn't ring and wake you at 2am, could I? We just talked and talked and lost track of time. Did you sleep well?' Her tone was so solicitous, he could almost have believed her.

'Where are you now?'

'I told you... I'm at Flicky's... in her guest room.'

When he put down the phone he sat for a moment, wondering whether or not to dial 1471, but he decided against it. Better not to know. All the same, they couldn't go on like this. Why was he shirking a showdown? He was descending the stairs when he admitted the truth: he feared a showdown would lead to her leaving and he wasn't sure he could live without her.

He was in the kitchen making breakfast and listening to the *Archers* on the radio when Diana returned. They spent the day making polite conversation, she produced a more than passable lunch, and in the afternoon he walked Max for miles. In the evening, he opened a good bottle and they ate sandwiches from a tray and watched television. They didn't talk much. Neither of them had anything worthwhile to say. It was a relief when he could plead an early start the next day and make his way to bed. This time he was the one who feigned sleep and, if she noticed, she did not show it or trouble him for a goodnight embrace.

He had promised to return to Twickenham at 11 the next morning. He went into the office beforehand, sorted his mail, conferred with Madge and with Peter Hammond, and then set out for the vicar's home. He was meeting with the executive directors to discuss the possibility of the Headey's bid, and Hammond was anxious to discuss tactics beforehand, but Ben made excuses. 'This afternoon. 2.30? That'll give us an hour.' The other man's face was a mask of disapproval. What could be more important than keeping the team informed in the face of a hostile takeover? But Ben stood firm. '2.30,' he said, and was out of the office on the stroke of 10.15. The visit to the old man was important but he knew too that it was an excuse, a chance to postpone unpleasant realities for a little while by delving into a safer past.

The Reverend Tulloch was not alone when Ben arrived. 'This is my granddaughter, Barbara,' he said. She was tall and slim, pale-faced because her red hair drained her face of colour. Her eyes were striking, a vivid turquoise blue. They were also hostile.

'I'm a little unsure about the connection here,' she said, when the formal introductions were over and they were seated. 'Your grandparents knew my real grandparents?'

Ben was about to say yes, when the vicar intervened.

'Barbara is a barrister.' He said it apologetically, as though to excuse her directness. So that explained the severe white shirt and black suit. He tried to imagine her in a lawyer's wig and felt his lips twitch. Until he saw her expression and realised that, whatever it was, it wasn't funny.

'My grandmother is very ill,' he explained. 'Quite close to the end of her life. She did know your grandparents, your father too, and his sisters. She is very anxious to know what happened to them. I want to put her mind at rest if I can.'

The turquoise eyes were unrelenting. God help anyone she faces in court, he thought. Aloud, he said, 'Your grandfather was telling me about the loss of your father.' She swung one black-stockinged leg over another, nodded slightly, and settled back in her chair as the old man took up his tale.

'David had been in Northern Ireland for quite a while when it happened. Perhaps that made him careless, I don't know. A car bomb exploded. Set off by someone watching with a remote control, they told me. He was dead when they got to him.' Barbara's eyelids drooped, but only for a second, and then her head became erect.

'They gave him a medal,' she said. 'For valour.'

'I'm sorry,' Ben said. 'But you must be very proud of him.' She nodded without a hint of relenting or the ghost of a smile. She neither likes nor trusts me, Ben thought.

'It must have been hard to lose a second parent.'

'Yes,' she said carefully. 'It was hard on Gramps too but we managed. My grandmother died two years later. I don't think she ever got over the loss of my father.'

The old man and the woman were smiling at one another, and Ben felt his throat constrict. This girl might not be flesh of the vicar's flesh but the love was certainly there. For a moment he contemplated telling Barbara the real reason for his intrusion, but decided against it. She was a barrister. If she scented any injustice, who knew what might happen. In fairness to Adele and to his grandmother, he must tread carefully.

'How did you trace my grandfather?'

'I employed a detective. It was relatively easy, much easier than I feared.'

'He wasn't an only child. You mentioned there were sisters.' It wasn't a question, it was a statement, but a statement that demanded an answer.

'Yes,' Ben said. 'He had two sisters. Margaret and Dolly. As yet we haven't traced Dolly but Margaret is alive and well. She's a widow living in County Durham.'

'She must be quite old. Daddy would have been 69 in November.'

'Margaret was the eldest of the three. She's 76... but quite hale and hearty. I've no news of Dolly at all, I'm afraid, but we're still searching.'

The old man in the wing chair was looking from face to face, as though seeking a guide to what was going on. 'I should go,' Ben said. 'I don't want to tire you out.' The old head shook in polite protest but the rheumy eyes were half-closed and Barbara rose to her feet. 'Yes, I think Gramps needs a rest. I'm in court at two o'clock but could we meet later? If I have a family, I'd like to know more about them. And I can fill you in on details of what happened after my father's death.'

'Of course.' Ben took out a card and scribbled his mobile number on the reverse. 'Ring me when you're free. We'll meet whenever suits you. I have a meeting, but I could be free by five o'clock.'

He made his goodbyes to the vicar and she came with him to the door. 'I'll ring you this afternoon.' He held out his hand but she ignored it. Instead, she held his gaze. 'I don't know what you're up to, Mr Webster, but I won't allow you to hurt my grandfather.' He was about to utter protestations of good intentions, but she had already stepped back and closed the door behind him.

Hammond was waiting for him when he got back to the office. 'The *FT* want something from you. They're doing a piece on the possibilities of a bid. They want you to say how you feel about defending a private family company against predators.'

Ben walked past him. 'I'm not doing it.'

'Why not?' Hammond sounded almost indignant.

'Because,' Ben said and shut his office door. It was a childish reaction, but how could he explain his reluctance to talk about a family company founded, partly at least, on theft from orphans?

Since he had come face to face with what remained of the Brewis family, the moral implications had come home to him. He had had a charmed life, at least until now. It had not been like that for those other children. Whatever Diana or anyone else said, recompense must be made. But when he sat down at his desk, reason overcame his initial distaste. Protecting the firm would benefit everyone. He picked up the phone and summoned Hammond and Madge. 'I'm sorry, Peter. I was wrong. I think we should take an aggressive approach, making it clear Webcon is not for sale and any bidder will have to pay dearly.'

Hammond was grinning now. 'Perfect,' he said. They hatched a statement together and Madge went off to despatch it. When Hammond left the office, Ben worked on his mail for a while, Madge plying him with tea and biscuits and offers to send out for sandwiches. 'You have to eat, you'll make yourself ill. What does that wife of yours think about your eating habits?' The tone of her voice implied what they both knew: that his nutrition was of little interest to Diana.

A call came in at 2.15. 'It's Hamish,' Madge mouthed. Ben nodded and she transferred the call. They chatted for a few moments about the marina and Ben promised to check up on one or two queries with the project co-ordinator, and then Hamish asked after Diana. 'She's fine,' Ben said, agreeing that, yes, they must come up to Argyllshire early in the new year.

'Are you holding out against Headey's?' The question came out of the blue. So that was why Hamish had telephoned. 'Yes,' Ben said. 'We're pretty confident of seeing them off if they make a formal bid.' There was a pause before Hamish spoke again. 'Well, don't forget to look close to home. You can never be sure just where your backing is. It pays to look close to home... in all things.'

Long after Ben had put down the phone, the phrase stuck in his mind. Four words repeated: 'Look close to home.' Perhaps Hammond was talking to Headey's. That would not be a total surprise. CEOs often contemplated sitting down with the enemy. But in the last few days he had felt a bond with Peter. He couldn't believe the man would betray him. In the end, he dismissed the conversation from his mind and got on with his work until Madge put a call through. 'It's Barbara. Barbara Tulloch.' They arranged to meet at the Landmark and he telephoned his home number to say he'd be late. Would Diana be home, and if she was, would she care whether or not he was delayed? 'Darling, do you want to eat out? Or there's heaps of M&S in the freezer,' she said. He settled for Marks & Spencer, smiling wryly at the thought that Diana had managed to reach the age of 29 hardly ever handling, let alone peeling, a real vegetable.

It was 2.30 now, time to talk with Hammond. He gave himself up to discussion and tried not to think about what, if anything, he was going to tell a rising barrister who already suspected his motives.

The meeting went well. The executive directors were gathered in the boardroom and he joined them. James Purnell and Nigel Gatsby were sitting upright and expectant. Neil Pyke was sprawled in his chair, twiddling something – a little metal object like a cocktail stick – between his fingers. The others were wary. Were they contemplating a management buyout? No, they could never mount the finance. Ben launched into his spiel, despite his worries. 'So if they make a bid, we fight it,' he finished, and this seemed to satisfy them.

'Just to say that we all back you. You can count on

us,' Peter Hammond said when he had finished. Purnell and Gatsby were nodding. Pyke looked faintly amused as usual and Ben felt a prickle of anger. For someone who might be facing the loss of his job, he was bloody casual. If Headey's took over, there would be a streamlining of staff and their own people would be favoured. Inevitably, Webcon people would lose out. He thanked them all and then went back to his own office.

Barbara had changed out of the severe white shirt and suit and was draped over a bar stool when he arrived at the Landmark, but she stepped down at the sight of him and walked towards a corner seat. 'What are you drinking?' he asked. 'Is it a Kir Royale?' He ordered two more and sat down beside her. It was Barbara who began the conversation. 'Please pay me the compliment of seeing through this story of your dying grandmother. It may do for Gramps, but I don't buy it. But for the life of me, I can't see why else you'd want to track down my family.'

Somehow her directness made it easier to be honest. 'Years ago, 1940, the start of the war, my grandfather was in partnership with yours. My grandfather had a gammy leg, a club foot. Your grandfather was a Territorial. He was called up and subsequently killed in France. His wife had taken their three children to the country to escape air raids. London was quite fiercely bombed that year.'

'I know,' she said. 'I've read my history. What was this partnership? Did they have a company?'

'It was a builder's yard. Quite small. A jobbing builders, I think you'd call it.'

'But it was owned in equal shares?'

Ben nodded. 'As far as I know. There are no records... Well, none I'm aware of... and everyone connected with it in those days is gone, of course, except my grandmother.'

'What about your parents?' Around them, the cocktail bar was filling with braying Hooray Henrys and a large number of Middle Eastern men. The one or two women among them were ornamental and doe-eyed. 'Shall we get out of here?' he said. 'I'll tell you about my parents then.'

They came out onto the Euston Road and went in search of a pub, not speaking until they were settled in a booth in a small, dingy establishment that nevertheless served a well-chilled wine and even threw in a dish of Japanese crackers. 'That's better. Now, you were asking about my parents. They were killed in a road accident when I was in my teens.'

'I'm sorry.' She sounded as though she meant it.

'Anyway, to return to the war. Your father, who I think was two, had two sisters. Dolly, who was four, and Margaret, the eldest at nine.'

'And they were adopted?'

'Two of them were. Margaret went into an orphanage and eventually into service. She married a miner, I think, was happy, no children, and is now a widow. That's all I know at the moment. To be honest, I didn't know of their existence until very recently.'

'So what happened to the business?'

'My grandfather kept it going. I don't think he had any expert knowledge. Your grandfather was the technical brain. But my grandfather was a good businessman. Shrewd. And the business prospered in the war. It was war damage that kept them going and then the boom in house building afterwards.'

'And now it's Webcon and worth £500 million.' She smiled at his astonishment. 'I looked it up this afternoon.'

'So they tell me. I... I must emphasise, I am not a business genius. What am I doing chairing a multi-million pound company? I sometimes wonder. My godfather took over when my father died. He groomed me to take his place.'

She was pursing her lips. 'So there was never any winding up of the original company?'

'Not as far as I know. Your grandparents were gone, the children were taken care of. I don't even know if there was a formal partnership, let alone a company. I think my grandfather just carried on. He could never have imagined how the business would grow.'

'We could sue for our share.' She said it provocatively but he knew she wasn't serious.

'You could, but with no records I don't fancy your chances.'

'Ah, but I would represent our side for free. You, Mr Webster, would have to pay for legal representation. It could cost you a fortune.'

'I hope it won't come to that.' He lifted the bottle and refilled their glasses. 'I liked your grandfather...'

'Gramps is a saint. My grandmother was a bitch. Don't look shocked. I could tell from your face today that you'd guessed as much. She made Gramps' life hell. My father's too, with her possessiveness and her grudging affection. My mother was putty in her hands. I survived because I stood up to her. But I don't want to talk about that. Tell me about Margaret. She's my aunt. It sounds quite strange to say that. And the other one: Dolly? Aunt Dolly! What a hoot!'

It was 8.30 when they left the pub. 'I'll set up a meeting,' he promised. 'As soon as we can. Perhaps we could bring her here? Your grandfather was relieved to hear she'd survived.'

'That would be nice.' She held out her hand before they parted and he felt a degree of satisfaction at the progress it represented.

'Where the hell have you been?' Diana said as he let himself into the hall. Her face was pale and two red spots of colour rode high on her cheeks.

'I had a meeting. I told you.' For some reason he didn't want to tell her about Barbara.

'A meeting. About the bloody takeover, I suppose.'

He walked past her into the kitchen. A frozen lasagne stood on the bench alongside a bottle of gin and a sliced lemon. He took the meal out of its wrapper and put it in the microwave. 'We haven't been taken over yet, Diana. It's just a rumour at the moment.'

'Why not let them? Don't pretend you have the slightest flare for the construction business. You're there because you were born in the right stable.' It was said contemptuously and it stung.

'At least I work!' The moment he said it, he regretted

it – or, rather, regretted its inevitable consequence.

'I suppose that means I don't work? Why should I? I am your fucking wife and, yes, I have had a gin or two before you remark on my language. I need something to make life bearable in this dreary, dreary house.'

He would have moved past her to get a plate but she barred his way. 'Go on. For once in your life, say what you think. Don't be such a bloody gentleman... Always a bloody gentleman, when what a woman really needs is a MAN!'

He forgot about the lasagne turning in the microwave. All he wanted was to get out of the kitchen and away from her voice, but it followed him up the stairs. 'Yes, run away. What a pity your sainted grandmother's pegging out. You used to run to her. Well there's only me now, sunshine. I am all you've got. So if you had any sense, you'd let Headey's take over and take oodles of cash, and then we could get on with our lives.'

He paused and turned on the landing to look down into the hall. 'How did you know it was Headey's?'

'You told me.' But he had never discussed the bid with her, not in any detail, and from the way her eyes dropped, afraid of meeting his, she knew it.

He had showered and retreated to his bed when he remembered Hamish's phone call. 'Look close to home. It pays to look close to home... in all things.'

Chapter Nineteen

'WHY ARE THEY SO KEEN?' Ben asked the question without lifting his eyes from the report in front of him. Headey's were getting ready to up their offer, according to Hammond's informant.

'Logistical and geographical presence?' Hammond offered. 'Enhanced reputation? And land. Especially land.'

It was the land which was swinging it, Ben thought. Parcels of land in areas ripe for development, bought at a reasonable price by Webcon, and now, with planning permission, worth probably half as much again. Aloud, he said, 'What will the outcome be if the offer is put to the board?'

Hammond shrugged. 'It's a good offer. You can count on family loyalty. I'll back you. But institutions will go for the cash. You could get a stand off at the board meeting, in which case it will go out to the shareholders...'

'...who will opt for the cash,' Ben finished for him. 'So either way we lose.'

'Unless we get a majority from the board – a definite

turndown. I've talked with most of them. They're cagey, but if you can count on your own people... You'll have your grandmother's proxy?' Ben nodded. 'And my brother-in-law will back me.'

After Hammond left, Ben sat at his desk thinking about the board meeting. If it went against him, would he care? If Webcon vanished in a takeover, he could take Diana around the world, make a fresh start. They had been happy once. He was thinking of hot sand underfoot when the phone rang.

'Darling, I'm sorry about last night. I was mean. Buy me lunch?' She sounded young and vulnerable. 'Where and when?' he said. They settled on L'Etoile and he buzzed Madge to book a table, then dialled his sister's number. 'Heaps to tell you,' he said. 'We've found the boy – or, rather, his daughter. He died in Northern Ireland, the IRA.'

'Come over for supper. Harry is home tonight. Bring Diana. I'll just do pasta or something simple.'

He felt good when he put down the phone. In the early days there had been lots of pasta nights. Harry playing his guitar, Adele in the kitchen, Diana sitting at his knee, looking up at him sometimes to signal 'Isn't this great?' Perhaps tonight it could be like that again.

Elena's welcome at L'Etoile was as warm as ever. 'I've put you at your favourite table,' she said, leading them to the secluded corner. As usual, her grey hair was immaculate, her figure trim, her energy unbounded. 'She makes me feel effete just looking at her,' Diana said, as the other woman moved away.

Diana was wearing black but had added red earrings and a red neckerchief to lift the outfit. She looked beautiful and he felt a familiar glow of pride as he realised men were looking at her and envying him.

They sipped wine and studied the menu. 'Smoked salmon blinis and scallops,' she said firmly. 'And some green beans.' Ben chose the warm chicory salad and a risotto and helped himself to an olive. 'Adele wants us to go for supper tonight. We need to talk things over but she particularly wants you, too.'

'Darling...' Diana's nose was wrinkling apologetically. 'Would you mind awfully if I didn't go? I feel really bushed and I promised myself an early night. 'Jamas at seven and a hot toddy. I think I might have a cold coming on and an early night could break it before it gets a hold.' He said he didn't mind and would explain to Adele, but there was a curious lack of disappointment in him which he couldn't understand. He had been looking forward to the idea of tonight, so why wasn't he choked that it would not go as planned? As the chicory salad was placed in front of him, he admitted the reason. He had never really expected her to go with him, so disappointment didn't enter into it.

He saw his wife into a cab at the end of lunch. He had told her he would go straight to Adele's from the office, but in fact he must call on his grandmother on the way. He hadn't been for two days. Sue would have telephoned if all was not well, but he should still see for himself.

Neil Pyke was leaving as he crossed the lobby. 'Everything alright?' Ben asked. 'Yes. Fine. I've put the

Essex specifications on your desk. I'm just off to the gym. Trying to keep in shape.'

Ben tried to look encouraging. 'Wise move. I'll join you one of these days.' Going up in the lift his brow wrinkled. Why had Neil felt it necessary to explain his leaving early? He was an executive director. He could come and go as he pleased. He ceased pondering when he sat down to a pile of letters needing a signature and the Essex specifications, which were technically almost beyond him.

At 4.30pm he pushed back his chair, switched off his desk light and made his goodbyes. 'I haven't heard from Sparrow for a couple of days,' he said to Madge as he passed through her office. 'I think he's having difficulty.'

'Needle in a haystack, that's the trouble. Still, if anyone can do it, he can.' She was trying to sound nonchalant but it didn't work.

Ben drove himself to Hampstead. 'She's had a good day,' Sue said as they mounted the stairs together, but when he came face to face with his grandmother he was shocked. She was visibly frailer, there were dark rings around her eyes and she seemed somehow smaller.

'Good news,' he said, taking her thin old hands in his warm ones. Her skin was dry and papery, but these hands had comforted him in childhood. He cleared his throat. 'We've found Billy. At least, we know what happened to him.'

She seemed to relax as he talked of the vicar and his love for the boy. 'So he did alright,' she said, nodding as she spoke. Her face clouded when he told her of Billy's death in military service. 'But he had a daughter. She's a barrister here in London.'

'A barrister!'

Her eyes widened and he smiled. 'A profession, Gran. Hasn't she done well?' She realised he was humouring her and freed a hand to smack his arm. 'You're a bad boy. Still, a woman barrister. They'd have liked that, Mollie and Jack. Jack prized education. That's why he thought so much of your grandfather. He was an educated man. A good man.' Of late, Ben had felt ambivalent about his grandfather, but he nodded agreement.

'Yes. She's quite something. Very imposing, very fond of the vicar.'

'Well, he's brought her up by all accounts. Losing her mother and everything.' There was a pause. 'Did you tell her...?'

'Did I tell her she was entitled to a share of Webcon? Not exactly. But I explained the circumstances.'

The old face suddenly looked even older. 'Was she alright about it?'

'She understood the difficulties. She's quite fierce. She can see there might be some liability – but it was all very amicable.'

'No news of Dolly?'

'Not yet. She's more difficult. Tracing the vicar was comparatively easy. There aren't too many of them around. All we know about Dolly was that she went off in a car. It'll have to be trawling through files, I'm afraid, but I've got a good man on it. You're not to worry.'

Her face lit up at news that he was going to Adele's

for supper. 'With Diana?'

'No, Gran. She's… not feeling a hundred per cent.'

Suddenly the old eyes were twinkling. 'She's not…'

'No, she's not pregnant. Soon, I promise. You'll have to make do with Adele's brood until then.'

'She looks a little fragile,' he said, as Sue accompanied him to the front door. The nurse sighed. 'Inevitable, I'm afraid. But the will's still strong. That's the main thing.'

He promised to come back soon and bring Diana. It was weeks, months since she had visited. If he hadn't realised, the look of polite disbelief on the nurse's face would have told him so.

He relaxed in his sister's home. She didn't seem at all put out that he had come alone. The meal was simple and simply served and they talked non-stop about the news of the day, her tribulations with Defra and the children's prowess on the sporting field. 'I know we're going to talk about the business,' Adele said over coffee, 'but do you mind if I just switch on the TV for a moment? I want to see who's expelled from *The House* tonight.'

'You don't watch that rubbish!' he said in mock horror. Half the nation was watching a group of wretches caught in reality-TV hell.

'Just to see who's out,' Adele pleaded.

'You're taping it,' her husband accused. 'You can watch it later.'

'I know… but just a little look.'

They watched as an alternative comedian was ejected. 'I didn't think it would be him,' Adele said as she switched it off. 'Everyone thought it would be Rocco.' She saw Ben's incomprehension. 'Rocco the wrestler. Horrible man.'

'They vote to keep the worst ones in,' Harry said. 'They make better telly.'

Ben was just about to launch into an update when his phone rang. It was Sparrow. 'Something's turned up,' he said. Ben signalled to Adele that there was news. 'About Dolly?'

'No. Not a whisper about her, I'm afraid. No, this is something rather unexpected. I'm going back to Yorkshire tonight. You haven't got half an hour later on, have you?'

They arranged to meet in a pub in Notting Hill at 10.15pm. 'It won't take more than half an hour,' Sparrow said, 'but I'd like to get your views.'

'Can't you tell me now?'

'It's nothing to worry about. I'll see you 10.15.'

'What is it?' Adele's eyebrows were raised.

'I don't know. Nothing to worry about, he says, but there's nothing on Dolly and that's more worrying.'

'You've found two of them. Well, traced them anyway.'

He wanted to explain why it was desperately important to find all three but he couldn't. Somehow what had been a quirky request from his grandmother had become a personal crusade.

He filled in Adele and Harry on the Billy story. 'That's sad,' Adele said. 'Losing both her parents. History repeating itself.' Her husband was nodding. 'Both fathers killed in pointless wars.'

A discussion on the merits of World War Two

followed, Ben contending it had hardly been pointless, the others secretly agreeing but arguing for the hell of it. 'I have enjoyed myself,' he said as he left. It was true. It had been a good evening in every sense of the word.

He drove back to the office and parked the car in the underground car park. He had had two glasses of wine and wine with lunch. If he was to have a pint with Sparrow, he would be over the limit. Better to call a cab to the pub and another home. English would pick him up if he rang early enough.

The pub was half-empty but warm and welcoming nevertheless. Sparrow was in a booth and two pints of beer were already on the table.

'Well,' Ben said. 'What's the secret?'

'This,' the detective said and pushed a photocopy of a newspaper cutting towards him. Ben looked down at a section from the classified page of a broadsheet. It was from last year.

'BREWIS,' it was headed. 'Would any descendants of John Leroy Brewis, killed in France in 1940, please contact Mlle Monique Bressier.' A contact address was given below; a village called Buerges in France.

'Leroy?' Ben's eyes widened.

'That was his mother's maiden name. It has to be him. Date's right, name's right. If it had been an ordinary second name, I wouldn't be sure, but Leroy's pretty distinctive.'

'What does it mean?'

'Who knows? Want me to follow it up?'

'I think you must. Could Dolly have married a Frenchman?'

'She could have done, I suppose. After the war. This Bressier woman could be a daughter, even a granddaughter.'

As Ben rode home in a cab, he thought about the cutting. Jack Brewis had been dead for more than sixty years. Why would anyone be trying to make contact now?

He had expected the house to be in darkness, but there were lights on and he could hear a radio upstairs. Diana was in the bathroom but she emerged as he got to the top of the stairs, pulling a towelling robe around her.

'I thought you were having an early night?'

'I tried, darling. But I started watching TV and I just got stuck. You know how addictive that dreadful *House* thing is.'

'Who got evicted?' As he asked the question, he couldn't believe his ears. Why had he asked for information he already possessed?

'Rocco... Rocco the wrestler. Well, everyone was expecting it.'

'Yes,' he said. 'I thought it would be him.'

She had lied, a trivial lie perhaps to cover up the fact that she had been elsewhere? Or that someone else had been here. In his bed?

Afterwards, he lay awake trying to concentrate on why anyone would try to trace a dead soldier sixty years after the war. It was easier to think about that than to think about his marriage.

Chapter Twenty

'So it's come,' Ben said. The formal bid by Headey's for Webcon was now on the table. The morning papers had carried their denials: 'Webcon Chairman denies bid as shares soar'; '"Takeover bid a rumour," says Webcon CEO.' One headline or other ornamented every business page – but all their denials had been in vain. The bid was fact as of 11am that morning. 'We need to call a meeting,' Hammond said. 'It'll take a day or so to get everyone together.'

Ben nodded. 'What will they do?' He had asked that question so many times before, but now it had added meaning. 'They'll go for whatever offers greater value,' Hammond said.

'We do.' Ben's reply was swift and vehement. Hammond's return was more measured. 'Long term, Ben. Long term. They'll go for a quick return, bird in the hand. After all, business could see a downturn if the economic climate changes. If the offer turns out to be good enough, they'll go for it.'

'They should know better.' Ben's tone was bitter because he knew there was reason in what the other man said.

Later that day, he tried to explain it to Adele. 'You know I've never had a head for business.' Adele's face was crumpled in earnestness. 'I mean, I want to help, offer some real support, but I don't understand what's going on. You're the boss. Why can't you just say "No sale" and that's that?'

Ben couldn't help laughing. 'If only it was so easy. But you have to try to understand, Del, because it affects you – and the kids. It's quite simple really. Headey's are another construction company, probably a little bigger than us, but not much. And they don't have the brown-field sites we have, that's the attraction. They've been buying our shares for a while. I knew that, but I didn't think they'd actually mount a takeover. However, they've put in a bid. Quite a good one. It's not acceptable to me because I don't want the company to fall into other hands, but I suspect it might be quite appealing to the bigger shareholders.'

'So what happens now?' Ben felt his lips twitch. Adele trying to put on a serious expression was something else. 'I have to persuade the board to turn the bid down. Our share price is rocketing because the news has leaked out. I'm hoping I can persuade them to sit tight.'

'Surely they'll back you. I mean, you know them all... Neville Carteret is your brother-in-law, for God's sake.'

'He's one vote, Del. I think the executive directors will

back me. The others will probably back the bid. And even if I carry the board, it might still go to the shareholders for a final decision. But I don't want you to worry. Even if Headey's succeeds, you'll get a good price for your holding.'

'But what'll happen to you? What will you do?' Ben stood up and stooped to kiss his sister's cheek.

'I daresay I'll find something. And Diana will be pleased. We might be able to get some time together, even go off somewhere for a while.' But Adele only pursed her lips at the mention of his wife. There had never been much love lost between the two women, Ben thought, as he made his goodbyes and stepped into the car. He waved to Adele until she was out of sight and then, as English negotiated the A40 and headed towards the city centre, he began to scan the contents of his briefcase. For the next hour he sat in his office, reading and signing the letters Madge put in front of him and scanning some specifications. 'Right,' she said at last. 'Now you can go to lunch.'

'I'm not going out.'

'You are,' she said. 'I've booked a table at Chez Gérard. Sparrow is waiting there for you.'

'He's got news about Dolly?'

'Get going and you'll find out.'

But it was not news of Dolly. 'I talked to a colleague of mine in Paris. He put out some feelers and came up with the goods. The woman – girl – who put in the advert is a hostess with Air France. Her mother was the illegitimate child of a British soldier – at least that's the story. Her grandmother imparted the information on her death bed and the mother...'

'The girl's mother?'

'Yes, the girl's mother wanted to find her father. They advertised but no one came forward, so the girl paid a detective agency. They tracked the father easily enough – she had his name and number – but when they found he'd been killed before the child was even born, they just lost interest. My contact knew their agency, that's how he got onto it so quickly.'

Ben let out his breath in a whistle. 'Could it be true?'

Sparrow shrugged. 'They did have his details. On the other hand, they could have taken the dog tags from a dead body. Who's to say what happens in war.'

'He was killed in France. Gran told me that.'

'Ah, well...' The detective looked thoughtful. 'If we know he was there... For the life of me I can't see how they could have got his name unless there had been contact of some sort. He was an ordinary squaddie, by all accounts, so they didn't choose him because he was rich pickings.'

Ben thought about it as he was driven back to the office. Another child! He had never bargained for that. And even if it was true, was he under any moral obligation? His grandmother knew nothing of the child's existence; must not know. He could just pretend he had never seen the notice and stick to his brief, which was to find the three children to whom his grandmother had made a promise. On the other hand, if the child was Jack Brewis's offspring, was she not equally as entitled to her inheritance as the others? Eventually, he decided to put the matter to one side. Sparrow had promised to talk to the air hostess, either in Paris or when and if she flew into London. For the time being, that was enough.

Back in his office, he summoned Hammond – but before he could speak, Hammond began. 'We're the object of a feeding frenzy now, Ben. Hecht and the Masters Group have suggested they're about to put in competitive bids. I've been expecting at least one other bid but two...'

His CEO sounded dejected and Ben seized the reins. 'Okay. Peter, I want you to prepare a paper setting out what we can achieve if we stay as we are and use our land for new projects. We need it for ammunition. Can you do that?'

Hammond's 'Yes' was decisive. Given something to do, he felt more hopeful. 'We need to show them we're still the better option in value terms. I'll get onto it straight away.' He was already moving towards his office when Ben said, 'Is Neil about? I want him to do some research into Headey's financial position.'

'He's gone out.' Hammond was already thinking about his task and his answer was vague. 'He said something about an appointment. I don't think he's coming back this afternoon.'

The phone rang and Hammond made his exit as Ben lifted the receiver. 'Barbara! Good to hear from you.' She was ringing to thank him and to ask when the meeting with her aunt could be arranged. 'I'll sort it,' he promised. 'Either here or in Durham. Give me a day or two to make arrangements.'

He turned the whole thing over to Madge. 'I want you to find out if Margaret Riley is willing to come to London. If she is, book her into a good hotel – central – and first-class travel. I could send a car for her if she'd prefer that to the train. See if she'll come for a week or so. That'll give them time to get to know one another as well as meeting Gran.'

Madge seemed to relish the prospect of organising Margaret's trip. 'Leave it to me,' she said. 'How was your lunch?'

Ben grinned ruefully. 'Interesting. Not the meal, that was okay. Your boyfriend's news was something else.'

'Never mind my "boyfriend". We're just friends.'

'His eyes light up every time he mentions your name. That's pretty friendly in my book.'

She flounced out of his office, but he could tell his teasing hadn't displeased her. She had never been married. Sparrow was a widower, remarried and divorced. Would it work? At least it wasn't his problem. That was one small mercy. He got back to work.

He cleared his desk by five o'clock and decided to go straight home. He had intended to visit his grandmother, perhaps even probe her gently for anything more she might know about Jack Brewis's death in 1940 or his time in France before that, but it would wait. Tonight he wanted to spend time with his wife.

He could hear her in the kitchen when he entered the hall and he walked though the open door. 'Only scrambled eggs and smoked salmon, darling. Will it do?' He felt a sudden wave of contentment engulf him. She was home. They would eat together, he would tell her about the day. The evening lay ahead, full of infinite possibilities. 'I'll just have a shower,' he said. 'Smoked salmon sounds wonderful.' He kissed the back of her neck as she stood by the stove, then raced upstairs to get rid of the grime of the day.

He had showered and was back in the bedroom reaching for a clean shirt, when he saw something gleaming on the bedside rug. He picked it up and turned it over in his fingers. It was the small gilt cocktail stick he had seen in the boardroom being twirled in the lean brown fingers of Neil Pyke. And suddenly it all came clear. Pyke's leaving the office almost every afternoon. Hamish's warning: 'Look close to home.'

He sat down on the bed, the towel that girded his loins falling to the floor. How could he have been so blind? Or was he being stupid? He looked at the cocktail stick. Mass-produced, value fifty pence. There must be hundreds, thousands of them. Hope sprang up but was extinguished when he remembered Diana emerging from the shower as he came into the bedroom last night. Washing away the odour of sex! He had gone to the bathroom and felt her towels, pink to distinguish them from his, which were white. They were damp, and when he had bent to kiss her neck her hair had been damp against his cheek. Funny how you could notice things and then not notice them at all until you had a reason.

He dressed carefully, taking comfort in the settling of a collar here, the knotting of a tie there. What was the cuckolded husband supposed to do? He knew what his inclination was: to smash his fist into Pyke's smug face. To sack him without recompense, to blacken his name to the four quarters of the earth. For the time being, however, he went downstairs and ate scrambled egg and salmon that turned to celluloid on his tongue.

Afterwards, he pleaded a headache and went outside for fresh air. It was cold and he almost turned back for a sweater but decided against it. The wind cut through his thin shirt and somehow that felt right. He deserved punishment for being a blind fool, if for nothing else. That night at the dinner party, Pyke must have been there at Diana's instigation, in which case their hostess knew. Hamish almost certainly did, hence the warnings.

He walked down the garden and out onto the path that circled their property. He would keep on walking in circles until he dropped from exhaustion and the dew fell on him at dawn. Except that he couldn't. He had obligations, duties, ties that demanded he cope. But not tomorrow. Not just yet.

'I'll sleep in the guest room if you don't mind. This filthy head. I don't want to disturb you.' She was solicitous, even bringing him lavender oil to anoint his pillow. 'That'll help, darling. You'll see.'

When he was alone, he took out his phone and dialled the detective's number. 'I'm sorry to ring so late...' Sparrow interrupted him. 'Don't apologise, I'm glad you rang. I think I'm onto Dolly. I only found out tonight or I'd have phoned your office. If it's her, and it's pretty certain, she's not far from London.'

'Good.' The news made it easier to say what he had intended. 'Don't bother chasing the French connection. I'm due in Paris tomorrow, I'll follow it up myself. You go after Dolly.'

Alone in the dark, he plotted what needed to be done to buy him 24 hours away. Madge would chase up flights, addresses, cancel his appointments. He could leave it all to her. He closed his eyes and, surprisingly, slept.

Chapter Twenty One

'LEAVE IT TO ME,' MADGE said sleepily when he phoned her at 6.30am. By 10am he was on an Air France flight out of Heathrow, a typed itinerary and all the relevant reservations in his hand luggage. 'Remind me to give you a pay rise,' he had said as she handed them over. This brought a sniff of contempt. Sinking back into his seat, he pondered, not for the first time, how old Madge was. She had worked for his father and known his grandfather, so she was at least sixty. He made a mental note to quiz her about the early days of the business. That there was a bond of sorts between her and the detective he had no doubt, but whether it was romance or camaraderie he couldn't be sure.

He accepted a gin and tonic and opened the documents. Monique Bressier lived in the Avenue Raymond Poincaré, which was not the address given in the original advertisement. He looked up the photocopy. The name had been Bressier but the address was Buerges, a village in northern France.

He was booked into the Le Parc hotel, which was also on the Avenue Raymond Poincaré. That was handy. More brownie points for Madge. He looked at the tiny map on the printout of the hotel brochure. The Avenue Poincaré was one of the spokes of a half-wheel with the Place du Trocadéro at its hub. He knew the district vaguely. As a boy he had stayed in Rue St Didier, which ran off Poincaré, so the Arc de Triomphe must be close by, too. He closed his eyes, remembering a holiday in Paris with Diana. They had walked hand in hand from the Trocadéro down to the Seine and had taken a boat to see the bridges. The bridges of Paris. And now she was probably preparing to ring one of his employees and tell him they had a whole 24 hours in which to betray him. For a moment, the hope that he might be wrong sprang up – but he quashed it. False hope was no hope at all.

Outside the plane window, white clouds came and went. Diana had worn white the first time he saw her. He was walking onto a tennis court and she was coming off, her cheeks flushed with exertion, her eyes sparkling with the thrill of a win. 'Who's that?' he had asked his partner. 'Diana. Diana Carteret. Don't drool, old chap. She's spoken for.' But he could no more walk away from her than he could have walked on water. In the end, she had broken off her engagement and they had been married four months later. With a pang he remembered her fiancé after the break-up. He had given precious little thought to the man he had supplanted. Now he knew exactly how that man must have felt. In a way, it was just punishment.

He went back to the folder Madge had given him. She had put all the logistics in place, but how was he going to handle the real purpose of his visit? A stewardess sashayed past in a wave of perfume. Pearls were threaded through the knotted scarf at her throat. A touch of the famed French chic. Monique Bressier was a stewardess, so presumably also chic, but was she a descendant of Jack Brewis and, if so, what the hell was he going to do about it? They were still flying through cloud, feather beds rolling past the window, endlessly comforting. If he wanted to, he could re-embark at Charles de Gaulle and forget Monique Bressier existed. He owed her nothing because he was hardly to blame for the present situation. There was not even a debt of honour owed by his grandmother. No promise to be kept. Except that if she was Jack Brewis's child, she was also entitled to a share of what had been filched. He put uncomfortable thoughts aside, accepted another G and T, and before he had finished it they were landing.

He reached the hotel at 11.30am French time and checked into a room which overlooked a tree-lined courtyard. There were tea- and coffee-making facilities in the room but he felt restless. Besides, he wanted to check out Monique Bressier's address, perhaps even leave a message. He couldn't just burst in on her unannounced. Suddenly the folly of what he had done washed over him. He had not come to Paris on an organised mission. He had run away from a private and professional life rapidly sliding out of control. His place was back in London sorting out the mess, so what the hell was he doing here? There were three messages from Peter Hammond on his mobile, but he ignored them. Time enough to confront that situation. He had come to Paris; there was nothing to be gained by turning tail to run now.

Number 14, the Bressier address, was down from the hotel, and he started walking towards the Place Victor Hugo. There were coffee shops there, if memory served him correctly. He would sit for a while and watch the world go by, marvel at the chaotic Parisian traffic which constantly threatened collision but seldom produced it. Number 14, when he reached it, came as something of a surprise. It was an apartment block, elegantly shuttered, a wrought-iron gate guarding a courtyard in which a fountain played. Paris was an expensive city. This was upmarket accommodation for an air hostess, who probably earned a few hundred euros a week. He looked at the names listed next to the bells, but no Bressier. The actual address had been apartment nine, number 14. But the name attached to nine was Deschamps. Perhaps Monique had moved. On an impulse he rang the bell. If she had gone, he would cancel his room and fly back this afternoon. It would be the sensible thing to do and half of him hoped it would turn out that way. A female voice sounded over the intercom: 'Oui?'

'I'm looking for Monique Bressier,' he said. And then: 'Je suis, um...' What on earth was French for 'looking for'? But the voice was speaking in perfect, if accented, English. 'Monique is out of Paris. Until this evening. Can you call back then?'

He stumbled out agreement, wondering what else he should say. Before he could decide, the woman spoke again. 'Who shall I say called for her?' An impulse to give a false name came and went. 'My name is Webster, Ben Webster. I'll come back this evening. Merci bien.' 'Ah, oui.' There was a click of the intercom and he continued towards the Place Victor Hugo, now in search of strong liquor. Coffee wouldn't do.

For the next two hours, he sat at a window-seat watching Paris go by. Every other face was black, but there seemed none of the racial tension he sometimes sensed in London. Traffic thundered in from the streets leading into the Place – for Victor Hugo was another, if smaller, hub, surrounded by tall, graceful, shuttered houses. He drank coffee after his first brandy and pondered the magnificent construction that was Paris. Planned by Napoleon, so they said, and hardly a false note struck. The Little Emperor had wanted to make the city the capital of Europe. Architecturally, he had succeeded. No other capital city could match the twelve avenues off the Etoile or the sweep of the Champs Elysées, although London's Mall might run it close.

At five he ordered a croque monsieur, aware that although he had no appetite, he had not eaten since breakfast, and who knew what the evening might bring. He checked his mobile. Two texts from Diana: 'Where are you?' at 9.45am and 'Where the hell are you?' at 1.15pm. She must have rung the office and discovered he was not behind his desk. He switched off his phone without replying, although he would have liked to have told her to take good care of Max. The dog was not getting a fair shake at the moment. He would have to make it up to him afterwards.

At 7.15pm he walked back to the hotel, showered and changed and then retraced his steps to number 14. This time the voice was different, but still young and female. 'It's Ben Webster,' he said. 'I called earlier. They said you'd be back this evening. If you're Monique Bressier, that is.' This time he didn't attempt to speak in French. She was an air hostess. She'd understand.

'What do you want?' It was blunt but not unpleasant.

'It's about an advert in the *Telegraph*. Last year. You were asking about a Jack Brewis.' There was a long pause and then, 'You'd better come up. Third floor.' There was a click, the wrought-iron gates opened and he stepped inside. The entrance was a marble lobby, the gilt chairs there obviously antique. The place reeked money. He took the elevator to the third floor and emerged onto pile carpets. A door was half-open at the end of the hallway and a girl was leaning out. She was young, pretty in a gamine way, and looking slightly apprehensive. She was also in a state of undress. A short robe covered the strategic areas but the long legs were bare and the feet shoeless.

'Come in,' she said. 'I've just come off a flight. Sit down. I'll be with you in a moment.' He sank into an armchair and looked around the room. Modern upholstery but a number of genuine antiques, unless he was much mistaken. A Lalique clock on the mantel and a Daum lamp in a corner. Monique was either a child of privilege or a kept woman. He eyed a sideboard groaning with booze and wondered if he dared pour himself the stiff drink he needed.

When she came back into the room she was wearing jeans and an angora sweater. 'There now,' she said. 'Can I get you a drink?' He settled for a glass of red wine and she sat opposite him, drawing her legs up onto her chair.

'Well,' he said, wondering where to start.

'Well,' she mimicked and smiled at him.

His tension eased. 'I don't know where to begin,' he said, and then it came out in a rush. 'I was looking for the children of a Jack Brewis, searching for them because they hadn't been heard of since the war. The detective I employed came across an advert – your advert – and I just wondered where you fitted in.' He could have added that had he not discovered he was a cuckold, he would never have come to Paris, but he didn't.

'Are you a relative?'

'No.' She was looking at him expectantly, so he launched into the tale of Brewis's death and his grandmother's promise, omitting any mention of a stolen business. 'She's old now and very frail. She wanted to know what had happened to them.'

Monique nodded. 'I see. You want to know about the advertisement. Why the advertisement? Well, it concerns *my* grandmother. Or rather, my maman...' The word 'maman' was said with great affection. 'She was born in 1941. A child of war. She was told her father was a British serviceman but nothing more. Her mother married in 1946, a Frenchman. He was good to her. She wondered, perhaps, over the years, but it seemed impossible to find out anything and so she let it go. My grand-mother died three years ago and maman inherited her possessions; papers, photographs. There was one, a snapshot, of a British Tommy with a name and number on the back. It looked as though he was the one – her father. I was flying in and out of London, so I put in the advert. I wanted it for her, some certainty.' She struggled. 'Bien... nothing! So we, an agency I used, tried your War Office. They told us he had been killed so...' She threw up her hands. 'Fini. It was closure of a sort.' She leaned forward. 'You said there were children?'

He told her then, of Margaret and Billy and Dolly, who was still a mystery. She listened, occasionally filling his glass, until he felt pleasantly woozy. 'I feel comfort-able,' he thought. 'Here in this strange room with a woman I met an hour ago. I feel at peace.'

'If it's true that he was my grandfather, I'd like to meet them... I suppose.' She was suddenly doubtful. 'It's a lot to take in.' She began to laugh. 'I came home for an early night and...' She blew out her cheeks. 'Wow!'

'I ought to let you get some sleep.' He suddenly felt reluctant to leave but he got to his feet. 'Are you flying tomorrow?' She shook her head. 'Not till Saturday.'

'Will you have lunch with me?' They settled on 12.15pm and he said goodnight. He held out a hand, but he wanted to lean forward and kiss her brow. That was the drink. She smelled of some perfume – rose, perhaps, but a little spicy.

He went down in the lift and out into the Paris street. Life was moving very fast. For the moment, all he could do was lie back and let the current take him wherever it chose.

Chapter Twenty Two

HE BREAKFASTED IN HIS ROOM. Melting croissants, salty butter, apricot conserve and coffee from an earthenware jug. Afterwards, he crossed to the window and looked out onto the quiet street. Down at the junction, there was teeming traffic. In this room, for the moment, there was peace. By the time he had showered and dressed it was ten o'clock. He packed his case and looked around him. One more anonymous hotel room. He went downstairs, checked the case with the concierge, paid his bill and wandered out into the Paris street. He turned right, afraid to turn left in case the lure of number 14 proved too strong. It wouldn't do to call on her before 12.30pm. 12.15pm at the earliest. He was booked on the 4.30pm London flight. He would have to leave for the airport at 2.00pm. Less than two hours. It didn't seem enough. He walked up to the Trocadéro, crossed the road and started down towards the Seine. A cold wind was blowing but it didn't seem to matter. He stood on the bridge for a long while, watching the traffic on the river, and then he turned and headed back to the Avenue Poincaré. There was little enough time as it was, he mustn't waste any of it.

She was ready when he rang the bell. 'I'm coming down.' She had jeans on under a belted trench coat and her hair was fastened on top of her head. 'Where?' he asked, but she simply took his arm and drew him towards Avenue Victor Hugo. Neither of them spoke until they were settled either side of a white-clothed table with a carafe in front of them and the odour of good food in their nostrils. They both chose mussels followed by filet d'agneau. 'Now,' he said, when they were left alone. 'Time is limited. Tell me about your grandmother.'

For the next hour they talked about young men far from home, fighting a losing battle, hungry perhaps for comfort. 'How old was your grandmother in 1940?' She shook her head. 'Twenty-one perhaps. She was 85 when she died. So, yes, twenty-one. Very pretty.' She looked down at her plate for a while. 'His wife. Was she pretty?' He had to confess he didn't know. 'I never knew them. Never knew of their existence until a few weeks ago. They were never mentioned.' Guilty conscience, he thought, but kept it to himself. 'My grandmother might have photographs. I could ask.'

In his pocket, his phone was vibrating but he ignored it. 'When are you in London again?' She was flying to London in three days' time. 'We could meet,' he said. He meant it to sound nonchalant but it came out intense. 'Do you like flying?' he asked hastily to cover his embarrassment.

She pulled a face. 'It's okay. It pays.'

'Well... I should think. You have a nice apartment.' Now she was laughing, throwing back her head. He felt again the desire to lean forward, kiss her throat, her mouth. 'I don't own it. We share it, four of us. We can just manage the rent.' Her hair was coming loose, wisping at her temples. 'I keep saving for a deposit on a place of my own but... Pouf! It's gone.'

His phone throbbed again, and again he ignored it. 'If you didn't fly, what would you do?' She was a florist. A trained florist but it didn't pay as well as flying. 'I prefer cooking to floristry but a cook doesn't earn much either. You have to do what comes.' The shrug of her shoulders was graphic.

It was 1.45pm. He signalled to the waiter and took out his Amex. 'Can we meet when you're in London? I want to arrange for you to meet...' He floundered. If she was Jack Brewis's granddaughter, that would make Margaret her aunt. '...to meet Margaret.' But he couldn't arrange a meeting until they were sure of her parentage. Never mind, it would do as an excuse because he had to see her again.

She came with him as far as the hotel and waited until the cab came. 'It's strange,' he said. 'But I feel as though we've known one another for a long time.' The cab was drawing up and she was reaching to kiss his cheek. 'My card,' he said, pushing it into her hand. 'Ring me.' He felt young and foolish and good. Above all, he felt good. Long after the car had whirled around Place Victor Hugo and was heading down towards Place d'Etoile, her face stayed in his mind's eye.

In the departure lounge, he took out his phone and scanned the inbox. Six missed calls: three from Hammond, one each from Diana and Barbara, and another from Madge. No one had left a message. He switched it off and put it away. He had two hours before he must face them. On the plane he closed his eyes and thought of Paris, but as England appeared below, reason reasserted itself.

He had been mad to take off for Paris on a whim. Madder still to moon over Monique like a lovesick idiot. He had a wife and a business, both in urgent need of attention. He rang Madge from baggage reclaim. 'How are things?' 'Pretty bloody but we'll cope. Get yourself in here.'

He went straight to the office and was paying off his cab when Pyke appeared. 'You're back.' There was no surprise in Pyke's voice. His welcoming smile was languid. 'Peter's been ringing all over.'

Ben couldn't resist a jibe. 'My wife too, I imagine. Unless she's been kept busy.' The blue eyes didn't waver. Instead, he said, 'You don't mind if I take this cab?' He moved easily past Ben into the cab's interior. 'If he gives my address, I'll deck him,' Ben thought. But Pyke gave the address of a lounge bar and Ben turned away and mounted the steps. Once round the corner, Pyke could change the destination and hurry to wherever Diana was waiting, but at the moment he didn't care.

Hammond's brow was set, his voice was furious. 'You're back. Well, thanks a bunch. I've had all the stockholders on to me... Well, it felt like that. They're panicking. We need to issue a statement.'

'Okay.' Ben tried to sound contrite when in truth he felt irritated. Between them, they concocted a defiant remittal of the offer and an assertion that shareholders would fare better if they kept faith in their board. 'I'll get this out straight away,' Hammond said, mollified. 'It might hold them off for a while.'

Madge brought him a cup of tea and a pile of mail. 'Margaret Riley's coming next week, if she can sort it out. I hope you'll stay put long enough to see her. And your wife's never been off the phone. "I'm not his keeper," I told her. She wants you to ring the minute you're back.' Her sniff implied that she was simply passing on a message and didn't care whether or not it was heeded.

He signed his letters and read the incoming mail before he telephoned Diana. 'Where the hell have you been, Ben? I've been frantic. So inconsiderate... Why didn't you phone me? You could have been dead somewhere.'

'Well, I'm not.' He hadn't meant to sound placatory, but he did. 'I have to make some calls. I'll be home about eight. Go ahead with dinner if I'm not back.' There was a gasp of anger and then the phone went dead. He replaced the receiver and went back to his work.

At six o'clock he told English to go, and took the wheel of the Bentley himself. He was emerging from the underground garage when his phone vibrated. It was Barbara. 'I was going to ring you. I'm on my way to my grandmother's. Are you free for a drink later? I've quite a lot to tell you,' he said. They arranged to meet in the Regent's Park Hilton at 7.30pm. Then he put his foot down and made for the Euston Road.

His grandmother was just finishing dinner. 'Only soup tonight,' she said regretfully. 'All I can manage at the moment.' Her eyes seemed sunken now and her scalp showed pink through strands of white hair. 'Gran, would you like me to bring you some fish? You used to like Dover sole.' She patted his hand. 'Next week perhaps. Now where have you been? It's been days and days since I saw you.'

He left out all mention of Paris. No need to complicate things. 'Margaret Brewis – Margaret Riley, as she is now – is coming soon. Barbara wants to meet her. And you too. Are you sure you're up to it?'

One hand clutched at the rug which covered her knees. 'Yes,' she said in a firmer voice. 'Yes. I want to see her. I want to say sorry. I want to make amends.'

They talked of the business. He would have skirted round the takeover bid but she had obviously heard about it from someone else. Sue, in all probability. 'I remember Headey's when it was a two-penny-halfpenny company.' Her voice was scornful and Ben smiled. 'Rather like Webcon when it began?' She grinned at him, her face suddenly animated and more like the grandmother he remembered. 'Don't be cheeky, young man. We were always a cut above the rest. Your grandfather made sure of that. Will they get you out?'

'I hope not. Hammond has all kinds of counter-plans, but it will depend on the corporate shareholders in the end.'

'If they do get us out, we'll be alright, won't we?' She didn't sound anxious, just curious.

'Yes,' Ben said. He put out his hand and covered her blue-veined one. It felt fragile and papery and he felt a surge of love for her. 'In fact, we'll be rich. What is it Diana says? Oodles of money. You can take off on a world cruise if you like.'

'I can't. I won't leave this house again. But you can... You should have travelled more. The business came down on you too soon.'

'Does that mean you wouldn't mind if it went?' He was surprised. He thought she would have been horrified, and yet she sounded quite sanguine at the prospect.

He kissed her fondly before he left and promised to come again soon. Back in the car, he got out his phone and dialled Barbara Tulloch's number. 'Ready for a swift half?'

'Make it a swift gin and tonic and I'll accept.'

As he put the car into gear and negotiated the drive, he acknowledged the truth. He didn't particularly want to see Barbara Tulloch. He just wanted an excuse not to go home.

They met in the same pub they had used the week before. As he waited for her, he thought how quickly life could change. Last time he had been in here there had been no Monique, no prospect of a trip to Paris. How much was he going to tell Barbara? In the end he opted for the truth. 'Good grief!' Her brow wrinkled in amazement. 'You mean there might be another cousin? Would she be my cousin? Two weeks ago, I was an orphan.

Now I have family coming out of the woodwork.

'Well, if it's true. Her mother was your father's half-sister. So, yes, she's your cousin. She might be your cousin.'

Tonight she wore a red corduroy coat, its neckline filled with a white fluffy scarf. She looked more feminine, less hostile than usual. And at the moment, she looked bewildered. 'It was complicated before. Now it's more complicated. If it's true, that is. I mean, there was a war going on, fighting, the Germans were all over them. Would he have had time to get a French girl pregnant?'

And suddenly they were both laughing. 'Yes,' she said dryly. 'They would have had time. All the same, we need to be sure.' She sipped her drink for a moment. 'Is she nice? You've seen her. Would I like her?'

'Yes.' Around them, the pub heaved with chatter and laughter and the clink of glasses. He thought of Monique, her hair escaping its bands, her bare feet tucked underneath her. 'Yes, I think you'd like her. Anyway, she flies in and out of Heathrow. We can arrange a meeting. With Margaret perhaps... But I don't want her – Margaret, I mean – worried until we know. If it's complicated for you, an arm of the law, imagine what it would be like for her? She's enthusiastic about meeting you, though. She remembers your father so well.'

'Dad never mentioned her. I knew he was adopted. My mother told me. It was never a secret, but I think she wanted me to know he wasn't Granny's child. Grandpa was different. He was really bonded to Dad. Anyway, she told me he was adopted, that his parents had been killed in the war. There was no mention of brothers or sisters. I think she'd have told me if she'd known.'

'Your father was very young when the separation came. Eighteen months, I think. Two at the most. He wouldn't remember – and if no one told him...' He was remembering the old vicar, still tortured by the little girl he had left behind. He had had his reasons for not saying there had been others. All the same, the boy should have been told.

He walked her back to her car and promised to keep her posted. On an impulse, he said, 'Do you trust me now?' It was an odd question and he wasn't sure why he'd asked it. Lamplight was falling on her head but her face was in shadow and he couldn't see her expression. There was a long pause and then she chuckled. 'I'm a lawyer, Ben. I don't do trust. But you're on probation.'

The house was in darkness when he got home. Max was waiting just inside the door. 'I've neglected you, haven't I, old boy?' Max's big head thrust against his knees and he fondled it. 'Big walks tomorrow, I promise.'

There was a can of soup and a tin opener on the kitchen table with a note which read: 'Presume you dined elsewhere. If not, tough.' He crumpled it up and put it in the pedal bin. At least it was better than a slanging match.

In the guest room bed, he tried to compose himself for sleep. He needed a good night's rest, but sleep would not come. Instead, he thought of battlefields and young men, separated from home by war, finding comfort with someone else. Just as he would have done with Monique if he had had the courage and she had been willing.

Chapter Twenty Three

H E HAD INTENDED TO LEAVE before Diana came downstairs, but he was still toying with toast and marmalade when she came into the kitchen. Would there be an outburst? In fact, she was positively sunny, asking if he'd like eggs or some fruit, offering to brew fresh tea. He wanted to say something incisive, a put-down, but the words wouldn't come. He wasn't afraid of Diana but he feared her tongue, those sudden flares of anger that took him aback. Today, though, he couldn't be bothered to placate her, so that was a small victory. He grunted refusals to her offers and left, cramming toast into his mouth and shrugging into his jacket as he went.

English was waiting outside. Good old Madge: he hadn't asked for a driver. He climbed into the back seat and leaned back against the headrest. 'I won't need you again today,' he said when they reached Farringdon Street. 'But can you put petrol in the Merc for me?' He paused. 'Does Neil Pyke keep his car here?' The chauffeur's face was impassive. 'I don't think so, Mr Ben. I think he uses cabs mostly.'

'I just wondered.' To his own ears, it sounded lame, but he couldn't think of a reason for his question – well, not one he was prepared to share. He felt able to be more honest with Madge. 'What do you think of Neil Pyke?' She went on putting letters in front of him for what seemed like minutes, but was probably only seconds. 'Not much,' she said at last.

'What does that mean?'

'What it says. I don't think much of him. I wouldn't trust him as far as I could throw him. If you're asking about where he'll stand in a takeover, he'll have his feet in so many camps, he'll be a centipede.'

Her words made him laugh out loud. 'Don't mince your words, Madge.'

'I never do. You should know that by now. Do you want a table for lunch?'

He assured her he had other plans and started to leaf through the various projects submitted for his attention. He tried to get interested in specifications and quantities, but his mind kept wandering. In Paris, Monique would be padding around in a shorty nightie. No, pyjamas. The ones with a smock top and panties. Or perhaps silk… Thinking of her made him uncomfortable. He tried to imagine her in safer tracksuit bottoms and a voluminous sweatshirt, but the mental picture wouldn't come. What the hell was he doing fantasising about a woman he hardly knew, when he ought to be thinking about his marriage? He sat for a moment contemplating his options, then he reached for the phone.

'Diana? I think I better go out to Adele's place this afternoon. I need to see her about business. I should be back for dinner, but don't worry if I'm a bit late.' When he put down the phone, he moved to the door of his office and crossed to the water-cooler. While he fiddled with cups and levers, he could see Pyke's office. Through the glass, he could see him sitting at his desk. If his calculations were correct, he would receive a phone call any moment now. Sure enough, Pyke reached for his mobile and put it to his ear. Ben saw him smile and nod, then look at his watch and speak to whoever was on the other end of the line. After a moment more, he put it down. He was smiling and Ben felt the cardboard cup, mercifully yet unfilled, crumple in his clenched fingers. So far, so good. Mustn't spoil it by going in there and smashing a fist into the man's smug face.

He left at 12.30pm, making sure Pyke knew he was going to Adele's. It was easy enough. The man who was almost certainly cuckolding him was in Hammond's office when he went to announce his departure. 'Okay,' Hammond said. 'But we need to talk in the morning. Please!'

'I promise,' Ben said. 'I'd talk later on but I won't be back till around seven or eight, so I'll go straight home.' Pyke's eyes never left the document he was studying, but Ben knew his words had gone home.

He collected his car and drove towards the Angel. In a corner pub he ordered beer and a steak pie. He wasn't hungry but he had at least an hour to fill. The pub was almost empty and the few drinkers kept nipping outside to smoke. He started to count. In an hour they averaged three exits apiece. Three cigarettes in an hour. Twelve waking hours. Thirty-six a day. Visions of lung cancer reared and were dismissed. Smoking was someone else's problem. He had enough of his own. But the pub pleased him. It had not been 'done-up', which too often meant 'done-in'. It was shabby and dusty and infinitely comfortable. If he wanted to, he could stay here all day. Except that he couldn't go on stalling forever. For weeks now, he had been escaping his responsibilities. Now they had to be faced.

At one o'clock he dialled his grandmother's number. It was Maya who answered. 'Hi, Maya. It's me, Ben. How are you?' For a moment they exchanged inquiries after health, wealth and happiness, and then he asked after his grandmother. 'She not well, Mr Ben. Not eat enough. I do thin sandwiches – thin, no end thin – she say too much.' He promised to come over soon and asked to speak to the nurse. 'She's holding up, Ben. That's as much as we can say at the moment. It's willpower with her. She's hanging on for something. I've seen it before. Usually it's a 100th birthday. They hang on for their telegram from the Queen, then they're gone.'

'Gran is only 87.'

'Same principle. She wants you to sort things out for her. She's waiting until you do.' He hadn't realised she had told Sue. He promised to come over later and hung up. If it was the need to know that was keeping his grandmother alive, he better check progress. He dialled the detective's number and got his answer phone. 'Any news?' he asked and rang off.

At half past two he went out to his car and turned it for home. He let himself into the house quietly and walked through to the living room. There were two spirit glasses on the coffee table with slices of lemon in them. Gin and tonic. Not exactly aphrodisiac but good enough. Pyke's jacket was slung on a chair. Ben was moving forward to look in its pockets when he saw the shoes, the suede loafers Pyke favoured. Kicked off as he relaxed with a drink 'and prepared to fuck my wife!' For a second, Ben feared he had shouted the words, but the house was mercifully silent. He was contemplating mounting the stairs and catching them in flagrante, when a better thought occurred. He picked up one of the suede shoes. Let the bastard hop home! He let himself out again, threw the shoe into the back seat of his car and drove away. For a little while, he felt positively euphoric.

It was 3.30pm when he reached his sister's house, and as he expected there was no one in. He settled down in his seat and waited for her to return from the school run. When her car roared into the drive, her face lit up at the sight of him, and the children erupted from the car and rushed to greet him. He felt his eyes prick at their warmth and then was filled with self-loathing. What a pathetic creature, hungry for comfort, he was becoming. It had to stop.

'Adele,' he said, when the children were settled with orange juice and toys, and he and his sister were sitting either side of the wood-burning stove. 'Can I stay here tonight?' He saw alarm flare in her eyes and he rushed to reassure. 'Just for tonight. I'll make other arrangements tomorrow.' She had been sitting on the sofa, her legs curled underneath her. Now she swung them to the floor and crossed to his side. 'Don't be an idiot. Of course you can stay here. I'm just worried about why.'

'Diana is having an affair!' It was out and the relief was huge. 'With Neil Pyke – you've met him in the office.'

'Are you sure?' She didn't sound surprised, just cautious.

'Yes. They're together now. I told them I was coming here. I was pretty sure they'd make good use of the time. I went over there after a while. They were upstairs but his jacket and shoes were in the living room. Actually, one of his shoes is in the back of my car right now.'

'You took it?' Her eyes were huge.

'I took it.' And suddenly they were both laughing, falling on one another's necks, wiping tears from their eyes. It was moments before she staggered back to her seat and he wiped his nose with the back of his hand. He didn't feel like laughing but he couldn't help himself. So that was what hysterics felt like, not unpleasant but definitely not normal.

'I love it,' Adele said when she had composed herself. 'But what comes next?'

Ben stretched out his legs in front of him and contemplated his shoes. 'Don't know. Wish I'd taken the other one now. They're bespoke. My size.' That set them off again until she begged him to stop.

Suddenly, she was serious. 'All the same, I have to admit I'm not sorry. That's the first time I've seen you laugh – really laugh – in a long time.'

He told her of Paris then, describing Monique, but skirting round his own erotic thoughts.

'Sounds as though you liked her.'

'I did. She's quite feisty, stands on her own two feet. I don't think she cares too much about flying but it's a job. Loves her mother.'

'What are you going to do about her?'

'I don't know. We must get proof one way or another.'

'Ah,' she was getting to her feet. 'So you've decided she should be treated as a Brewis.'

'She is a Brewis… Well, she may be. Anyway, we don't have to settle that tonight. When I have time, I could check out whether his regiment was in northern France at the right time: nine months before the grandmother's birth. I suppose they could tell me that after this lapse of time.'

'Get her DNA tested,' Adele said. And then, shocked at her own statement: 'My God, I'm clever!' He put an arm around her shoulders. 'Never doubted it, sister mine. Never doubted it. You got the brains, I got the beauty!'

'In your dreams,' she said and hugged him close.

They moved into the kitchen and Adele began to prepare the evening meal. Harry came in at six o'clock and they ate with the children around the kitchen table.

'Ben is staying tonight,' Adele said as she handed out the plates. 'Good,' Harry said and asked no questions. But his eyes on Ben were reassuring. 'Thanks,' Ben said. 'I need to go home and get some things but I won't be late back.'

'Take your time.' Harry reached in his pocket and pulled out his key. 'Take this, I've got a spare.' It was a symbolic gesture and both men knew it.

As Ben drove back into London, he reflected on his brother-in-law. He was a man of few words, he was hardly a money-maker, but when the chips were down you couldn't ask for anyone better.

There was the smell of cooking fish as he entered the hall. 'Is that you, darling? It's your favourite tonight. Dover sole.' He walked into the kitchen, the suede shoe in his hand. 'Dover sole,' he said. 'You're spoiling me. I've got something for you too. It's got a sole as well.'

She swung round, anticipation on her face, and he held out the shoe. 'Nice, isn't it? One of a pair, I think, but quite impressive on its own. Bespoke, obviously. Perhaps I'm paying him too much.'

She looked stunned for a moment, then puzzled and, at last, aghast. Ben smiled. 'Shut your mouth, Diana. Being lost for words doesn't become you.' He turned on his heel, mounted the stairs to their bedroom and packed enough to tide him over for a few days. She was not in the hall when he came downstairs and he was glad. He got in the car and headed for pastures new.

Chapter Twenty Four

IT SEEMED STRANGE TO BE driving into London from another direction. Around him, morning traffic swirled and eddied. No wonder Harry had shirked this rat race. His sister and brother-in-law had made him more than welcome but he couldn't stay there forever. As soon as he reached his office, he was straight with Madge. 'I've moved out. I need a place. Can you find me something for a while? When we get this thing – the Headey's thing – over, I'll look around for something permanent. For now I need something central and convenient.'

'Leave it to me.' That was all she said. Impulsively, he bent and kissed the top of her head. 'You're a treasure.'

'Get off.' She armed him away but he could tell she was pleased. He had just settled behind his desk when there was a tap at the door. It was Neil Pyke and for a moment Ben felt panic. What did you say to the man who was fucking your wife? In the event, it was Pyke who began the conversation.

'Look, I want you to know...' There was a patronising tone to his voice that roused Ben to fury.

'And I want to know nothing from you. Get out of my office.'

'There's no need to be like that. We can be civilised, surely.' It was still there, that patronising 'let's be grown up about it, old boy' thing. Ben rose and came from behind his desk. 'Get out. Now. Or I'll show you just how bloody uncivilised I can be.'

For a second, Pyke was taken aback – but only for a second. 'We have to work together. Being childish won't help.'

That was too much. 'We don't have to work together. I want you out of here now. Permanently.' Pyke was spluttering about his contract, his rights, as Ben armed him through the door.

'You'll get your rights, not that any right-minded person would think you had any. I want you out of here in the next five minutes. Peter Hammond will contact you. Don't come here or ring. You're finished, Neil, and if you think that's me abusing my position, you're dead right.'

Something changed in the man opposite him. Before he had been prepared to placate. Now he was defiant. 'I'm out, you're in? For how long, Ben? How long?'

He left the office, walking past startled faces which suddenly became intent on their consoles as he drew abreast. Ben went back to his seat and sat down. That had been a mistake but he didn't regret it. There would be repercussions. Pyke could possibly claim wrongful dismissal but what the hell! As for the staff, they would know sooner or later – had probably known for months – so why worry about it now?

For ten minutes or so, he tried to concentrate on the papers in front of him. One was a paper from Peter Hammond detailing the fluctuations in the share prices since first news of the bid. For a while, the shares had risen sharply as people anticipated a windfall. But as the takeover had hung fire, the price had declined. Today it was a penny up, so perhaps the fall had been halted. He was turning to a pile of tenders which needed a signature when Hammond knocked and entered. He looked taken aback. 'You've heard,' Ben said. Hammond nodded. 'He's just told me. There'll be fall out, Ben...'

'I know.' He paused for a moment. 'You don't sound exactly sorry he's gone.'

'No, I'm anxious about the handling of it, but he's no loss.'

Ben was surprised. 'I thought you rated him.'

'Technically, he's brilliant. I doubt his probity.'

'What do you mean?' Ben sat up. This was news.

'Someone was feeding Headey's. Our land deals, cash projections, future spend. It was him or me. It wasn't me.'

Suddenly it made sense. Hamish had said, 'Look close to home – on all fronts.' He must have meant at work and at home. Pyke had not only shagged his wife, he was shagging his business too – or at least selling it down the river.

Madge brought in coffee and he and Hammond discussed tactics: what they would do at the meeting and what they would do if they lost the vote. By the time Hammond went back to his own office, they had both grown thoroughly morose over the present state of business ethics. It was a relief when a text message came through on his phone. 'I fly in to Heathrow at 20.06. Will I see you?' The flight number followed and he made a note of it. He texted a reply, suggesting they meet in the arrivals hall, and sat back in his chair, feeling suddenly relieved, almost buoyant. When, at last, he reached for his phone, he was whistling under his breath. The tune was 'J'attendrai'.

The detective rang back as Ben was finishing a sandwich lunch. 'Got your message. Actually, I was going to ring you. I've found the missing link. She's in Chigwell.'

'So she's alive.'

'Alive and kicking, apparently. I'm going there tomorrow to make sure it's kosher, but she was very cagey on the phone. Said there was no way it could be her, she didn't have siblings, absolutely no connection. But the files say different.'

'Well, keep me posted.' It would be a pity if it was indeed Dolly and she wouldn't co-operate, but two out of three wasn't bad. For a second, he contemplated ringing Barbara to tell her about Dolly. In the end, though, it was his sister's number he dialled.

'I'm going to Gran's when I leave the office, Adele. After that I'm meeting friends. Don't worry about dinner. I'll probably eat with them. And we may have word of the missing Dolly. I'll fill you in later.' When he put the phone down, he wondered why he had not said it was Monique he was meeting. Adele would have understood.

His grandmother looked dreadful when he arrived. Her eyes seemed to have sunk even lower in her head and her voice was faint. As they talked, however, he noticed an improvement. At the end of half an hour, colour had come back into her face and she was sitting more erect.

He didn't mention Dolly but told her that he had made contact with someone who had known Jack Brewis in France. She assumed it was another serviceman and he didn't disabuse her. She was more animated now and anxious to talk.

'He was a Terrier, you know. Went off to camp every year to keep his hand in. I used to think she was mad to let him, leaving her with three small children. But she didn't seem to mind. I expect the money came in handy.'

'They were paid then?'

'Oh, yes. I don't know how much, but it wasn't coppers.'

He decided to probe a little. 'Were they happy?'

She looked startled. 'Of course they were. Three lovely children – and he knew the business would take off with your grandfather guarding it. He was clever, your grandfather. That's where you get your brains. Adele takes after your mother.'

Ben didn't feel very clever. In which area of his life could he report progress? Aloud, he said, 'So she didn't have to worry about him… With other women, I mean.'

The old head shook vigorously. 'No, nothing like that. Well, we didn't in those days. Not nice people anyway.

And the Brewises were nice. Lived for their children.'

Her face clouded and he knew she was thinking about those children and the way they had been let down.

'Cheer up,' he said, getting to his feet. 'You'll see Margaret soon – and Billy's daughter. You'll like her, you'll like them both.'

He had been waiting for ten minutes when he saw Monique walking towards him. She was in uniform and he felt suddenly shy. But when she reached him and smiled up into his face, he relaxed. The girl who loved jeans and sweaters was still in there.

He took her to L'Escargot and they laughed their way through three excellent courses and a bottle of fruity Viognier, which she said was her favourite wine. At times he felt as though they had been dining together for a lifetime. There was no artifice about Monique, or if there was, she concealed it well. Her face clouded or beamed depending on the conversation and she ate enthusiastically, explaining that she didn't often dine at this level and wasn't going to waste it.

Over coffee she produced the photograph. 'That's him,' she said. On the back of the faded snap was written, 'Jack Brewis, Buerges, 1940' followed by an Army number. Ben turned the photograph over. His first impression was that the man in it was unbelievably young, and yet he had been the father of three. He was in his shirtsleeves, laughing and squinting up into the sunshine. His feet were bare and planted in a tin dish. A towel was slung over one shoulder. 'He was happy,' Ben thought. 'And then he was dead.' Aloud, he asked, 'Do you feel as though he's your grandfather?'

She shrugged. 'Maybe. Maybe not.'

'There's a test,' he said tentatively.

'DNA. I know and I want it. If I have a family, I want to be sure they are family. You know them. Are they nice? Are they rich?'

'Not really. Your Aunt Margaret, if she is your mother's half-sister, she's quite poor, I think. There's a girl not much older than you. She'd be your cousin. She's...' Something made him cautious. 'She's got a profession, so she's probably well-paid but not rich.'

'Pity. If they were rich and I was their family, they could give me enough money to stop racketing around the world.' She was laughing as she said it and he could see that whatever she was after, it was not monetary gain.

They walked through the streets towards her hotel, pulling her wheeled travel bag behind them. She chatted away but Ben's thoughts were elsewhere. Jack Brewis had been in his late twenties when he died. Younger than me, Ben thought, and a wife and three children at home. Had he been afraid of the remorseless German advance? Written a farewell letter? Made his peace with his maker? Or had he fallen in love with a pretty French girl and planted his seed a fourth time? 'I have done nothing with my life,' Ben thought. 'If I die tomorrow there will be nothing left of me.'

'We're here.' Monique was tugging his arm. He was preparing to wish her goodnight but she was having none of it. He found himself in the lift going upwards to the fifth floor. The room was a typical, anonymous hotel room. She threw down the key and turned towards him. He knew what she intended even before she said his name, very softly.

It was a long time since a woman had wanted him and he felt a degree of embarrassment. What if he couldn't perform? He kept his mouth on hers as they struggled free of clothes and then he was lifting her from the ground and her legs were wrapped around him and he was entering her and being made welcome in a way he had forgotten existed. After a while, they made love again on the bed and then lay back, sated.

'I think we need a drink,' she said, and was on her way to the mini-bar when he stopped her. 'Champagne,' he said, reaching for his wallet. 'Nothing less will do.' But she waved the money away and rang room service. The champagne was dry and crisp and made them both inclined to giggle. After a while, she said, 'More?' but when he held out his glass, she took it from him and placed it down on the bedside table. Her mouth came down on his and travelled down throat and chest into the space between navel and groin. He groaned with pleasure as she roused him until they could once more move together to a climax.

Afterwards, they put out their respective lamps and lay like spoons until they slept. He woke before daylight with money on his mind. She had put the champagne on her bill. Air France might be a good employer but he doubted their generosity extended to Moët & Chandon. He slipped from the bed and felt for his wallet. Three twenties should do it, more would be tacky. Her handbag had been on the second bed. He felt his way to it and carried it to the window. There was enough light from the streetlamps for him to open it and look for her wallet. Best put the money there rather than tuck it in the top of the bag where she would see it straight away. The wallet was red leather with a purse compartment and a space for notes behind. But it was not the purse or the note compartment that held his attention. It was the photograph, behind plastic in the flap. It was of a handsome, rather serious man whose uniform bore the insignia of a pilot. He was young, assured and very French. She did not have a brother so this was a lover. Ben tucked the notes away and crept back to bed, and lay still till dawn.

Chapter Twenty Five

'Do you want the good news or the bad news?' Madge's face was, as usual, impassive.

'The good news. You can file the bad news.'

'I've got you a flat. Very nice, very pricey.'

'Is that the bad news?' She shook her head.

'No. The bad news is there are three messages from board members. They want to meet ASAP.'

He told her to check his diary and arrange it and went on into his office. The phone was ringing and for a moment he contemplated ignoring it. If it was someone else worried about the bid, they would have their meeting soon enough. But the ringing went on until he could stand it no longer. 'Webster.' There was a little snort of annoyance at the other end. 'Diana.' She was mimicking his terse greeting. His heart sank. It was nine-thirty in the morning and he was not in the mood for a row. 'Yes, what do you want?'

'We have to meet, Ben. Thanks to your spiteful behaviour there's no point in even discussing a reconciliation…'

'My spiteful behaviour? Do you mean my refusal to share an office with your lover?'

'If you're going to be childish, Ben, I'll just have to hand everything over to my lawyer. I was prepared to talk but you seem determined on aggression.' He stood, phone in hand, as she began listing his failings.

'You've never pulled your weight in our marriage… no emotional support… begrudge me having fun… not like other husbands…' Her claims were so outrageous he found himself smiling wryly, until she touched a nerve.

'As for the way you dance attendance on your grandmother…'

'Diana, go to hell.' He had clashed down the receiver before he added, 'and take Pyke with you.'

He went to look at the flat, anxious to get out into the fresh air. It was in Margaret Street, just off Oxford Street. 'It'll do,' he told Madge when he got back to the office. 'No, it will more than do. They say I can move in in about two weeks. I'll need bedding, that sort of thing. Can you fix it?'

'Do I ever fail you?'

'Never. Clever girl.'

'You'd do badly without me. Now, I've arranged the meeting for tomorrow. Eleven sharp. They'll all be there. Peter wants an hour with you beforehand.'

He tried to concentrate on the project files in his tray, but he kept on thinking of the photograph of Jack Brewis Monique had shown him. Jack had been a simple joiner.

He could never have envisaged a company of the complexity of Webcon springing out of his builder's yard. As if on cue, the phone rang. 'It is Dolly, or Dorothy Graham, as she prefers to be called. I'm certain of it, but she still maintains we're making a mistake. My guess is she doesn't want any links with the past.'

'What would change her mind?'

'Not money. She's got that. Million and a half's worth of property, maybe more, knuckleduster diamonds, staff. She's sitting very pretty.'

'Have you told her you've found her sister?'

'Told her that, and the niece. Wrung her heartstrings but no dice. And even if it was true, she says, the past is the past. She's had it hard, I imagine, but now… She's rolling in it now. She may be scared they'll want something from her. I don't know, but she's adamant.'

When he had put down the phone, he thought about Margaret Riley. She wouldn't ask anyone for a penny however rich the sister was. Neither would Barbara, unless she felt it was her due. Sponging off an aunt, even a rich one, would not be her style.

He looked at his diary. No meetings before tomorrow. He ought to talk to Peter Hammond but they could get together this afternoon. He picked up the internal phone and set up a meet, then he dialled the detective. 'Give me the address. I'm going over there.' The detective repeated his assertions that the woman wouldn't be budged, but he handed over the address just the same.

Ben was ready to leave when the phone rang again. 'It's Diana – and don't you dare hang up on me.' He saw

Madge hovering outside the door and waved to her to come in. 'Speak to my PA,' he said into the phone. 'She'll see if she can fit you in somewhere.' Diana's gasp of outrage cheered him up all the way out of the office and down to the underground car park.

He stopped in a lay-by once he left the city and looked up the address. Buena Vista, Arundel Drive. No house number, so it must be a residence of some importance. He couldn't help contrasting the lifestyles of the two sisters. Margaret had had a life mostly of hardship. She had put a good face on it, but it was plain that she had had to work all her life. Dolly, on the other hand, seemed to have had a cushier life. If Margaret had been adopted, would it have been different? If his grandmother had kept her promise, if his grandfather had not been an opportunist? The list of 'ifs' was endless.

Buena Vista was straight out of a child's picture book. White-painted walls, green tiles to match the green bricks that framed the windows, chequerboard-fashion, a Tyrolean number-plate, and even roses round the door. Or what would be roses, come summer. He rang the bell.

There was a yapping from inside the house but no sign of life. He rang again. He was just about to give up and return to the car when he saw activity behind the frosted glass. A moment later the door opened.

His first thought was that this couldn't be Dolly. Dolly would be 71 by now. The woman looking enquiringly at him was fifty, no more.

'Mrs Graham?' he inquired, half-expecting a denial. Now he noticed the eyes, pinkish behind the well-applied mascara. The cheeks were lined beneath just the right amount of rouge, and the hands which clutched a designer handbag were ever so slightly gnarled. 'I thought you were the window-cleaner,' she said, snapping her bag shut. 'But you're not.' The 'who the hell are you?' was implied but not spoken.

'I wonder if I might have a word. My name is Ben Webster. I believe you knew my grandmother... Well, she knew you, many years ago.'

The door, which had been open a foot, did not widen in welcome. 'Who was your grandmother?'

'Gwen Webster.' Her face was clearing now but the door didn't budge.

'Are you something to do with the man who came yesterday?'

'Yes. He came on my behalf... I know you said you didn't want to be involved but I wonder if I could just come inside for a few moments. I promise not to take up too much of your time.'

'You can come in, but I said all I wanted to say yesterday. Never live in the past, my husband used to say, and he was right. And this isn't even my past. You've made a mistake.'

The hall was eau de Nil. Completely eau de Nil, down to the picture frames. The dog which padded at her heels was a Bichon Frise, off-white all over, apart from the rhinestone-studded collar around its neck. Magnolia dominated the sitting room, everything perfect, looking untouched by human hands. He sat gingerly on the magnolia settee she indicated with a be-ringed hand and wondered what the hell he was going to say. She sat opposite him, the dog curled in a ball beside her.

'Do you smoke?' The question was unexpected and he began to nod before he collected himself and shook his head. Even if he had been an inveterate chain-smoker, he wouldn't have dared to light up in a room which seemed straight out of a Mappin and Webb window. But Dolly was producing what looked suspiciously like a cigarillo from a soapstone box and lighting it with an onyx table lighter. 'Well,' she said, when she had exhaled the first plume of smoke. 'Say what you've got to say. Just don't expect me to change my mind. I've never heard of Dolly Brewis. I was a Mayhew before I married. I've got a birth certificate to prove it.'

'Okay. Well, the parents of the woman I'm seeking were killed in the war. The father died in France, he was in the army. The mother died in an air-raid – in London.'

The pencilled brows raised slightly. 'He said they were dead. I didn't know they died in the war. I should have known, I suppose, him mentioning 1941.' Her hand moved to caress the watchful dog.

'1940,' Ben said. 'It was 1940. You had a brother and a sister. He was the baby, she was five years older than you. Do you remember them at all?'

'Of course I don't remember them, because they never existed. Well, not in my life anyway.'

'But you were adopted?' For a moment, he thought she was going to deny it but her gaze dropped to her lap and she nodded instead. 'Yes, but I wasn't the child you want.'

'Do you remember anything about the adoption?'

'Not really. Well, you don't at that age, do you? I remember crying a lot at first. Wanting to go home, that sort of thing. But you get over it...No choice.' She laughed, but it was a laugh without merriment.

'Did it work out?'

'Were they good to me, you mean? Yes, in their own way. I went to good schools, I had nice clothes. She was a good cook, we had good meals.'

'But...?'

'No buts. They took care of me. You could say I had every advantage.' She was holding something back, but he wasn't going to get anywhere. He changed tack. 'I'm sorry to tell you that your brother died in the 1980s.'

'Very sad for someone, but not my brother.' She sounded totally disinterested. Ben pressed on.

'But your sister Margaret is alive and well. She's widowed, no children. She lives in County Durham.'

'Can we stop this foolishness? I don't have a sister. Or a brother, dead or alive.' The ash from the cigarillo was tapped into an onyx ashtray. She had crossed her legs when she sat down and now one cream suede court shoe began to bob-up and down. She wants me to go, Ben thought, disconcerted, but he gave it one more try. 'I think she'd like to see you.'

The elegant blonde curls were shaking now. 'There's no point in carrying on with this conversation since you can't take a telling. I'm sorry if this woman wants to find her sister but it's nothing to do with me. Besides, what would we have in common after more than sixty years?

She's not in want, is she?'

It was Ben's turn to shake his head. 'No, that's not the point at all. She wants to know what happened to you, that you're safe and well. So does my grandmother. That's why I instituted the search.'

She rose to her feet. 'Well, you can tell them I'm fine. I'm not their sister but I'm fine. I had a good marriage. We never had children... but Eddie left me well provided for.' She looked around. 'As you can see, I've got a nice home. I have a daily help. I can travel when I want to. No worries. And, frankly, I don't want any. So if you're finished...' She put her be-ringed hand on his arm.

He got to his feet, as if impelled by the force of her words. 'If you change your mind...' he began, fishing for a card. She took it from him but her smile said, 'I won't'. The dog put its head on one side as if to say 'So there!'

He was on the doorstep now and relief made her more expansive. 'Good luck with your search, though I doubt you'll find anything. Too much water under the bridge, Mr Webster. Far too much.'

The door had closed behind him before he reached the gate, and when he looked back, the house had once more resumed its picture-book quality, as though no one at all lived there. It was just an illustration in a fairy story.

Chapter Twenty Six

Dolly's Story, 1940

THE BOTTLE WAS DARK BLUE and contained something called Evening in Paris. It stood on the dressing table in the big bedroom and the woman would dab it behind her ears with her finger and then shake some onto her hanky. It smelled nice. The woman smelled of it and she smelled nice. When Dolly cried the woman would cuddle her and the smell was overpowering but comforting. Every day she asked when Maggie would be coming and Billy, and the woman would shake her head and say 'Shh' and 'Never mind'. Once, desperate for a proper answer, she lay down on the floor and screamed for her mother, which was strange because her mother had been gone a long time. Longer than yesterday.

Then the man came into the room and after a while the woman with the spectacles came. She sat on the settee and the other woman pushed Dolly towards her. 'Dolly,' the glasses woman said. 'I explained this to you before. You have a new mummy and daddy now. Your sister and brother have gone somewhere just like you, somewhere where they'll be very happy. Now you have a forever mummy and daddy, so you must be a good girl and not ask silly questions. Can you do that?' Her voice was kind but very firm. She wouldn't take no for an answer, so Dolly nodded, and then, when the woman kept staring into her face, she said 'Yes'. The woman who smelled nice was crying and the man had his arm round her, but when the woman with the spectacles went away, he lifted Dolly onto his knee and asked what she would like for tea. She said biscuits because she couldn't think of anything else to ask for.

The next day, men came and dug a hole in the garden. Dolly was allowed to watch them. The woman said it was for an Anderson shelter. 'Somewhere to go if there's an air raid. But you're not to worry, Dorothy. Daddy will keep us safe.' Dolly nodded. She knew now that if you nodded at whatever they said, it made them happy. She didn't ask about Maggie or Billy any more or cry for her mother. She knew Maggie would come for her one day because Maggie always managed something. So she nodded when the woman asked her to call her 'Mummy' and the man was to be 'Daddy'. For some reason this pleased them a lot. The woman would put her hands under her chin and give a little wriggle of pleasure when she did it, and the man's eyes would crinkle up as though he was going to cry.

Sometimes she took a dab from the blue bottle and dabbed it behind her own ears, and when the man smelled it on her he smiled and called her 'a little tinker'.

They bought her a puppy, a black and white dog with fluffy hair. They said it was a collie but she knew it was a dog and she loved it so much that sometimes she didn't remember Maggie for a whole day at a time. She called the dog Billy but Mummy said a dog couldn't be called a boy's name, and anyway the dog was a girl, so they called it Lassie instead.

Sometimes there were air raids and they would go down the garden to the Anderson shelter. Lassie would bark if there was gunfire but mostly she slept on a blanket in the corner. Everyone else had a bed with blankets and a little pillow. Everything in the shelter smelled damp even though Mummy hung the blankets on the line every day so they got some fresh air.

Mummy and Daddy were keen on fresh air. It was something to do with Daddy being in a place called a sanatorium. 'They got him better,' Mummy said. 'Now wasn't that clever?' But Dolly had a funny feeling that he mightn't be as better as they said because if he gave a cough, even a little one, Mummy got agitated and suggested a trip to the doctor. Then Daddy would laugh and shake his newspaper and say, 'Don't panic, May. I'm fine. Aren't I fine, Dorothy?' And Dolly would nod.

That Christmas she got three books and a doll with eyes that closed when you laid it on its back. 'Nothing from your mother?' Daddy said to Mummy and Mummy bit her lip. 'Give her time, Tommy. She'll come round.' Dolly knew this was something to do with her, but like most other things, when a nod didn't seem appropriate, she said nothing at all.

Mummy's mother came to tea sometimes but she didn't speak much and never to Dolly, not even when Mummy would speak in a very high voice. 'Say hello to Grandma, Dorothy.' Dolly would say an obedient hello but the old lady would just turn her head away. So Dolly would go into the garden and play with Lassie until she heard the front door bang shut and she could go back into the house.

When it got nearly to Christmas, she had her fifth birthday party. Little girls and boys came with their mothers and every one of them gave her a present. The children hardly glanced at her in their haste to get into the garden and play, but the mothers seemed to inspect her. 'Tragic,' one woman said and patted Dolly's head, but two mothers told her she was a very lucky girl and must be very good. That night Daddy told her she would see the boys and girls again. 'Next month, when you start school.'

Dolly knew about school. Maggie had told her you got a book called a jotter and if you made a mess in it, you got smacked. 'But not hard.' She asked Mummy if she would be smacked when she started school and Mummy laughed and said it was a 'private' school and no one ever got smacked there. Mummy told Daddy when he came home that night and he laughed too and said 'As if we would let anyone smack you'. That night she gave Mummy a kiss at bedtime, which made Daddy, who was holding Lassie, wipe his eyes with the back of his hand. Dolly snuggled down in the bed and decided there was no point in trying to understand people. They liked it when you kissed them but it made them cry. Not much point in asking questions either because you seldom got sensible answers. When she fell asleep she dreamed she was in school and Maggie was waiting at the gate to take her home. She remembered the dream the next morning but in the cold light of day she accepted that Maggie was not going to come for her. It wasn't fair because she had stayed with Billy instead of coming with her, but life here was alright. She could do without Maggie. And Billy too for that matter, because he had always been a little whinge.

Just before she started school, Mummy's mother died. 'She was your grandmother,' Daddy explained. Dolly pondered this. She knew about grandmothers in storybooks and this one hadn't been anything like them. In storybooks they gave you sweets and they had cheeks like apples and smelled of flowers. This grandmother never gave anyone anything and smelled of wee. Mummy cried all the time and kept drawing Dolly to her and weeping against her hair. 'I loved her, Dorothy,' she said one day. 'She was a hard woman in some ways but I loved her.' This seemed the time for a question. 'Why didn't she like me?' This brought fresh tears but it also brought forth an answer. 'It wasn't you, darling. She thought Daddy and I shouldn't have children because Daddy isn't strong. If I'd had a baby I dare say she'd have come round, but it didn't happen. When we got you… Well, she didn't agree. But you mean everything to Daddy and me. You know that, don't you?' Dolly nodded.

School was just an ordinary house, which came as a

bit of a surprise. She had always thought schools were big places. Her school was one room with one teacher, a lady called Mrs Williams, who smelled of mint humbugs and sometimes made them recite aloud while she went into the kitchen to see to her oven.

But as spring came, Dolly began to understand words. She could read to Daddy, moving her finger from word to word on the page. By the time Mr Churchill said the church bells could ring again because the Germans would not be coming after all, Dolly could read the newspapers and had a shelf of books in her bedroom. But she was always called Dorothy now because Mrs Williams had suggested that Dolly was a silly name for a big girl and wouldn't do when she went to the big school.

The big school would also be 'private', mummy told her, and would give her 'every chance in life'. Dolly nodded at this and started to write 'Dorothy Mayhew' in her exercise books because that was her name now.

Daddy listened to the wireless every evening after tea. They had high tea, which looked more like a dinner to Dolly because you ate it with a knife and fork. If the war news was good, Mummy and Daddy would laugh a lot. Sometimes she would sit on his knee and put her arms around his neck. Dolly had a vague feeling that she had seen someone do that before, but if she had it was a long time ago and she couldn't remember their faces. When it happened now, though, Daddy would put his arm out and let Dolly climb up too and they would all cuddle. Sometimes a woman called Vera Lynn came on the wireless and sang songs. Mummy said Vera was 'sincere' which was obviously good because Mummy cut a picture of Vera out of a magazine and put it up in the kitchen. Vera had a dress on but a soldier's hat too, which looked a bit strange to Dolly. There was also a lot of talk about Japs. Japs had slitty eyes, Daddy said, and Mummy would click her tongue against her teeth and say, 'Not in front of the child, Tommy'.

After a while the air raids got worse. Daddy said it was revenge for the RAF flattening Germany and meant we were winning the war. Mummy bought Dolly a siren suit 'just like Mr Churchill's, only pink'. For Dolly's eighth birthday she had a party. 'You have a clever Mummy,' Daddy told her. 'Making this lovely cake without butter.' The cake tasted oily and Mummy said that was the liquid paraffin, something else Dolly had never heard of. She was not sure what 'rationing' meant either but everybody said it was a 'bugbear', which Mummy said meant something which got on your nerves. Dorothy always remembered that birthday because they took her to the cinema, which was a big place like a palace with echoing halls you had to walk through before you got into the place where the picture was, which was pitch black. The film was *Lassie Come Home*. It was about a dog exactly like her own Lassie and made Mummy cry, but Daddy produced a bar of chocolate and cuddled them both on the bus home. 'You're a big girl now,' Mummy said when she put her to bed. 'You've been to the pictures.' After that they sometimes went to see Disney films and any film which had Greer Garson in because she was Mummy's favourite.

Daddy said Mummy was a sentimental little idiot, which was why he loved her.

Not long after Easter in 1945, Daddy began gathering wood. Other fathers did it too, piling it on a bombsite two streets away. 'We're going to have a bonfire to celebrate victory, Dorothy.' It was funny to see her father, dressed in his office suit, dragging wood along the street in broad daylight. The pile of wood grew higher and higher but it was August before the war ended and it could be lit. They had a party in the street, a feast such as none of the children had ever seen, and then they all got a mug with crossed flags on it, one for America and one for Britain. 'They should have had the Russians on too,' Daddy said. 'We'd never have done it without them', but Mummy just laughed and went on piling plates with jam tarts. The jam had been hidden at the back of the pantry, saved for this special occasion. Somehow, seeing it ladled out like that made it seem certain that the war was over. For a brief moment Dorothy wondered if that meant they would all go home now, back to the house with the backyard she could only dimly remember. But she didn't wonder for long. Someone was playing Vera Lynn records on a wind-up gramophone and Mummy and Daddy were dancing in the street in broad daylight. Or nightlight, because it was eleven o'clock and only the moon and streetlamps to see by, lamps that had only been lit a month before to signal that the war was nearly over.

Dolly wasn't quite sure what she had expected of peacetime but she knew she didn't get it. The weeks and months that followed the street party were disappointing. Food was still short, clothing coupons ran out. There were queues everywhere and no petrol to run the car. When the summer came, bread was rationed for the first time. 'Fancy,' her mother said. 'We had bread all through the war. Now it's going to be rationed. It would never have happened if Mr Churchill had still been in power.'

Dorothy didn't mind about bread. She was full of plans for her move to the big school that year. 'You'll do well, Dorothy,' Mrs Williams said. 'You're a bright girl and the Church High will give you every advantage. I hope you're grateful.' She had counted the months till the move. January, February, March, April, May, June and then the summer holiday to get her uniform and all the things you needed to be a high school girl. At first the school was a bit scary, the mistresses stricter. In the end, though, it made her feel safe. You knew what you had to do and if you did it, you didn't get wrong.

At Christmas that year Daddy bought her a watch. It had a leather strap and 22 diamonds in the works. Well, he said it had diamonds in so she was inclined to believe him. Her first Christmas at the high school was magical. They had a Christmas play and she played a snowflake. Mummy made a white dress edged with tinsel and she had tinsel in her hair. 'You were the best one in the whole thing,' Daddy told her on the way home. 'Everyone thought so.' They had a car now, a Morris 8. Sometimes, when she rode in it, Dolly pretended she was a princess and waved to people though the window. Mummy would say 'Dorothy!' and tut tut, but only slowly, which meant she wasn't really cross. And Daddy would call her 'Princess' and help her out of the car as though she was a real one.

In February the snow started. 'Four million men idle,' her father said gloomily. Her mother worried constantly about power cuts. 'They're sitting in the dark in half the country,' she warned. 'It'll be our turn next.' Daddy went out to work each day, but even when he had petrol the snow made use of the car impossible.

One day he didn't come home at five o'clock. Dorothy kept watch at the window and for once her mother didn't grumble about displacing the lace curtain. At seven o'clock, with the snow still swirling, they set out to look for him, holding hands against the wind that tore at their clothes and drove the snow into their open mouths.

The found him slumped on a pile of snow someone had shovelled away from their gate. His eyes were closed and when Dorothy touched his wrist where it showed between glove and cuff, it was very cold. She began to cry but then his eyes opened and she knew it was going to be alright. 'Run for Mr Dickinson, Dorothy. Tell him we need help.' Mr Dickinson was their next-door neighbour. He shrugged into coat and cap and followed her along the street. 'For God's sake, Tommy,' he said. 'Let's get you home.'

For two days Dad lay in bed upstairs and then an ambulance came and took him away. Dorothy went to stay with the Dickinsons. 'Why can't I come with you?' she asked. But her mother just told her to be a good girl for Mrs Dickinson and not to worry.

'It's his lungs,' Mrs Dickinson explained. 'Your dad had consumption. That's why he was exempt in the war. He's got something called pneumonia and it's serious. Still, they're clever nowadays.' But if her tongue said 'clever', the tone of her voice said something different. Dorothy tried to remember what that other mother had said when she went. 'I'll be back directly.' Or something like that. And she had never come back. And Maggie had promised to keep her safe and then let her down. People lie, Dorothy thought.

It was two days before her mother came back. 'You'll have to be a brave girl, Dorothy. Daddy thought the world of you. The world.' In the corner, Lassie suddenly started to howl. 'Is he dead?' Dorothy said, but she knew the answer to her own question.

She wore her school uniform to the funeral and tried to sing the hymns, although her voice sounded strange. Beside her, her mother wept quietly into her hankie. She hugged Dorothy at the grave and helped her throw some earth onto the coffin. The snow had ceased while they were in church but now it started again. Dorothy wondered what would happen when they all went away. And then she saw the men leaning on their shovels a little way off. Wild thoughts of Daddy not being dead after all but covered with tons of wet soil and snow entered her head, but she shut them out. Instead she decided he was not in the coffin, had never died. He had gone out like her mother and was somewhere else, living in another house, perhaps with another little girl. She didn't realise she was smiling until she saw her mother's shocked face and then she decided she had better cry. This was too serious for a nod.

For a while strangers came and went from the house. Mrs Dickinson made tea for them and sometimes carried in casseroles and pies. But her mother didn't eat and there was no comforting smell of Evening in Paris. The funeral had been over for a week when she came into Dorothy's bedroom one morning. 'Things are going to be different now,' she said, sitting down on the edge of the bed and fingering the silk of the eiderdown. 'We'll have to make some changes. I'm afraid we can't afford school fees... but you'll be fine at Broad Street. We'll manage somehow, won't we? You and me. Just like Daddy would want us to.' Dorothy nodded. She couldn't think of anything else to do.

Chapter Twenty Seven

MUMMY HAD SAID THINGS WERE going to be different and they were. The paperboy didn't come any more, but sometimes Dorothy would be sent to the newsagents to buy a copy of the *Daily Express*. Meals were sparser but, as her mother pointed out, everyone was suffering as rationing became more severe.

'I'm glad your father isn't here to see this,' Mummy said, as the tinned meat ration was cut to tuppence worth per person per week. Dolly didn't care too much about the meat ration. She was too busy trying to escape the bullies at Broad Street, who thought anyone who had been to private school was a snob and therefore an enemy.

And then an announcement came from Buckingham Palace. Princess Elizabeth, the King's daughter, was to marry Lieutenant Philip Mountbatten. 'He's not an ordinary lieutenant,' Mummy said. 'He's a Greek Prince and ever so handsome.'

For a while it seemed everything cheered up. The

wedding was still four months away but no one talked about anything else – at school, in the shops, even at church. Norman Hartnell would make the dress and it would be embroidered all over with pearls and beads. 'Where will she get the clothing coupons?' Dolly asked, but Mummy just gave her a knowing look. 'But where?' Dolly persisted.

'They're royalty,' was the answer, as if that explained it all. Seeing Dolly's puzzlement, she elaborated. 'The world's not fair, Dolly. It should be, but it isn't. Some people have everything, others have everything taken away from them.' She sounded half-angry, half-sad. Dolly wanted to say something to cheer her up but she wasn't sure what it should be. 'I could make you a cup of tea,' she said at last. But that didn't cheer her mother up, it made her cry. People were very strange, Dolly decided.

She had a day off for the royal wedding and listened to it on the wireless. It had been a cold, wet November night but soon after she got up, the rain stopped. When at last the coach came out of the palace gates there was a thunder of cheering from the radio that almost hurt Dolly's ears. Mummy told her the wedding dress was made of ivory silk and had a thirteen-foot train. 'As long as our back garden, Dolly, and it took 350 girls to sew on ten thousand seed pearls. Two hundred extra clothing coupons, that's what she got from the government. Two hundred! But every bride gets that, she didn't get more than her share.' There were six kings and seven queens among the 2,500 congregation. The man on the wireless told them that and Mummy said it was because Britain had saved the world in the war. Prince Philip was a Royal Highness now, Mummy said, and that was only right because he was a hero who had fought in the war. Wedding fever just went on and on. Dolly and her mother went to the cinema to see the film of the wedding and Mummy read the list of wedding presents aloud from the newspaper. 'Two thousand five hundred, Dorothy, silver and jewels and even cases of tinned pineapple and salmon – and us on one ounce of bacon a week and eating snoek. We were born in the wrong bed.' Dolly didn't understand what beds had to do with a royal wedding but she just widened her eyes to express astonishment and that seemed to satisfy her mother.

It was the day after the wedding when her mother told her about the lodgers. 'We're going to have people living here, Dorothy. Nice people, professionals. You'll have to move into my room and they'll have the front room, but it'll work, you'll see. And we won't have to worry so much about bills.'

The first lodger was a grey-haired woman who worked at the Labour Exchange. She had the front bedroom and paid £1 a week for the room and ten shillings extra for an evening meal. Weekends she would spend with her sister in Bolton. Miss Emmet, for that was her name, hardly ever spoke and kept her radio tuned to the Home Service at all times. She didn't like dogs and Dorothy was under orders to keep Lassie out of her way. Mr Stainsby, who moved into the dining room, was quite the opposite. 'What a nice dog,' he said, even before his bags went upstairs. On her mother's birthday, Mr Stainsby opened a bottle of wine. 'Can she have a sip?' Mr Stainsby asked and after a moment's hesitation her mother nodded. 'Just a sip as it's a special occasion.' The wine was a disappointment. Girls at school had told her about the effects of alcohol, so she held the wine in her mouth for as long as she could before she swallowed it, but absolutely nothing happened. But for the first time since her father died she heard her mother laughing. Her cheeks went quite pink and when it was time for Dorothy to kiss her goodnight, she smelled it. Evening in Paris. Quite strong.

Three months later, her mother and Mr Stainsby announced a wedding of their own. 'It'll be better, you'll see,' her mother told her. She had brought cocoa up to the bedroom and now she sat on the edge of the bed. She had taken to curling the front of her hair and she looked a little foolish, a bit like a girl but grown-up. 'It'll be better, I promise you. Miss Emmett will be leaving and there'll be more money. You can have your own room back. And you like him. I know you do. And he likes you. You'll have a daddy again.' Dorothy nodded. What else was there to do? 'Besides,' her mother continued. 'He says he'll pay for you to go back to private school. Isn't that kind of him?'

Dorothy went to stay with a friend of Mr Stainsby while the newlyweds honeymooned in Southport. 'You'll see some changes, I expect,' the woman said. There was a smirk on her face and it made Dorothy uneasy. 'A man in the house and all. Still, you'll soon be up and off their hands.' Now Dorothy was frightened. She wanted to say that she was still quite young and didn't want to go off anywhere, but instead she nodded and accepted another piece of Madeira cake.

They brought her a satin headsquare from Southport. It had a pattern of flowers and a plaque in one corner that said 'Southport'. Dorothy said a dutiful thank you and Mr Stainsby bent to give her a peck on the cheek. She was halfway out of the door, taking her scarf upstairs, when she heard Lassie whimper. 'Get this damned dog out of here, will you?' He said it pleasantly enough, but when she reached for Lassie's collar the dog was shaking.

Upstairs she got ready for bed. It was still light outside but she wanted to go to bed. You were safe in bed. Her mother looked in to say goodnight but she didn't seem surprised that Dorothy was so early to bed. In fact, she seemed relieved.

For the first time in a long time Dorothy thought about Maggie. When she had been scared before, Maggie had read to her. They only had one book. It had been blue with a shiny fabric cover with a picture of a girl on it. Three names. The girl in the book had had three names. She tried and tried but she couldn't remember them. She felt a tremor as Lassie leapt onto the bed. She moved a hand over the dog's fur and felt her eyelids droop. It would all be alright in the morning. Maggie had told her that. Except that she couldn't remember Maggie's face. Only the face of the girl in the book, the girl with three names.

But it was not alright in the morning. 'I'm afraid it has

to go, Dorothy. I know you're attached to it but this is partly your...' There was a hesitation and then her mother went on, speaking more firmly. 'This is half your father's house now and he can't be doing with dogs. They affect his chest. Besides, dogs cost money.'

They had not affected his chest up till now and surely they had more money now, Dolly wanted to say, but she knew it was useless. 'You won't put her to sleep? Please say you won't put her to sleep. They electrocute dogs no one wants.' A girl at school had told her that. If they wanted to electrocute Lassie, she would run away.

'Of course not.' She felt a wave of relief so strong that it almost took her breath away. 'It's going to a man your father knows. He only lives two streets away so you can probably visit, as long as you don't make a nuisance of yourself.'

The return to private school never materialised but the promised visits to see Lassie did take place. Ernest Leighton had grey hair but quite a young face. 'Come anytime,' he said when Lassie was handed over. 'I can see she's attached to you. Come whenever you like.'

It was on the fourth visit that Ernest touched her chest. 'You're growing up,' he said and smiled. She had noticed her chest getting bigger. Some of the girls at school had breasts. One called Maureen wore a bra, even when they did gym. She had never thought about having breasts or wearing a bra, but now that touch made it difficult to think of anything else.

She had looked forward to her visits to Ernest and Lassie, largely because home wasn't home anymore. It was Mr Stainsby's house. Increasingly, what he said went and her mother seemed jumpy, especially at mealtimes, because Mr Stainsby liked his food just so. Now, though, she felt a curious reluctance to go to Ernest's house. She spent a long while trying to work out how she could train Lassie to unlatch the gate and come to her, but she knew it was useless, so she kept on going. The second time he touched her, his hand stayed and then pinched a bit. She winced at the pain of it and Ernest laughed and said, 'Touchy, are we?' He turned her round to face him and looked her in the eye. 'You know what would happen to Lassie if she had to leave here?' Dorothy nodded. 'I want to keep her, Dorothy. I really do. And I will. But I expect you to be nice to me in return. You will be nice, won't you?'

Behind him, Dorothy could see Lassie's eyes on her, trusting her to make everything alright. 'Well?' He sounded irritated now. Dorothy nodded. She kept looking at Lassie even when his hand moved down and pushed her legs apart. 'You mustn't tell, Dorothy, because if you do I'd go to prison and what would happen to poor Lassie then?' It was alright as long as Lassie held her gaze. In fact, she felt a kind of peace sweep over her. She was making it safe for Lassie and it would be alright. He was trying to kiss her now and he was shaking, shuddering even. 'Do you understand, Dorothy? Why you mustn't tell?' She nodded but the expression on his face told her he wanted more. 'I understand,' she said.

Chapter Twenty Eight

SLOWLY BUT SURELY, BRITAIN MOVED away from war. The last of the black paint applied in the blackout was scraped from windows; bomb sites bloomed first with rosebay willow-herb and then with scaffolding; uniforms ceased to be a familiar sight on the streets and very slowly food came back into the shops.

Life for Dorothy did not move forward, or if it did she was unaware of it. She had shut down thought and feeling except when it came to Lassie. With her dog she felt safe, warm, loved. Enduring Ernie's onslaughts, which increased in fervour as she matured, was a price to be paid and she paid it willingly. No use doing anything else. At home Mr Stainsby – thankfully her mother had abandoned attempts to make her call him daddy – continued to complain and control. Her mother chatted away brightly like an agitated little bird that realises it is being eyed by a tomcat. They both accepted her frequent visits to see her dog – 'That damned dog,' according to

Mr Stainsby. In fact, she thought they were relieved to see her go, leaving them their home. Ernie demanded two visits a day, one before she went to school and one after. Sometimes he held her jammed against the sink while he 'made her happy'. She watched the dog over his shoulder and tried to pretend his intrusive fingers were a bad dream. Then it was her turn to make him happy. When it was done and he had retreated to his chair, she would take down the lead from its place behind the door and escape into the open air, Lassie at her heels.

For her thirteenth birthday Mummy took her to see *The Red Shoes*. Mr Stainsby was away 'on a course', whatever that meant. 'This'll be our little secret,' Mummy said. 'Your father doesn't approve of spending money in the cinema, not with the pound devalued and everything so dear. I saved the money out of the house-keeping, so it's not really waste, is it?' But she didn't sound sure. The film was lovely and the music the best Dolly had ever heard. On the way home, Dolly tried going up on her toes like the ballerina in the film, but she couldn't do it and nearly fell over, which made Mummy laugh. 'We've had a lovely evening,' she said. 'I'll make cocoa when we get home but not a word to your father. This is just between you and me.'

The day after her birthday, Dorothy had penetrative sex for the first time. 'Was that nice?' Ernie asked. She nodded and reached for the lead. She knew what had happened because there was no shortage of sexual know-alls in the lavatories at school. Knew too that she would not have a baby, for Ernie had dangled the French letter in front of her eyes, expecting praise for his precautions. It was the school nurse, summoned by a teacher who saw blood seeping through the skirt of her tunic, who explained to her that the flow of blood that had started two days later and went on for a week was nothing to be worried about. Merely a sign that she was growing up.

In some ways it was easier after that. The act of sex was over more quickly than all the fumbling that had gone before. She lay beneath Ernie as he laboured away and made her thoughts a kaleidoscope of things she liked. Dogs, principally, and peaches and the feeling of suede, and toast hot from the fork with best butter. Sometimes memories intruded but they became harder and harder to bring into focus. There had been a mother and a father once, and a big sister who bossed her about, and a baby brother who wet his pants and sent warm waves into the bed when his nappy was soaked. But that was a long time ago, so she made her thoughts spin them out of the picture and concentrated on her dog. 'I love you, Lassie,' she would whisper when at last they were free and out in the open air. And the dog would lick her hand and then run ahead of her, drunk with freedom.

School was something else to be endured. 'There must be something you're good at, Dorothy,' her teacher said. It was a statement of despair, but not unfair, so Dorothy nodded. 'It's no good nodding,' came the exasperated reply. 'You have your way to make in the world. Nodding won't get you anywhere.'

Mr Stainsby had already told her this. 'Don't think you can sponge off us indefinitely, my girl. I've borne the burden long enough.' Only that time, Dorothy and her mother had nodded in unison – or perhaps her mother had shaken her head? It didn't matter anyway.

Lassie died on October 3rd 1950. She didn't run to rub noses when Dorothy arrived in the morning and that was strange. She walked through to the living room and Lassie was there, curled in her basket. 'The dog's gone,' Ernie said from the kitchen. 'Went in the night. She's had a good run for a collie. They don't make old bones.'

As she walked past him to kneel at the basket, it struck her that she was free now. She touched the fur. It felt warm and silky, as usual. But the eyes, which were normally alight and alert, were strangely yellow and opaque. 'What will you do with her?'

'The binmen come tomorrow. They'll take her.' He was standing up, loosening his belt.

'I want a funeral.' Her voice sounded strange but firmer than she felt. 'Can't do that.' He was moving towards her, reaching out.

'Not unless we bury her.' She backed off a step and folded her arms across her chest. For a second he eyed her.

'Alright but I want it first.'

'No.' This time she knew she had the upper hand. 'I want her buried in the yard, under the rose bush. And deep. Then we'll do it.' He was looking at the clock. 'There won't be time, you'll be late for school.'

'I won't go in today. We can have extra time, do anything you like...' She stood by as he shovelled earth, then she wrapped Lassie in her school jumper and stood as he lowered her into the earth. 'You'll get wrong for that jumper,' he said. Dorothy nodded. 'I know.'

When he was done with her she walked home, her knees trembling at what she had just endured and at what was to come. Her mother swung round as she entered the kitchen. 'Dorothy...' She held a bottle in one hand, a glass in the other, and she looked as though she'd been crying. 'What are you doing home?'

'I have to get some things,' Dorothy said and walked past her to the hall and stairs. She took only what she would need for a few days, emptied the coppers and silver from her money box and packed them all in a holdall. When she came downstairs, the bottle and glass had vanished and her mother was peeling sprouts. 'Will you be home as usual?' she asked. Dorothy nodded and let herself out of the back door.

It took her two days to get to London. The first lorry driver took her as far as Peterborough, gave her all the loose change he had and strongly advised she go home. 'Or at least ring your mam.' Dorothy nodded. It was eight o'clock. At nine she stopped trying to thumb another lift, curled up in a hedge and tried to sleep. She did sleep, fitfully, but it was a relief when the dawn came. The first car she thumbed was local. 'You look all in,' he said. 'I'm just going to the next village but there's a transport café on the way. You'll do better there.' He dropped her among the lorries and vans and wished her good luck as he drove off.

She bought a thick bacon sandwich and some tea and felt contentment flood through her with the warm liquid. She was going to survive. The second lorry driver offered to take her right into London, but at a price. She submitted to his attempts to have sex and thought about London. Buckingham Palace, The Mall, golden coaches... He didn't speak the rest of the journey, neither did she.

For the next few weeks, she slept rough in an alley behind a church. By day she looked for a job, in between scrounging food where she could. She avoided the men who tried to pick her up until hunger drove her to accept. 'A fiver?' the man said. Dorothy nodded. After that she had sex only when there was no alternative and she always insisted they used a French letter. If you didn't do that you had a baby. The girls at Broad Street had told her that, and what would she do with a baby and no place to lay it down?

And then Eve came into her life. Eve was seventeen, streetwise, pretty and had a Liverpudlian accent broader than the Mersey. At night they slept like bookends, back to back. 'Safer that way,' Eve said. Eve had found an alley with an air vent that gave out warm air. They had thick cardboard under them and an old eiderdown for cover. As soon as they got under it and she felt Eve's back against her back, Dolly felt safe. By day they ate well, the food expertly lifted from stalls and counters by Eve. 'Hang in there, kid,' she said when Dorothy feared for the future. 'The Festival starts in two weeks. We'll all get jobs then.' Seeing Dorothy's unbelieving face, she hugged her and said she loved the bones of her, but if she didn't cheer up, she'd be history. Dorothy cheered up as Eve outlined the wonders of the coming festival. 27 acres of bomb-damaged London had been transformed into a wonderland. There would be a Dome of Discovery and a floating thing called a Skylon, which would be floodlit from every angle. There would be a huge concert hall and, down the river at Battersea, a sculpture exhibition and pleasure gardens. 'So?' Dorothy said, bemused.

'Jobs, numbskull. Jobs. Thousands of people needing feeding, cleaning up after. It'll be a doddle.'

'How old do you have to be to get a job?' The revelation that Dolly was still short of her sixteenth birthday shocked Eve to the core. 'Fifteen? You look thirty if you look a day.' But from then on she was more protective, less critical. 'You'll have to say you're sixteen. Look them straight in the eye. They'll be too short of staff to do any checking.'

The Festival was a doddle, as Eve had predicted. Dorothy got work in the kitchen of a restaurant; Eve donned a cap and saucy apron to dispense coffee from a booth.

'Nine pence a cup,' she said, scandalised. 'Nine pence a bleeding cup.' They shared a room in Bow with two other girls now, which meant they had money left over to visit the funfair in the Pleasure Gardens. Life, Dolly decided, was on the up and up.

When the Festival ended at the end of September, so did their jobs, but they had a toehold now. 'I can't sign on,' Dorothy said when Eve talked about dole. 'There's no such thing as can't,' Eve said firmly, and sign on they did. It meant a lot of lies and tales of lost documents, but it worked. They found jobs eventually, working together in the warehouse of a department store. But with the spring of 1952, Eve's longing for Liverpool overcame her. 'It's been great, London. I wouldn't have missed it. But I'm going home. You should go home. They'll be glad to have you back. They say good riddance when you go but they come round in the end.' Dorothy nodded.

With Eve gone, life was lonely. She went out occasionally, slipping into pubs and ordering a half of lager and lime. Barmaids were openly hostile to her, barmen kinder. And there were men, drinkers. When they asked her for sex, it was easier to go along with it than say no. Besides, she felt a curious pity for them. They couldn't help themselves. Men never could.

Chapter Twenty Nine

SHE WAS SIXTEEN WHEN THE King died. Around her, people cried in the street or stood on street corners to swap stories of what a good King he had been and his stoicism in the war. She tried to feel patriotic but it wasn't easy. She was too busy trying to keep body and soul together to care much about the monarchy.

The King had been dead for a few weeks when she got a new job. It was in a club not far from the Ritz hotel, but the Rendezvous bore no resemblance to its prestigious neighbour. The proprietor was a Cypriot named Renos and the clients were mostly Japanese. They were small and polite until the night wore on and they got drunk and boisterous. Then they vanished upstairs or to a back room with one of the hostesses.

Dolly had been engaged as a waitress but had ambitions to be a hostess herself. They got commission on any drinks ordered by their customers and the mark-up was huge. There were three grades of drink. First came the sealed bottles that were served up at the beginning. When the customer was pleasantly inebriated, he would be served drink two: wine with water added and the cork reinserted. Only when they were close to insensible was it time for drink three: coloured water with a nip of spirits added. All three drinks were charged at the same eye-watering price. 'Serves them bloody right,' Rebecca said when Dolly wondered aloud. Rebecca was Jewish, a redhead with a faint patina of freckles under her skin and eyes the colour of emeralds. Dolly liked Rebecca, who would share her makeup, her fags and even her clothes. But she was adamant that Dolly should not become a hostess. 'You've got a lot going for you, kid, with a face and a body like that. Don't waste it on *drek* like this lot.'

Dolly could not work out why Rebecca was so willing to waste her own talents on *drek*, which Ruby, another hostess, explained was a Jewish word for shite. 'It's her habit,' the girl explained. 'She's a bloody fool, that Becky. Lost her family in Ravensbrück. Now she's trying to drown her sorrows with stuff. Never works. You have to move on, don't you? She can't – or won't.'

In June 1953 Dolly stood on a London pavement to see the Golden Coach carry the new Queen to be crowned. That night she put on the slipper satin gown Renos gave her and took Rebecca's place at the bar. Rebecca had died that morning of septicaemia following a botched abortion. 'Poor cow,' Ruby said. 'I could have given her the name of a proper doctor, certificated and everything. Only charges a pony and he's dead kind.'

Now, by night, Dolly hostessed, plying the men with drink, slipping the dollars they sometimes gave her into her brassiere and then going upstairs or to the back room, whichever was unoccupied at the time. She felt a curious detachment about it all – some things just had to be endured. By day she haunted the cinema. Alone in the dark, she felt emotions she never felt in real life. Her favourite star was Grace Kelly, cool, unapproachable and dignified, all the things that she would be one day when the ship came in. She never tried to identify the ship or from whence it would come. She simply clung on to the knowledge that such a ship existed and would appear on the horizon one day.

She cried when her screen idol, James Dean, crashed his Porsche Spyder on a road outside Los Angeles. He had been wonderful in *East of Eden*. When *Giant*, the film he had completed just before his death, came to the cinema in the Edgware Road, she wept copious tears for what might have been if he had lived and she had crossed his path one day. She cried again when a hollow-eyed Princess Margaret renounced Peter Townsend. The princess's face, seen through a car window and splashed across the newspapers, was a picture of a life gone wrong and happiness denied. She knew exactly how that felt.

The following day she went off to have the first of two abortions. It took place in the back room of a house in Notting Hill, and when she cried out in pain, the woman abortionist told her she should have thought of the consequences sooner. By now she was accepting money for sex from men she met through an agency called Glen

Modelling. The money was fair, though fairer still for the agency, and it allowed her to give up her job at the club. By day she went to the cinema or walked in one of the London Parks. Hyde Park was her favourite. By night she made up her face, tonged her hair and studied details of her night's assignment before she sallied forth.

Her second abortion brought tsk-tsks from the agency but they paid for her to go to a private hospital where she was treated with contempt by the nursing staff, but still given tablets for the pain.

Sometimes, especially on the nights when she slept alone, she would lie and try to make sense of it all. Other people had families, grandparents, uncles and aunts. She had never had a family, not one she could count on anyway. Faint memories would occur then, of laughter and warm bodies next to her in bed, and the sweet taste of chocolate on her tongue. There was one memory – she had fallen on a cinder path and someone had sat her on the kitchen table and bathed the wound on her knee after they had picked out fragments of cinder. There had been no cinder path at her adoptive home, so it must have been before, in that other world that was hidden now even from memory.

One thing she never did was drugs. She remembered that poor cow, Rebecca, who hadn't been able to move forward. It wasn't that she had a moral objection to drugs, it was that they took away what little control you had over what was happening to you. She saw that all around her, drink and drugs making puppets of people for someone else to push around. No one was doing that to her. She meant to keep her wits about her and that meant hanging on to them at all times.

Somehow the years sped by. Governments came and went, black faces became more common in London streets, a war erupted over the Suez Canal and ended in a humiliating defeat for Britain. 'Tail between its legs' was the phrase on the lips of Londoners. Dolly didn't mind. She had a television set now, bought second-hand in Petticoat Lane, and it was a source of endless pleasure. She saw man go into space and worshipped Jacqueline Kennedy in her pillbox hats and stand-off collars. And she cried when Marilyn was found dead of an overdose in her Hollywood home. She was 27 when the Profumo scandal erupted and Christine Keeler's picture was in every paper. She was beautiful, but as the days went by photographs showed her more and more haggard. It made Dorothy think of her own situation. Sooner or later she would lose her looks. Already she had tiny crows' feet. She could get to thirty, even 35 if she kept herself trim. But forty? At 27 she was one of the older women on the agency's books. She started to worry about it, lying awake on the nights she did not work. There could be no going back to Otley. Her mother was probably dead of drink by now. She could go back to the club, they had been sorry to see her go, but she had a nice flat now. The rent couldn't be afforded on the commission the club paid.

One day, in the bath, she had a panic attack. 'Mammy,' she called out, half under her breath, and wondered where that word had come from. After that she tried not to think about it for fear that fear itself would overtake her. Time enough to do something about it next year. Or the one after. There was still time. And then, one night, there was Eddie. He was stout but nimble on his feet, and he didn't have her flat on her back two minutes after she hit his hotel room. In the bathroom afterwards he was whistling 'She Loves You' and looked pleased when she said she liked the Beatles too.

He counted out her money and offered her a drink. 'Would you like a bite to eat?' he said. 'There's a nice little Italian round the corner. And you look as though you could do with a good feed.' When she didn't get to her feet, he said: 'Come on then, lass. I'm ready to eat shoe leather. Don't just sit there nodding.' After that he came to London every weekend. He paid well and she began to decline other assignments. They didn't always have sex. Sometimes they went to the pictures, even to the theatre. She had never been to the theatre and Eddie laughed at her awe of it all. 'You're a funny one and no mistake, Dolly.'

They married on November 25th 1963, while the world mourned John F Kennedy, gunned down in Dallas. On her honeymoon, she cried at television pictures of her heroine Jacqueline Kennedy crawling over the back seat of a car to cradle her dying husband's bloodstained head in her hands. It just proved that everyone died, even Presidents.

Eddie was a widower and had no family. 'I like a laugh, Dolly. That's what I miss about the wife. She was always up for a giggle. You're a good sort. I could see that right from the start.' They honeymooned in Southport, a four-star hotel on the seafront, and dressed for dinner every night.

'You'll never want for anything, Dolly,' Eddie told her when he opened a bank account for her – and she never had. She was Dolly again now, not Dorothy. She lived in a redbrick bungalow in Birmingham with a paddock on the side and a fountain in the garden. Eddie owned a factory which made electrical components. He was in Rotary, gave generously to any good cause which asked and was kind in bed. Dolly thought she had died and gone to heaven. She didn't love him at first. It was simply another business arrangement with a greater degree of security attached and jokes into the bargain. In the end, though, she was waiting for his key in the door, liking the warm bulk of him in her bed, the look of admiration in his eyes whenever he saw her. 'How would you feel about kids?' she asked one day. She saw pleasure flare in his eyes but all he said was 'Up to you, Dolly'.

She wanted to give him a child, or children – a boy to inherit his business and a girl to make a fuss of him. But her attempts to get pregnant ended in failure. 'I'm sorry,' the gynaecologist said. 'There was an infection. There's extensive scarring.' She remembered the back room in Notting Hill and felt ashamed. Eddie, however, was philosophical. 'If we have none to make us laugh, we'll have none to make us cry,' he said, and bought her the first of many poodles. And then, when the tears still threatened, 'Never look back, lass, never look back.' He made her laugh, he gave her a lush life, he took her to far-off places, but most of all he made her feel safe, and when he died in 1998 she found he had provided for her every need. 'I want my wife to enjoy the years which remain to her in token of all the enjoyment she has given me,' his will said. So she had enjoyed life, although there had never been another man. There could never be another Eddie. She left the Birmingham bungalow and moved nearer to London. She had access to the shops and the theatre and there was a garden for whichever dog she had at the time. She had been quite happy, very happy really. Eddie had said never look back and she never had. Until a young whippersnapper with a posh accent had arrived on her doorstep to stir up the past.

Chapter Thirty

O<small>N HIS WAY BACK INTO</small> London, Ben was aware of planes criss-crossing above him. Monique would be somewhere up there by now. He thought fondly of her now but he had felt awkward when she awoke yesterday morning. She had turned to him, wanting to be loved, but the photograph he had glimpsed in her purse had intruded. 'Never mind,' she said contentedly when he failed to respond, and settled for snuggling into his arms. It had been unutterably pleasant to lie with that warm, slim body entwined with his. Making no demands but not withdrawing either. It made him realise how barren life with Diana had become. They had had sex regularly but compared with what he had known with Monique, it was as cold and clinical as flu jabs. Diana had never said, 'There, that's done' in the manner of a nurse carrying out an injection, but the words had hung in the air. But sex with Diana was in the past and suddenly the uniformed photo ceased to matter and all that mattered was to enter Monique and feel her respond. Remembering the intensity of that moment now made his hands clench the wheel. He felt the engine surge and moved his foot off the accelerator. Couldn't afford to crash now with so many balls in the air.

Monique had stood in the doorway of the room to watch him go down the corridor. 'A bientôt,' she had called and he had turned at the lift door and lifted his hand in salute. Was he in love? And if he was, was he part of another triangle? Pyke/Diana/him. He/Monique/some René or Jacques? It came as a relief to feel the office close around him, to know that it was time to concentrate on business. But not before he took a call from his sister. 'Where were you last night?'

'I stayed over with a friend. Well, not a friend...' He was about to stammer out an explanation but she stayed him. 'Don't bother. I was worried you'd gone back to Diana. You're a big boy, bruv. Where you sleep is your own business.' He promised to arrive in time for dinner and she rang off. Leaning back in his chair, he thought over what leaving Diana had meant. Had he missed her? He certainly hadn't missed the tension that had existed in the last few weeks, the terror of not knowing whether or not he was loved. Knowing that he was not was somehow easier to deal with than uncertainty. He missed the familiarity of his own place, that was certain. However welcoming Harry and Adele had been, their place wasn't his home. He missed Max, missed the warm head thrust against his knee, the pleading eyes, the wagging of the tail at his approach. Yes, Max was a huge miss. The one consolation was that Diana was generally good with animals. It was only people for whom she had no room. Max would miss him but he would not be ill-treated. All the same, he wanted his dog eventually. When he had a place of his own. At that moment, he realised that he had no intention of trying to repair his marriage. It was over.

When he arrived at his sister's home that evening, there were no questions and he was grateful. How did you explain to your sister that you were having unbeliev-ably good sex with a comparative stranger five minutes after you had walked out on your wife? Except that he hadn't walked out on Diana. It was she who had walked away from him.

He enjoyed the evening spent with Harry and Adele, watching their children laughing, squabbling, enjoying their home. He helped to take them up to bed and stood by as father or mother settled them for the night. This is what family life should be, he thought. This is what I want some day. With someone.

The following morning he felt less confused. It was a fine day and that lifted his spirits. When he reached the office he went through the post with Madge and then rang through to Peter Hammond. 'Can we meet at three? I'm popping out for lunch but I'll be back by then.' He had intended to grab a pint and a pie, but on a whim he dialled Barbara Tulloch's number. 'I know it's short notice. I don't expect you'll be free... but have you lunched yet?'

They settled in a booth at a pub she recommended

near to her chambers. 'Have the casseroled chops,' she said. 'Glorious gravy.' He followed her example and the chops were indeed glorious. 'Now,' she said, wiping her lips and aligning her knife and fork. 'Bring me up to speed. Have you been in contact with the French girl again, Monique?' He told her he had seen Monique again but was sketchy about details.

'And you still like her? She's nice?' He gave her a cautious opinion of Monique's 'niceness' and added 'not that I've had a chance to get to know her'. To his horror, he felt his cheeks grow warm and knew he was blushing at the lie. Mercifully, she appeared not to notice, so he hurried on. 'And we've found the third child. Your Aunt.'

'Dolly?'

'Dolly herself. Well, we've found her, except that she doesn't want to be found.'

'How old is she? Younger than the other one?'

'Dolly is 71, I think, nearly 72. Maggie is 76, although you'd never think they were so close in age. Dolly is very well preserved. Patronises a good beauty parlour, I should imagine.'

'So she has money?'

'Oodles of it, if appearances are anything to go by. Everything in the house is white. Well, magnolia. Even the dog!'

'It's not a poodle...'

'No, it's a bichon frise and pampered into the bargain. But she's adamant that she is not the Dolly we're looking for. I'm sure she is, but at the moment she won't admit it. She doesn't want to know about the past, though she did ask if you were all provided for. My guess is she'd have written a cheque if I'd said no, but she doesn't want contact so she won't admit… Which is a pity because it would be nice for the two sisters to be reunited. And to meet you.'

'Would it do any good if I made contact?' She was looking at him expecting an answer. Her eyes were green, not greenish, but a clear dark green. Unusual, but good with the red hair.

'Well?' He brought himself back to the question in hand. 'I don't know. Let's leave it for now. If all else fails, you could try.' They discussed the coming meeting with Margaret. 'I'm half-scared, half-keen,' she said and he nodded understanding. He bent to kiss her cheek when they parted in the street. She smelled faintly of soap. Monique smelled of the expensive Chanel that stood on the bedside table. As he walked on from Barbara's office he was half-smiling. If Diana thought he was bereft of female company, she was wrong.

Madge brought in tea as he settled down with Peter Hammond. 'Full complement,' the executive said. 'No apologies.' The shares had gone up another penny as the City scented profit and all the board members would be at the meeting.

'Any better idea of what will happen?' Ben asked.

'They'll be playing their cards close to their chest. You can count on four votes: mine, your own, your brother-in-law, Cyril Evans perhaps – he's not after quick returns. About the rest I'm not sure. The institutions won't think about the workforce or tradition. Can they do better by selling or not? That's the only criterion.'

'Will Pyke turn up?' Ben's uncertainty must have shown in his voice because Hammond, when he replied, was reassuring. 'I wouldn't worry about it. He's got the brass neck to turn up and technically he's got the right to vote because he hasn't been dismissed by the board and no proper procedures have been followed. But my hunch is that he'll stay away. The only thing that might tempt him is wanting to assess the board's mood, but that'll be all round the city by teatime so I don't think he'll bother.'

They supped their tea after that, business over. 'What would you do if Headey's won?' Hammond asked. Ben shrugged. 'I'd find something, I expect. I can't twiddle my thumbs for the next half-century.'

'You'll be able to afford to laze around with what you'll get for your shares.' Hammond dunked a biscuit and conveyed it hastily to his lips.

'What will you do?' Ben asked. Then he realised what he'd said: 'I'm talking as though it's all over.'

'Me?' Hammond licked in a stray crumb. 'I'd buy a yacht and sail round the world... No, seriously, I'd hope to get something else. Construction still, but not as big as Webcon. I need a rest.'

Outside the light was fading fast. 'Round the world on a yacht,' Ben said. 'That's an enticing prospect.'

Madge came in to clear the tea things. 'Solved all your problems?' she asked. The words were sarcastic but the tone was kind. 'They're only just beginning,' was Ben's reply. A few weeks ago he had been a vaguely happily married man with a secure job. Now his life was starting to resemble a television soap.

'About this meeting,' Madge said when she had disposed of the cups. 'I've talked to Margaret Riley on the phone, as you know. She's apprehensive about coming to London, doesn't like trains for some reason, but she wants to meet her niece. She appreciates the girl can't get away from work. Anyway, a trip to London would do her good.'

'Get her a good hotel. First-class travel.' A thought struck him. 'I did suggest we could send a car for her.'

'It's a long journey by car,' Madge said doubtfully. 'It's an option. Leave it to me. And I thought I might have her to stay. More homely than a hotel.'

'God, you're a treasure. But spare no expense. And copy Barbara in on everything.'

'Barbara?' She was making eyes at him now. 'It's Barbara, is it? And Monique? I'm working for a philanderer and me an ex-Sunday-school teacher.'

'Look who's talking. I know all about you and your detective friend.' He pretended to duck as she threatened to hurl her files at him. 'Well, it takes one to know one,' she said. They were both laughing as she let herself out of the office. Afterwards, he stood at the window gazing out on the city, which was now almost dark, strings of lights springing up as far as the eye could see. Whatever he did in the future, it would have to be in London. The city held him in its thrall. He could never leave it. He turned to gather up his things and got ready to join his sister's family once more.

Chapter Thirty One

'STAY HERE AND HAVE YOUR coffee,' he said when Madge carried in his tray. Madge considered for a moment and then went in search of her own special cup. They sat either side of the desk in companionable silence and then Ben put down his mug. 'I'm thinking of moving into the flat next week. Will I have everything?'

'Yes. Linen, utensils, enough for you to exist. It's better that you decide what else you need once you're on the spot.'

'I suppose I could leave it till we get this visit over, not to mention the board meeting.'

'The visit will be no problem. She sounds a nice little body.' The white blouse beneath Madge's navy suit was pristine, her waved hair immaculate. Come to think of it, he had never seen her looking anything but out of a bandbox in all the years. Whatever crises she had had in her life, she had kept them well hidden.

'I'm very grateful,' Ben said. 'For arranging it all. I hope you know that.'

'I've rather enjoyed it. And she's looking forward to it. She's nervous but she wants it just the same. It sounds as though she's missed her brother and sister. It's a shame about the boy. "Our Billy" she calls him. What are you doing about the other one, this Dolly? "Very pretty, our Dolly," according to her sister.'

'Yes, I can see she would have been pretty, and she's well preserved even now. What can I do? She says she's not the Dolly we want. We know she is, she knows we know, but there it ends. I can hardly bring her to meet her sister by force.'

'Well, it's a pity just the same.' She was rising to her feet now, gathering up the coffee things. 'Now, if we could squeeze in a little work before lunch...'

He grinned and turned back to signing his letters, but the mention of lunch made concentration difficult. He was meeting Diana at 1pm at The Ivy. It had been her suggestion. No, her order. 'We need to talk. I've booked at The Ivy for 1pm. Don't be late.' Wild thoughts of claiming a previous engagement had come and gone. They would have to talk some time. But he would not have chosen The Ivy, that haunt of has-beens and would-bes and gawpers. He went down to meet English without much of an appetite for what lay ahead.

Diana kept him waiting for fifteen minutes. He sat sipping an aperitif and trying to marshal some reasoned arguments. But without knowing what she was going to say, that was difficult. What if she suggested reconciliation? But it was not reconciliation she was after.

'I want to put the house up for sale.' That took him

by surprise and he concentrated on the menu to give him time to think. 'Scallops, I think. And some green beans.'

'Always so predictable. And please, not a Chardonnay.' So she was going to be a bitch. Well, if that was the way she wanted it.

'Why do you want to sell? I thought you liked that house.' She was silent until the wine was poured. 'I did like it. I still do. I just don't want to live there anymore. I want to be more central. Besides, it will make my settlement easier to work out.'

Around them the restaurant buzzed with laughter and idle chatter. Odd that they were interring a marriage. 'So you expect a settlement.'

Out of the corner of his eye he could see Cilla Black in animated conversation with a grey-haired man. No one he recognised. And Stephen Fry was being ushered to a corner table with a deference that wouldn't have looked out of place in the Vatican.

For the next hour they toyed with food and drink while discussing the end of their relationship. 'What have you done about those orphans?' she asked at last.

'I've found two of them, certainly; three probably.'

'What are you going to do about them?'

'Arrange some sort of settlement, probably.'

'Well, I think you're mad. And they're not getting a penny of my money. Let me make that clear right now!'

He changed the conversation by asking about Max. No point in arguing with her. 'The dog's fine. Which is more than I can say about you. You look paunchy. You need the gym.'

'I haven't had oodles – that favourite word of yours – I haven't had oodles of time for working out in the last few weeks.'

'Well, make time. Not that it's any of my business if you go to seed.'

'Will you move in with Pyke?' The moment he asked the question, he regretted it. The delicate arch of her eyebrows was raised slightly. 'Do you care?'

'Not really.' It was a banal answer but he was proud of the steady way he delivered it. After that, conversation was sparse until they exchanged details of lawyers and rose to leave.

'Can I drop you anywhere?' he said when English drew up at the door of the restaurant, but she was already moving away, her kiss on his cheek a token gesture of times past.

He worked steadily through the afternoon. In a day or little more, Webcon might no longer be his concern. If the worst happened he would want to walk away. Better to tidy loose ends now wherever possible and while he had the chance. At four o'clock he phoned Adele. 'Don't worry about dinner, Del. I had lunch at The Ivy, with Diana. I'll tell you about it tonight. I'm going to see Gran when I leave here but I won't be late.'

He put down the phone and went back to work. His shoulders began to ache after a while and he moved to the window. Six months ago – less –life had been on an even keel, the future stretching out as neatly planned as a kitchen garden. 2.4 children, some sort of decoration for services to industry and large donations to a political party, early retirement and then a life of affluent idleness. Now there would be no children – not with Diana – and he doubted he would marry again. Webcon was slipping from his grasp, hordes of hitherto unknown people were invading his life and everything was fucked. He turned back to his desk, cleared things away so as not to impede the cleaners and went off to visit his grandmother.

'Darling.' She looked even smaller and frailer but she was smiling. 'Come here, beside me. Is Maya bringing you a drink?'

'I asked for sherry. I thought you might have a small one too.'

'You're a naughty boy. Her hand on his was cool, the skin papery. 'Now, tell me all the news.'

'We've found Dolly. At least, we're pretty sure we have. She says it's not her.'

'Why would she say that?' He had never noticed before but the hair at the nape of her neck was golden, almost ginger, against the whiteness of the rest. Had it been like that years ago? He couldn't remember what she had looked like, only that she was always there.

'I think she might be fearful we're after her money. She's quite rich. Well, comfortable. Nice house. Widow of a businessman. She's just being cautious.'

'You'd think she'd want to meet her sister. Perhaps if the boy had still been alive. They were very close as children.'

Maya arrived with glasses and a decanter. Ben sipped appreciatively. 'You forget how good a dry sherry can be.'

His grandmother smiled. 'We can't bribe her then, if

she's got money.'

'I don't think so, but I haven't given up. Let's get Margaret here. You'll like her and Barbara is rather a splendid young woman. Very intelligent, no nonsense.'

'You said she was a barrister. They'd've been proud of that, having a professional in the family.'

It was eight o'clock when he left. The old lady was visibly drooping and Sue was hovering. He had watched while his grandmother picked at her meagre supper and refused Maya's entreaties to eat himself. 'How is she?' he asked as the housekeeper accompanied him downstairs. She didn't speak, just shook her glossy head, and when he turned in the doorway he saw that her eyes were bright with unshed tears.

He was halfway home when he felt his phone vibrate. Safe in a lay-by he answered it. 'Chéri?' It was Monique, nervous about the coming DNA test. He undid his seatbelt, settled down in his seat and gave himself up to the pleasure of conversation.

Chapter Thirty Two

THE TRAFFIC WAS AS THICK as ever as he drove himself into London. Ken Livingstone's congestion charge had achieved little or nothing except to pour more money into the maw of the authority. It was 8.35am when he reached the underground car park. At 9am Monique would be giving her DNA sample at a clinic in Bloomsbury. He tried to expunge speculation from his mind and concentrate on the meeting which lay ahead, but the Frenchwoman was hard to forget.

'The share price is steady,' Hammond told him once they were seated either side of his desk. 'That should be on our side. But it's still in the lap of the gods.' In an hour's time they must persuade the board to back them in turning down the bid. If they succeeded, Headey's could go over their heads and appeal to the shareholders, but a successful outcome today could buy them vital time in which to persuade all the shareholders to turn down the bid. A vote against them today would mean an immediate acceptance and the end of Webcon as an entity. Inside him a little voice whispered freedom – but was that just a euphemism for desertion? His father and his grandfather had built this company. Should he be the one to lose it if it was humanly possible to prevent it?

Again he and Hammond went over the list of who could be counted on and who could not. 'We should swing it,' Hammond said at last. 'If everyone we can count on holds firm, we should swing it.'

Madge brought in coffee after Hammond left. 'Margaret Riley arrives on Monday,' she said. 'Sparrow and I are picking her up from King's Cross, so lay on the niece for Tuesday.' She was trying to take his mind off what lay ahead and they both knew it. 'Drink up,' she said as she left the office. 'I'm tired of finding half-full cups in here, stone cold.'

When he was alone he dialled Monique's number. 'How did it go?' It had been easy and he leaned back in his chair, relieved. Then it was her turn to sympathise with him about the meeting. He promised to let her know what happened and rang off. As he sipped his coffee, he dialled Barbara's mobile, half-expecting to get the answer phone. 'How are you fixed on Tuesday? Your aunt arrives on Monday, so if you're free...' She had no engagements she could not break. 'But you'll be there, won't you?' For once she did not sound angry or dogmatic. She sounded uncertain and he warmed to it. He found himself telling her that today was the day of Monique's DNA test and felt reassured by her reaction. 'If she's his grandchild, she's his grandchild, just like the rest of us.'

When he put down the phone he felt comforted. He liked Barbara. Given time, she could become like a sister, someone with whom he could be at ease.

He was still musing on Barbara's virtues when Madge appeared in the doorway. 'It's time,' she said, advancing on him, clothes brush in hand. He submitted to a tidy up, half-expecting her to spit on her hanky and wipe his dirty face. 'Done, mum?' he asked when she stepped back, and received a dirty look for his pains. As he walked to the door, Neil Pyke came into his mind. Would he have the nerve to turn up? If he did, Madge would deal with him.

Once ensconced in his chair at the head of the board-room table, he surveyed his fellow directors. The executives looked scared – or as near to scared as high-flyers could ever be. The directors representing the major shareholders were not meeting his eye and that was not a good sign. He resisted the impulse to yell 'Geronimo!' and instead cleared his throat.

He had just launched into his introductory remarks when Madge appeared in the doorway. Her very appearance was scary enough. Board meetings were sacrosanct. But her face was even more alarming. Something was very wrong. 'I'm sorry, Mr Chairman.' Even in a state of agitation her address was formal. 'You're wanted on the phone. It's very urgent.' He excused himself and went to the outer office. Madge's face told him not to question.

'I think you need to come now.' The nurse's tone left him in no doubt of the urgency of the matter. He didn't bother with questions. 'I'm on my way,' he said and put down the phone. When he got back to the boardroom the faces around the table were apprehensive. 'I have to go, I'm afraid. My grandmother has taken a turn for the worse.'

There was a moment of total silence and then murmurs of sympathy. Hammond rose from his seat. 'Off you go. This can wait.' But it was Neville Carteret, his brother-in-law, who accompanied him to the car. 'Don't worry, Ben. She'll be sitting up asking for tea when you get there. Don't worry about this place. We'll see to everything. I'll see that Diana is told, leave her to me.' He had never really liked Neville but you learned who your friends were when the chips were down. Diana was entitled to know – she was technically his wife – but Neville would make sure she stayed clear.

He leaned back in his seat and tried to stop memories of his grandmother crowding in. Outside the traffic was sluggish. Why didn't someone do something? Getting there in time was all that really mattered. Suddenly he realised he ought to tell Adele. He dialled her mobile but all he got was her message service. The house phone was on answer phone. He tried Harry then but his phone too was switched off. He gave up trying and concentrated on the road ahead.

His grandmother seemed to be sleeping when he entered the room. He looked towards Sue, hoping for comfort, but there was only a shake of the head. He sat down beside the bed and reached for the thin hand that lay on the coverlet. Blue veins stood out like cords, the skin was paper thin and dry, the broad wedding ring loose beneath a knuckle it would never again pass in life. 'I'm here, Gran.' The eyelids flickered and then the eyes, still amazing blue, were open and fixed on his. 'I love you, Gran.' Why had he never said that before? She had been more than a mother to him and now he was giving back too little, too late.

'Margaret Riley... Margaret Brewis is coming to London on Sunday. Remember, I told you. You have to get well so you can meet her.' For a moment there was no response and then the thin, pale lips curved in a smile. She was pleased. 'I'm going to bring her here. And Barbara. She's Billy's girl. They want to meet you.' Again the faint smile but then the eyes closed. 'She knows,' he thought. There would be no tearful reunion but at least she knew he had tried to make good her promise. He wondered if he should make up some lie about Dolly in order to complete the circle but the old woman's breathing had grown louder. Once it seemed to stop and he held his breath until it started again. 'Not long now.' The nurse was feeling her patient's pulse. 'Do you want to be alone with her?'

'No.' He did not say it out of fear. The woman opposite was the woman who had cared devotedly for his grandmother. She had a right to be there to the last.

They sat in the room, listening to the hoarse, shallow breathing until at last it ceased. 'That was a good end,' Sue said. 'But no more than she deserved.'

Ben made the necessary phone calls: Adele, the family solicitor, his grandmother's doctor, Madge and Peter Hammond. His own composure amazed him. How could he sound so calm when there was a scream inside him? He could not bring himself to ring Diana. She had a right to know but it would have to be up to someone else. But he did ring Barbara. 'I'm so sorry,' she said. 'I know how much you loved her.'

When he had done his duty, he let himself out of the now silent house. A light rain was falling and he turned up the collar of his coat. He couldn't get behind the wheel of a car. Not yet. Memories were crowding in. Holidays with his grandparents, time spent at their country cottage. They had called it a cottage but it had seemed as big as a castle to him as a child. She had always been there for him: when he had been bullied at prep school; his first days at his public school, when he had wanted to come home and had only been consoled by the lovingly prepared tuck boxes she had provided; she had listened when he confided his feelings for Diana and, if she had had doubts, simply advised him to follow his heart. 'I love you, Gran,' he said aloud, letting rain mingle with his tears. And then he turned and made his way back to the car.

Barbara was waiting in the pub when he got there. He had telephoned her on his way into London and she had suggested an immediate meet. 'I'm sorry,' she said when he had settled in the booth beside her. 'I know she meant the world to you.' She listened as he spoke of the past and his frustration that he had not brought about a reunion in time. 'You did your best,' she said, putting a hand on his arm. 'You did your best and she knew you were making it happen – that's what counts.'

He was halfway to Adele's when he remembered
Monique. She had been flying out at noon, so no point in
phoning her now. Suddenly he wanted to be in a warm bed
with a naked body next to him and death a million miles
away. But there were things to be done. He put his foot
down and drove to where his sister awaited consolation.

'What happened?' Adele's eyes were swollen, her hair
damp on her forehead. 'I'd turned my damned phone off
because I was going over the farm accounts with Harry.'

'It didn't matter. She was unconscious when I got
there. You wouldn't have made a difference.' It was a
little lie but it was what she needed to hear.

'Gran gone... I can't take it in.' She shook her head as
if to clear it. 'There's only you and me now, the lid on the
family.'

It was true, Ben thought. However helpless his grandmother had been latterly, she had still been there, above
them, a shield against fall out. 'It'll be alright, kid,' he
said, resorting to the old address of childhood. 'She
didn't suffer. She had a good life. She knew she was
loved. That's all that matters.' He didn't add that she had
died with a weight on her conscience. It was not the time
to remind his sister of that.

Chapter Thirty Three

THEY PLANNED THE FUNERAL CAREFULLY. '"All Things Bright and Beautiful" was her favourite,' Adele said firmly. 'No.' Ben was smiling as he shook his head. 'She said that because it was *your* favourite.' In the end they settled on 'Oh Love That Will Not Let Me Go' and 'Amazing Grace' because they agreed she had loved that. The vicar would read from John 14, 'Let Not Your Heart be Troubled', and Sue, if she agreed, would read something of her own choosing. 'We have to do something for Sue – and Maya,' Adele said anxiously.

'We will – if we have to. My guess is Gran will have seen to that herself.'

'There'll be a will, I suppose. I hadn't thought of that.'

'Oh yes, there's a will. According to Simon Ellis, the longest one he's drawn up.' They both smiled then, remembering their grandmother and her love of knick-knacks. 'Bet she's left you the Crown Derby,' Adele said. 'I'll get the Beswick horses, all 53 of them.'

They began to talk about other things. 'Were the board all right about postponing the meeting?'

'Yes. They understood. It would have been all the same if they hadn't. I was leaving anyway. We're reconvening after the funeral. Peter says they're all okay about it.'

'Will the Headey's offer wait that long? Could the board act without you?'

'Yes to the first, no to the second. Not with Hammond watching my back.'

Adele shifted in her seat. 'You trust him – after Pyke? He was on your side once.'

'They're different animals. I trust most of the board to be honest with me. They may not go with me but they won't deceive.'

'And you can count on Neville Carteret.' It was half a statement, half a question.

'I suppose so. Diana will want to protect my interests, to make a bigger cake for her to slice.'

But as he drove towards the office, Ben began to wonder. Diana was greedy, yes, and would want as much as she could get out of their marriage. But if Headey's won out and took Pyke as part of the bargain, her future interests might well lie with him. In which case, which way would Neville Carteret jump?

He looked for Madge when he came out of the lift, until he remembered she was meeting Maggie off the train at King's Cross this morning. He sorted through his post and then dialled Barbara's number. Madge had been ahead of him.

'She's taking my aunt – God, that sounds strange,

rather nice, I think, but strange – she's taking her to her place. I'm going round there at three.'

He promised to see her there and was about to replace the receiver when another call came through on Madge's line. It was Simon Ellis, his grandmother's solicitor.

'You're an executor, of course. You knew that. It's fairly straight-forward, although I have to admit to being a little taken aback at the content.'

'I think I can guess what's coming. The shares in Webcon: my guess is they go to the heirs and assigns of one John Brewis, lost in France in 1940.'

'How did you know? Are they family? Can't be an old sweetheart, surely. She wouldn't say.'

'Not a sweetheart,' Ben said. 'It's a long story. I'll tell you when we meet.'

'Okay. Well, you and your sister get her house and possessions and the balance of the estate, apart from sums of £100,000 to Sue Davis, her nurse, and the same to Maya Marcos. Smaller sums to other staff and the Webcon shares to the Brewises, whoever they are.' There was a pause as Ben tried to assimilate the details.

'You're not disappointed?' The solicitor's voice was a little anxious and Ben chuckled. 'Am I contemplating contesting? No. And neither will Adele. It was pretty much as we expected.'

'Do you know the whereabouts of these people, the Brewises? Otherwise I can have them traced.'

'No need. I know the whereabouts of all of them.' Ben glanced at the clock. It was five to one. Time to get something to eat and then make for Madge's place.

As he drove towards Madge's bungalow, he did sums in his head. His grandmother had had a three per cent stake in Webcon. At current values, that would represent around fifteen million pounds. Nice for Dolly, if she claimed her share, and opportunities for Barbara – but for Maggie Riley it could mean a total change of lifestyle. Unless she opted to stay safely in her tiny house and will it all to a dog's home.

His thoughts drifted to that other player in the drama. If Monique was Jack Brewis's child, she could also claim a share. He wasn't sure about the laws on illegitimacy, but if her DNA proved her a Brewis she would have a good case. And neither Barbara nor Maggie would begrudge her. About Dolly he couldn't be sure. Anyway, they would know tomorrow. He put his foot down as the traffic eased and hurried on his way.

They were there together in the tiny sitting room, tea on a table between them. 'It's good to see you again,' he said, smiling at Margaret Riley as he eased himself into a chair. 'I'll get you a cup,' Madge said suddenly and got back to her feet. He was about to point out that there were three cups already on the tray, when something stayed his words. Madge never got things wrong. If she was leaving the room it was for a reason. What did she want or expect him to do in her absence? He was still trying to decide when she re-appeared, cup in hand. As she passed the sideboard, she reached out and straightened a vase of chrysanthemums, moving it a few inches to the left. It was done effortlessly and then she was at the table, clutching the spare cup and saucer to her and tut-tutting over her own foolishness. 'Silly me, of course I'd already set for you.'

'You can keep the extra cup. Barbara will be here soon.' What was she up to? He sipped his tea and bided his time. It was difficult to make conversation with Margaret. She was obviously tense, awaiting Barbara's arrival. That was not surprising: a blood relation, possibly her only living kin, was about to walk into the room and she would not even recognise her. Opportunity came when the doorbell rang and Madge went to answer. He got to his feet and crossed to the sideboard. When he returned to his seat he was chuckling. What Madge had been at pains to hide with the vase was a photograph of her and Sparrow, arm in arm and squinting into the sunshine. The old foxes! And then Madge was ushering Barbara into the room and the old woman was setting down her cup and attempting to rise.

'Don't get up!' Barbara's voice was pitched higher than usual, a sign of the emotion she too must be feeling. But Maggie was already standing, looking suddenly old and frail. 'You're like our Billy,' she said, her lips trembling. 'Except for the hair.'

'That's my mother's fault,' Barbara said, and then suddenly she moved forward and took the older woman in her arms. They hugged for a moment and then, arms still around one another, the two heads moved back for a better view of each other's faces. 'Hello aunty,' Barbara said lightly to diffuse the tension.

'I might have known you'd be bonny, pet. Your dad was always a bonny bairn.' The tears flowed then, copiously from the old lady and merely a suspicious brightness in Barbara's eyes. Ben felt his own throat convulse and was relieved when Madge diffused the tension.

'I'll put the kettle on again,' she said and scuttled for the kitchen. It was a further relief when Ben felt his phone vibrate and could make his excuses and escape to the hall. Those two deserved a little time to themselves. It was Monique on the other end of the line. 'Are you missing me?' She was teasing and he responded in the same way. 'Madly, truly, deeply.' They spoke of his grandmother's death and the forthcoming funeral. 'I'll have flown out by then or I would have come,' she said. 'I know,' Ben replied. Neither of them referred to tomorrow's decision until the last moment.

'You'll come with me?'

'Yes,' Ben said, feeling a comfortable certainty that however it turned out, it would be okay.

The two women were close together on the settee when he came back into the room, chatting away as though they were related, he thought – and then he smiled to himself because, of course, they were. He broke the news of his grandmother's death to Maggie. 'I'm sorry to have to tell you this, but my grandmother died two days ago. Quite peacefully, but it's a great shame she couldn't hang on till you got here.' It occurred to him that perhaps his grandmother had willed it that way. She had wanted the children found and compensated but perhaps she had shirked meeting them face to face.

'I'm sorry. I wanted to meet her again.' Margaret Riley looked genuinely sad.

'And she you... but she knew you were coming. That gave her a lot of satisfaction. My sister too. She wants you all to go over for supper tonight. Is that okay? She would have come over this afternoon, but she thought it might be too much for you, all at once.'

They all said yes, except Madge. 'I've got things to do,' she said. 'Adele will understand. She's a good girl.'

'Yes,' Ben said. 'She will understand. I do too. You're going to wash your hair.' Beneath the faint coating of powder on her cheeks, he detected a tinge of red but she met his eye.

'Yes,' she said. 'You could say that.'

Would she leave him if the private detective made an honest woman of her? Would he have a job to offer her after the meeting? He made an effort to put all thoughts aside, except a wish for the night to go well.

Barbara opted to go home to change. He left Maggie – she had insisted he call her that – with Madge and went into the office for an hour. There were letters of condolence from business acquaintances piled on his desk together with letters to sign. The building was almost silent now and he sat for a moment, pondering. If Webcon went, if Headey's took over, this building would be obsolete. Headey's had its own huge headquarters out at Twickenham. This office had been built in his father's time, so it was hardly the birthplace of the business, but it had been his father's pride and joy and he would have minded its demise. What would it become? And no less important, what would become of Webcon's Chairman? 'I am equipped for nothing more than to live off income and dine out at the club,' he thought. It was a relief when it was time to stop thinking and collect the women for the evening ahead.

Settled in Adele's living room, the kids trooping in to be kissed goodnight before bedtime, he broached the subject of Dolly. 'So she doesn't want to meet up,' Maggie said when he was finished. Her voice was flat.

'I haven't given up.' Ben put out a consoling hand. 'She has a very safe, comfortable lifestyle. She's... not young. She's probably afraid of change...' He said the consoling words, but there had been nothing vulnerable about Dolly. She had known exactly what she wanted and opted for it.

Barbara stepped in, soothing things over. 'It would be a lot to take in. She may simply need time.'

'She likes Maggie,' Ben thought and felt a surge of relief. It had never occurred to him that they might have hated one another on sight, but in retrospect it might well have happened. They came from completely different worlds and yet barriers seemed to have melted away.

'I like her,' Adele said as they carried dishes out to the kitchen.

'Maggie? She's a bit of a star, isn't she?'

'Not Maggie. Well, her as well, but Barbara, I mean. What is she to me?'

'Nothing,' he said firmly, trying to balance plate on plate. 'No blood relation. You can be friends though. She's not as old as you... Well, who is? But she's knocking on.'

'Pig.' He ducked the tea towel easily and was halfway

back to the dining room before he realised that he had
not thought of Diana at all today.

'Are you going to tell them about the will?' Adele
asked when he went back to the kitchen. 'Not yet. I want
to see it all in black and white and make some kind of
assessment first.'

They tucked Maggie into the front seat for the return
journey, but not before Adele had hugged her and made
her promise to return. 'You're coming to the funeral?'
she said before the door was closed. A look of uncertainty crossed the old lady's face and she looked at Barbara
for guidance. 'Yes,' the younger woman said. 'We'll be
there. After all, without her we might never have met.'

Ben felt a twinge of conscience. Without the Websters'
inaction the children might never have been split up, but
that had to be water under the bridge. The two women
hugged and then Barbara was in the back seat and they
were gliding away.

'I like your sister,' Barbara said from behind.

'It's mutual,' he answered. In the rear-view mirror he
saw she had leaned her head back against the headrest
and her normally stern expression had softened. Beside
him, Maggie sat, gloved hands folded on the handbag
that sat in her lap, her face half-shadowed by the brim of
her felt hat, but she too looked content. 'It had been a
good night,' he thought. For a second, thoughts of the
outside world intruded: Diana and Pyke and the
hovering menace of the Headey's bid. But only for a
second. The road ahead was clear and the night sky full
of stars. That was enough for now.

Chapter Thirty Four

B EN TRIED TO CONCENTRATE ON the papers in front of him but it wasn't easy. He could see people moving around in the outer office, the life of Webcon going on as if its world was not rocking on its axis. They must be anxious about how many of them would retain their jobs if Headey's took over. He had his own anxieties, chief among them the thought that Pyke could be sitting in this very chair under the new regime. The thought was so unsettling that he pushed aside the papers and buzzed Madge.

'Coffee,' he said. 'Four spoons of sugar. I'm feeling low.'

'Coffee and sweeteners coming up,' came the reply. He smiled. Madge would do most things for him, but letting him ruin his waistline was not one of them. He was sipping his coffee when Peter Hammond knocked and entered. He had a fat brown folder in his hand.

'Got a moment?' Ben signed to a chair and pointed to

his cup. 'No thanks, just had one. Is that the Braintree specifications there?'

They talked plans and logistics for a while and then turned to the subject neither of them could dismiss from their mind: the board meeting rescheduled for Friday. 'I know that's only two days after the funeral. I'm sorry, but they're getting restive and we don't want to...' Ben held up a hand. 'Don't apologise. In many ways I want to get it over with. Any more thoughts on how it will go?'

Hammond shook his head. 'No. As we've already said, the institutions will vote for acceptance. The execs will say no out of self-preservation, if nothing else. You and I will vote no. That leaves Cyril Evans and your brother-in-law. They were both your appointments. Will they be guided by gratitude?'

Ben thought for a moment before he answered. 'Cyril, yes, he's a good old stick. About Neville, I'm not sure. I'll try and have a word with him beforehand. In the end, though, he'll do what his sister tells him.'

'How is Diana?'

'Are you asking after her welfare or wondering if she's behaving herself?'

Peter smiled. 'Was my dislike of her so obvious?'

Ben shook his head and put down his cup. 'I never thought you disliked her, just that you were wary of her. Would that I had been. Anyway, we've hardly spoken since the split. There'll have to be negotiations but they haven't begun yet.'

'So it's final?'

'Very final.'

When Peter Hammond had left, Ben leaned back in his chair. It was 11.15am. In a little over an hour, he was meeting Monique. They would have lunch and then go to find out about the DNA, whether or not she and Barbara were cousins, or not even remotely related. Barbara had been willing when he asked if she would provide the comparison, but ambivalent about the outcome.

'Do I need a half-cousin? Growing up I always felt completely happy with my own company. Do I need complications? Besides, my French is not only lousy, it's non-existent.'

'Not even a *petit peu*?' he had teased. Now, suddenly, it wasn't a teasing matter. In an hour or so, both girls could find their lives changed inexorably. His own life had changed immeasurably in a few short weeks. And yet he did not totally regret the tidal wave which had overtaken him. His grandmother's death, certainly. The discovery of treachery at home and at work. Having to leave his home, perhaps. Not having Max by his side. But the influx of strangers into his life was somehow energising. As for the loss of Diana, it was failure but it did not hurt as much as he would once have expected. Perhaps he had never loved her. As Madge entered the room, he acknowledged the truth. He had loved his wife deeply. It was simply that, like anything which is not nourished, his love had died.

'This flat,' Madge said. 'You get the keys on Friday. You can move in any time next week. I've arranged for cleaners, got you basic furniture, sorted the utilities.

There'll even be food in the fridge. And, yes, I am a bloody marvel. You'll get the bills in due course.' He confessed himself lost in admiration of her talents and was still smiling when he pressed the button for the lift.

Monique was twenty minutes late at the restaurant. 'I'm so sorry. We didn't get in until 2am and I overslept. I just pulled on some clothes and ran.'

'For someone who threw themselves out of the house, you look pretty sensational.' It was true. Her blonde hair was scooped into a smooth knot, the make-up, if she was wearing any, was flawlessly natural, her pale grey suit the perfect foil for the white T-shirt and gold hoop earrings. 'Are you nervous about this afternoon?' he asked as they ate pan-fried sole and wilted greens. She shook her head. 'Not nervous. Hopeful, perhaps?'

Around them the restaurant buzzed with conversation. Could any other table be talking about anything as life-altering as finding yourself part of a family? Or not, as the case might be.

'Hopeful? What are you hoping for? Do you want to be a Brewis? Find a family? You'd like Barbara. She's just about your age.'

'Will there be any money for me if I am his child?'

'Yes.' Ben thought of his grandmother's will. 'The heirs and assigns.' That would include all offspring, even the illegitimate ones. 'There would be money. What would you do with it? If you got it, that is.'

She was looking down at her plate. 'I would open a restaurant, a bistro. In Provence. In Aix... Do you know Aix-en-Provence?'

Ben nodded and then he posed a question. 'A restaurant. You said you liked cooking, but what about the business side? You'd need someone to keep the books.'

For some reason, she was still staring at the plate. 'I don't... Well, I have a friend...' She was definitely uneasy now. Ben smiled.

'A friend? Would he be a member of an Air France crew?' She looked up, eyes widening in surprise. 'You knew?'

'I saw the photo in your wallet, in the hotel. He looks like a nice guy.'

She put out a hand. 'He is nice. But that doesn't mean I didn't...'

'Didn't mean that what happened between us was real? I'm sure it was. And I'm grateful. It came at a bad time for me and I'm grateful.'

In the cab on their way to Harley Street he tried to analyse his own thoughts. He didn't mind that Monique had a man in her life. Sex with her had been wonderful but she had not penetrated his head. Or his heart. Did hearts exist except as utilitarian organs? Perhaps Diana had put him off women forever. Perhaps he was incapable of love at all. They were nearly at their destination now.

'How much would you need for the restaurant?' The answer had obviously been well thought out. '30,000 euros. Not a fortune, but beyond us at the moment. We're saving but...' She shrugged.

30,000 euros. Just over 20,000 pounds. A pittance by most standards. He helped her out of the taxi. If the

DNA was a match, she would be too rich to want a Provençal restaurant. And that would be sad.

They sat in upholstered chairs side by side, waiting for the consultant. He came at last, sober-suited, apologising for being a little late. 'I have the results. I don't know whether or not they will please.'

'Get on with it,' Ben said, but only in his head. Monique's hands were clasped in her lap but he could see her knuckles were white where each hand gripped the other.

The consultant shuffled his papers. 'I compared the two samples. There were no points of resemblance.'

'So they're not related?'

'No. The two samples submitted to me are very definitely not kin.'

'No fortune then,' Monique said when they were back in a cab.

'No fortune. Are you disappointed?'

'Yes.' That was one of the things he liked about her. She did not dissemble. 'I would have liked some money – so we could stop flying in and out of one another's lives and settle down. But, who knows? There would have been other things, relatives, complications.'

He took her to The Landmark for tea. 'Will you stay in Paris? Keep flying?'

She shrugged. 'For the time being. C'est inévitable!'

'What made you become an air hostess?' Now she laughed aloud.

'Le glamour! I trained in a flower shop but always wanted to fly. My teachers suggested other things.

Boring! But flying around the world, I thought that would be formidable.' The emphasis was on the last syllable and she rolled her eyes too.

'And it wasn't?'

'For a while it was wonderful. But it's mostly airports and pandering to rich people. You get stopovers, you see places, but after a while you want something more...' She was searching for a word.

'More substantial?'

She nodded and then shrugged. 'For the time being...'

'It's doors to landing?' They both laughed and sipped their tea.

He got out of the cab when it reached her hotel.

'Are you coming up?' Her eyes were on his, questioning.

'You need to rest.'

'I'm fine. If you want to come up...'

'You know what will happen if I do. And, as I said, he looks like a nice guy, so better I don't.' He kissed her on the forehead and then again on the mouth. 'Remember what I said. You helped me through a bad time.'

She was smiling. 'C'est rien, monsieur. A bientôt.' He twisted in his seat as the cab pulled away. He could see her there, smiling, until the cab turned the corner and she was lost to sight.

When he got back to the office he looked at the clock. She was flying out at nine. It was 4.30pm now. No time to wait. He made out the cheque for £30,000. That would leave her with around £10,000 to spare. 'Can you have this biked round to the Excelsior in Southampton Row?' he asked Madge. 'Now. She leaves at 7pm.'

He went to the window when he returned to the office. It was growing dark and lights were springing up everywhere. London at nightfall. If the meeting went against him, would he stay here or would he go? For a fleeting moment, he thought of Provence in springtime. Fields of lavender, vineyards, olive groves and, in the distance, the hills of the Luberon. He could almost smell mimosa and pine trees, taste the peaches plucked and eaten while they were still warm from the sun. Wonderful if you were French, perhaps, but not for him.

Chapter Thirty Five

THEY GATHERED IN THE DRAWING room of his grandmother's house, spilling over into the wide hall as the
crowd increased. There were business acquaintances of his
grandfather, old and frail now, and people from the church
where his grandmother had worshipped. They all seemed
to know him but he had to busk every greeting, nodding
enthusiastically if they said 'Nice to see you again'. If was
a relief when Adele and Harry arrived, their unusually
subdued children in tow. 'They want to come,' Adele had
told him last night. 'I thought not but Harry says they'll
only imagine worse things.' Now he looked at his niece
and nephews, wide-eyed and close to their mother but
missing nothing. He looked and he envied his sister. If only
he had children to comfort him now – or anyone, come to
that. Sue was virtually holding Maya up. The Filipina
looked old, her tiny frame suddenly drooping, the eyes
swollen with weeping. I must make sure she's okay in the
future, Ben thought. One more thing to fix.

Maggie Riley entered, with a be-hatted Madge in attendance. 'I didn't know you did hats,' he whispered. 'Behave yourself,' was the stern reply. He embraced Maggie and saw to it that she had a chair. It felt odd to be dispensing sherry and finding chairs for new arrivals. In the next room his grandmother lay swaddled in white and looking infinitely tiny. When he was a child, particularly after his parents' death, she had seemed a huge woman, a safe refuge from all the ills of life. Now, at this last moment, she seemed to have reverted to an almost childlike state, the wrinkles gone from her face, leaving it girlish once more. Thinking of her, he felt his eyes prick and it was a relief when Barbara appeared and he could draw her into the circle and introduce her as a family friend. And yet even that struck a false note. The Websters had not befriended the Brewis children. They had done them down and if his grandmother had tried to make amends, she had left it perilously late.

There was time for him to take Barbara aside before they went out to the cars. 'We got the DNA results yesterday. Monique is not your grandfather's granddaughter.'

'Is that certain?'

'A hundred per cent.' He couldn't be sure whether her expression was one of relief or disappointment. Had her poker face been born with her or cultivated for court appearances? But it was time to file out to the waiting limousine, as names for the following cars were intoned behind them. He was about to climb in beside Adele when he heard a demur. He turned. Maggie and Barbara were shaking their heads as the undertaker tried to usher them into the second car, alongside Sue and Maya. 'Please,' Ben said. 'It's what my grandmother wanted.' Barbara still looked hesitant. He bent to whisper. 'You're mentioned in her will. She'd want you to be with us today.' Maggie was looking from one to another, in total incomprehension. Barbara's eyes were on his, questioning.

'Please,' he said again. 'Get in the car. I'll explain later.' And then he was in the limousine and it was purring down the drive and out onto the road.

He was more than halfway down the aisle, his eyes on the coffin borne aloft in front of him, when he heard Adele's sharp intake of breath. As he turned his head towards his sister, he saw what had caused her surprise. Diana stood in one of the foremost pews, Neville Carteret at her side, her head defiantly erect. He looked ahead again, conscious only of gratitude that the man at her side had not been Neil Pyke. She had a right to be there. She had been part of his grandmother's family – still was, in a way.

They sang 'Oh Love That Will Not Let Me Go' and then the vicar read from John 14, verses one to three. 'Let not your heart be troubled. Ye believe in God, believe also in me. In my father's house are many mansions...' Strangely, at that moment, he thought of Webcon. His father and his grandfather had built mansions, brick upon brick till they had built an empire. And now it might all slip away. He turned his attention back to the vicar's homily. 'Gwendoline was a woman of faith. She believed that The Father had prepared a place for her and now she has gone to it.' A tear slid down

Ben's cheek, but inside him calm grew. His grandmother had believed and in the end she had done her best to make amends for any wrong she had done. They sang again, although he only mouthed the words, and then Sue stood up and moved to the lectern. Her voice rang out, calm and amazingly clear in view of the bond she had shared with her patient.

'Remember me when I am gone away, gone away into the silent land, when you can no more hold me by the hand...' His grandmother had held him by the hand once and now she was gone. The air above the altar seemed to shimmer and he struggled to concentrate on the words. 'For if the darkness and corruption leave a vestige of the thoughts that once I had, better by far you should forget and smile than that you should remember and be sad.' As Sue was returning to her seat, he mouthed 'Well done'. It was for much more than the reading and he hoped she knew that.

The crowd stood respectfully aside outside the church. He tried to speak to those faces he knew, old friends, staff who had worked for the family, ex-employees of Webcon brought here by loyalty to the firm which had once employed them. Thoughts of that firm disappearing intruded and were banished. He had evils enough for the day.

It was a relief to be back in the car and gliding towards the cemetery. The ground was wet as they threaded their way between graves to the newly dug mound of earth at the side of his grandfather's grave.

'Benjamin Webster, a dearly beloved husband and

father.' Next to it was the stone inscribed for his parents. Beneath their names was a familiar text: 'They were lovely and pleasant in their lives and in death they were not divided.' That came from David's lament over Saul and Jonathan. His grandmother had picked it and explained why, and the idea of his parents being together in death had comforted him. Now he scattered a handful of earth on that same grandmother's coffin and hoped to God he would not break down. He was the head of the family now and the thought terrified him. His grandmother had been weak and dependent latterly but she had been there. There was no one now, only him.

It was amazing how the mantle of grief was cast off back at the house. People commiserated, yes, but swiftly moved on to marvel at how well old acquaintances looked or swap accounts of holidays blissful or vile.

'She has a bloody cheek,' Adele hissed in his ear, nodding to where Diana was holding court for all the world as though she was still the mistress of this newly acquired house. 'Any moment she'll look around and say, "Mine, all mine",' Adele said. Ben nodded. 'You know what, sis? I don't give a toss.'

It was harder to be so lofty when Diana at last approached him. 'We need to talk, Ben. I've filed for divorce, you'll get the papers any day.'

'Not here, Diana. In case you hadn't noticed, this is a wake.'

'I know and I'm very sorry she's dead. I know how much she meant to you. I'm merely saying we need to get things straight.'

'You mean you want your pound of flesh.'

'If you want to be like that, yes, I want what's mine. And now that she's dead, I hope you've dropped that ridiculous orphan thing.'

'I think that's my business, Diana.'

'Just as long as they don't get a penny of my money. I want my full share.'

He was about to say she could have the lot when he thought of something more important. 'I want Max.' For a moment, defiance flared in her eyes to be immediately replaced by speculation. He could have laughed aloud because he knew exactly what she was thinking. How good a bargaining tool could the dog be?

She was saved from a reply by Barbara appearing at his side. 'Barbara Tulloch, Diana Webster, my soon to be ex-wife.'

Diana's lips tightened. 'Unless my husband has acquired a paramour, you must be one of the orphans.'

Barbara smiled graciously. 'Not quite. My father was alive and well the last time I heard.'

'Good for you,' Ben murmured as Diana melted into the crowd.

'I did wonder if you'd regret the split,' Barbara said. 'I don't anymore. Anyway, to more important things. I think Maggie is desperately disappointed Dolly's not here. Can't she be made to change her mind?'

He promised to see what he could do but didn't hold out false hope. 'She's quite a character. If she's made up her mind, it'll take some changing.'

In the distance he saw Diana taking her leave of a

stony-faced Adele. At that moment Neville Carteret appeared at Ben's side. 'We're off, old chap. Lovely service. About Friday's meeting, you can count on me.' So Diana wanted to keep Webcon in the family, Ben thought, as he voiced his thanks. That was something to be grateful for, even if a little hard to believe. There was something else to be grateful for today. In the last few days, and against his will, happy memories had intruded. Diana splashing in the surf in Barbados, her squeals of pleasure when he had brought Max home as a puppy, the fun they had had on the Grand Cornice in an open-topped car with wind whipping her hair around her face, or that same face, softened in the aftermath of love-making, eyes half-closed, mouth slack and vulnerable and sated with kissing. In the future he would remember the set of that mouth as she had attempted to deny a single penny to the Brewis children. If, indeed, he ever remembered her at all.

Chapter Thirty Six

THEY GATHERED AT MADGE'S HOUSE to bid farewell to Maggie. Adele and Harry had made their goodbyes at supper the night before, but Barbara was here today. Ben was slightly surprised that Sparrow was not in evidence. He had been the man who had found Maggie, after all, and he had seemed genuinely concerned for her. Besides, he seemed to treat the place as home, knowing just where the sugar was kept and how to turn up the central heating. Were he and Madge living together? Ben half-hoped so, but would only get a flea in his ear if he asked. Perhaps Madge had bundled him out of the way specially? He tried to imagine Sparrow and Madge in a clinch but the picture wouldn't come and he had to subdue a giggle at the thought. But he hoped Madge did have love in her life. She deserved it. What would he do if she upped and left Webcon? Except that if tomorrow's meeting went against him and Webcon vanished into Headey's maw, there might not be a job for her. He turned his attention back to what was happening around him. Barbara was perched on the window-seat. Maggie Riley was sitting upright on the settee, obviously ready for the off. She had seemed to enjoy her time in London but he could see she was keen to get home.

'You don't have to go back yet,' Madge had said yesterday, when Maggie was enthusing about her stay. The reply had been swift. 'Thanks pet, but I have to get back. They call for the rent on Fridays. And the window cleaner – and I collect my neighbour's pension for her.' She had made her life sound full, but Ben was remembering the silence of the little house, broken only by the ticking of the clock. Her life could change now, if that was what she wanted. As if on cue, Madge departed for the kitchen on the pretext of making coffee.

'While you're both here,' Ben said, suddenly feeling nervous. 'The solicitor will be contacting you officially, but as executor I can probably explain in advance. My grandmother had shares in Webcon. It's worth several million pounds. Difficult to be exact at the moment.' Barbara's eyebrows moved fractionally but he could see that it was going over Maggie's head. 'She left her shares to you – or, rather, to you and Dolly, Maggie, and to Barbara's father, so of course it comes to her.'

'Why would she want to do that?' Maggie sounded bewildered. Here it was, Ben thought, the awkward question. He cleared his throat.

'When your father... your grand-... When Jack Brewis went off to war, my grandfather, his partner, ran the business single-handed. It was tiny. I believe they didn't

317

even have a lorry but used handcarts. My grandfather was born with a thing called talipes. A club foot, it used to be called. They cure it quite easily now, I believe, but in 1940 it meant he wasn't fit to join the forces, so he stayed behind. He was clever. What had been a tiny business grew. Especially after the war, when there was so much damage to repair. By then, though, your parents – or grandparents – were both dead and you three had been adopted. You and Dolly and Barbara's father. I mean, Dolly and Billy were adopted, and you grew up in care.'

'But half of the business was theirs,' Barbara said. She already knew the truth; this was a statement given for Maggie's benefit. 'Yes. But half of a business worth perhaps £500 in those days. It was my grandfather who built it into the company it is today. However, my grand-mother always felt that Jack and Mollie's children were entitled to something – hence the legacy. Which will amount to some several millions, I should think.'

'A million pounds,' Maggie said, shaking her head in wonder.

'Several million,' Barbara corrected her.

'That's a guesstimate,' Ben said hastily. 'At the moment, another firm is attempting a hostile takeover.'

'So there may be nothing,' Maggie said. She didn't sound too disappointed and Ben chuckled. 'Oh there'll be something. It could even be more.'

'You don't want the bid to succeed?' Barbara's eyes were on him, their expression unfathomable.

'No. It's been in the family for three generations. I don't want to be the one who loses it.' Madge came into the room, bringing cups and a jug of cream. She looked abstracted. There was even a wisp of hair which had escaped from her coiffeur. Now that really was unusual. 'Can I do anything?' Barbara's offer was met with a shake of the head, but the older woman didn't speak.

There was a moment's lull in the conversation as she clattered cups and then the sharp ring of the doorbell. Barbara was making for the door until Madge's voice rang out. 'I'll get it.' She went out, closing the door behind her. Ben could hear voices in the hall. What was going on? A moment later the door re-opened and Madge reappeared. Behind her, Ben could see Sparrow and, at his side, another smaller figure. It was Dolly! How had they managed that? Outside of her own setting, she looked smaller and less certain of herself. Ben sought desperately for something, words that would ease the tension in the room, but it was Maggie who spoke. 'Dolly? Is that you, Dolly?' And suddenly the made-up little face was crumpling as Dolly moved towards her sister. 'Maggie? Let's have a look at you... Now don't cry... Two silly old women.'

Instinctively, Barbara and Ben had drawn closer and he felt her hand slide into his and grip as the two older women embraced. 'I'll get some more coffee,' Madge said, her voice suddenly husky, and she and Sparrow vanished into the kitchen.

'What a carry-on,' Dolly said at last, standing back to examine her sister's face. She put up a be-ringed hand to pat her immaculate hair-do, a little disarranged now.

'You always did have lovely hair, our Dolly,' Maggie

said, but Dolly was throwing back her head to laugh. 'This lot's not mine, pet. Mine went long ago. You can thank Monsieur René for this lot, a thousand pounds a go.' And suddenly the tension was eased and they were all laughing, even if the laughter verged on the hysterical.

'You used to have plaits,' Maggie said wonderingly as they subsided onto the sofa.

'And you had a fringe and shoes with Snow White on and you used to read to us... What was that book? Our Billy loved it.'

And suddenly they were both remembering their baby brother and Maggie was reaching out to his daughter. 'This is our Billy's bairn, Barbara.' Barbara's hand reached out to the work-worn hand of her aunt, as though to draw confidence. 'They like one another,' Ben thought and was glad. Dolly was looking uncertainly from one to another. 'Billy's bairn?' Her voice trembled and Barbara stepped in. 'My father died when I was quite young,' she said. 'He was a soldier in Northern Ireland and very brave. You'd have been proud of him.' Now she held out a hand to Dolly. 'I never knew I had aunts but I'm glad I do.'

Ben turned away, feeling like an intruder, and tiptoed into the kitchen. 'You don't think she changed her mind because of the money, do you?' Ben asked as they rustled up coffee for six.

'She doesn't know about it,' Madge replied. 'She came because she wanted to.'

'What changed her mind? She was adamant last week.'

'Fill that sugar bowl; it's in the cupboard. I changed her

mind, me and Sparrow. And don't ask how. It wasn't easy.'

'The immovable object and the irresistible force?'

'Something like that,' Madge said. 'I haven't dealt with three generations of your lot without learning how to deal with unreasonable people. Now let's get this coffee in before it's stone cold.'

After that it was a welter of recollections, of filling the spaces in the family history and for exulting in the possession of a niece.

'We never had children,' Dolly said.

'Neither did we.' But Maggie's voice was less certain, Ben thought. She had faltered in the middle, as though she didn't want to admit it.

'Fancy you living in Durham, Maggie.' Dolly's voice had a faint Cockney twang to it and was infinitely posher than her sister's, but there was warmth in her tone. 'I want to hear all about how you wound up there. I came back to London when my Eddie died. Eddie was my husband. Well, we were born in London, weren't we? Although I never knew that until Mr Sparrow came. It was all too much for me at first, I don't mind admitting. A brother and sister. I did remember, I realise that now. But like a dream, you know, something you're not quite sure of.'

'I remembered you.' Maggie's voice was firm. 'Well, I was nine, wasn't I? You were a picture then. You still are. Mam used to put rags in your hair on bath nights, to make ringlets. I used to envy you, Dolly, curly hair. Our Billy had curly hair as well. I used to think it wasn't fair.'

Dolly was smiling, luxuriating in things long forgotten, now remembered. 'You had a cotton reel with nails in and wool, and you could make this long knitted thing come out the bottom. I thought you were so clever!'

'French knitting,' Maggie said. 'I'd forgotten I could do that.'

'We need to be making tracks if you want to catch that train,' Ben said, when it was time. 'But we can so easily change the arrangements if you want to stay.' This time it was Maggie's turn to be adamant. She was going home but she would come back. 'I've done it once, it'll be easier now.'

'Of course you'll come back.' Dolly put a proprietary hand on her sister's arm. 'You'll stay with me. I'll come up to Durham. And you, Barbara, because I'm new-fangled with a niece. You're not like your dad. Well, perhaps about the chin. He was a little beggar when he liked, unless I've remembered wrong. We'll sort it all on the phone. I want to hear everything – from both of you.' There was a pause and when Dolly spoke again she was looking directly at her sister. 'Why us, Maggie? Why did we lose all that time together?' Maggie simply shook her head and Ben found the gesture more poignant than any words. Why had they been separated? He had no answer – and no excuse.

'Should I tell Dolly about the money now?' he wondered and decided against it. She was still in full flow. He thought of the apple-pie house. She had had no wants, but neither had she had anything to live for. Now she did. Whether or not she quite realised it yet, she had a family.

'You'll come back, Maggie, and we'll phone. You'll come over, Barbara. You're not five minutes away. I've got loads of room. I'll look after you, our Mags. For all the grief I gave you back then. I was a little brat. No, don't shake your head. Little Miss Prima Donna...' Suddenly her voice tailed off. 'Who used to call me that?'

'Our Dad,' Maggie said quietly and two sets of eyes grew bright with tears. Barbara stepped in, lifting the conversation. 'You must come and meet my Grandpa, once we get sorted out. You'll like him and he'd love to meet you.'

'He was good to our Billy.' Maggie was speaking to her sister now. 'And he's a vicar!' The way she said this, as though she was speaking of the Pope, made Ben's lips twitch and he didn't dare meet Barbara's eye. He knew she too would appreciate the joke.

Maggie was climbing into Sparrow's car, Barbara beside her, when Dolly called out. 'It was *Milly-Molly-Mandy*, that book, the one you used to read every night. Our Billy's favourite.'

As the car drew away, Ben saw that tears were streaming down Maggie's face. 'You'll see her again,' he said to Dolly but she didn't seem to hear. The blonde wig was ever so slightly askew from hugging her sister, the mascaraed eyes were wet. He wondered if he should shepherd her back inside. Instead, he left her standing with her thoughts.

'Maggie was crying as she left,' he told Madge once Dolly had been installed in a chair with a fresh cup of tea and he and Madge were alone in the kitchen. 'She should have stayed longer.'

'She has every right to cry,' Madge said. 'It's got

nothing to do with saying goodbye to Dolly. It's something else. She had a baby, a boy. She was taken advantage of in the war. When she was in service. They wouldn't let her keep the baby. She's never got over it.'

One more misdeed to chalk up to the Websters, Ben thought, and felt ashamed. 'But why is she crying now?'

'It was the mention of that book – that "Milly, Molly" whatever. It was the only possession she had. She put it in the baby's cot when she said goodbye.'

He thought about the three women as he drove home to Adele's. It was already growing dark and he thought of the wartime blackout. Those children must have felt desolate, clinging together in a strange place, waiting for a mother who never came back and a father gone to war. What would have happened if his grandmother had kept her promise and come back for them? Their lives would have taken a completely different course.

'You look whacked,' Adele said when he let himself into the house. Tonight would be the last night he would spend there. Tomorrow, after the meeting, he would move into the Margaret Street flat. 'Yes, it's been quite a day. Dolly turned up – and before you ask, she didn't come for the money. She came out of love. None of them seemed to care about the money. It wasn't what mattered to them, not at all.'

Chapter Thirty Seven

Downstairs, Ben could hear the sound of children's voices. He reached out for the travel clock beside his bed. 6.30am. Too early to join the mêlée. He turned on his side and thought about the day ahead. The meeting would commence at 11am. By noon he might be out of a job. He would do well out of any buy-out, so would Adele and the other shareholders. But what about the people who made up the Webcon workforce? Yesterday he had signed a card to go with a gift to a bricklayer who had served his father and his father before him. Forty years' continuous service. How would he fare in a Headey's regime? New brooms had a habit of sweeping clean. One way or another, he had to stave off the takeover.

How many of the directors would stay faithful, and could he even count on Neville Carteret when Diana would be pulling his strings? It amazed him that he felt so little for Diana now. Only a short while ago he had longed for her favours, responded to her every whim –

now she was simply something to be dealt with by lawyers. Perhaps he was lacking in depth if he could lose faith like that? But in his heart he knew the real reason. Monique had shown him what it was to be desired. Diana had never desired him. Not even in the beginning. He had been an acceptable meal ticket and now Pyke had taken his place. Except that Pyke was not rich, not by Diana's standards anyway. What did he have that was so desirable?

In the shower he thought about Monique, remembering her in the shower at the hotel, soaping him lovingly, kissing the space between his shoulder blades and letting her lips travel down and down as the water splashed around them. And yet all the while she had loved her French pilot. Did that make her cheap? Whether or not it did, he owed her a great deal. She had helped to set him free, for he did feel free. Stressed as he was, he felt freer than he had felt for years. He stepped out of the shower cubicle and set about preparing for the day.

Adele wished him luck as he left. 'You know Harry and I are behind you.' He nodded and then, because of the lump in his throat, he patted her arm and moved on.

He sat with Peter Hammond to hammer out a strategy. The Headey's offer would have to be formally put to the meeting. Ben could have his say, then Peter would support him. After that he would throw the matter open for discussion and thereafter put it to the vote.

They were gathering up their papers when the phone rang. It was Barbara. 'I don't know if this will come in time, but I've talked with Maggie and I rang Dolly this morning. Such shares as we have, when we get them, are at your disposal.'

'You don't need to do that for me,' he said, taken aback. There was a snort from the other end of the line. 'Isn't that a typical male reaction. Three intelligent women decide on a course of action but a man has to think they're only doing it for him. Chauvinist!'

She sounded genuinely put out and he tried to mend fences. 'I didn't mean it like that – and I'm grateful, I just didn't think you... Well, they... knew much about business.' This time there was a chuckle from the other end. 'Stop digging, Ben. You're only making matters worse.'

As he waited for eleven o'clock, he thought about her offer. If the vote went against Headey's today they could appeal to the shareholders. His shares, even added to Adele's and his grandmother's bequest, amounted to a mere drop in the ocean compared to the mass owned by the institutions. No, if the vote didn't go his way today, it was over. All the more reason why he must win. He gathered up his papers and made for the boardroom.

All the board members were there, with the exception of Pyke. Technically he was still a director, as Peter had pointed out. Only the board could dismiss him and Ben had already considered the possibility of his turning up. But he had not and that was to the good.

He waited until everyone was settled and then opened the meeting by recapping on the Headey's offer. 'I strongly recommend that we reject this offer. Webcon has paid high and reliable dividends for more than half a century. In my opinion, it will continue to do so. I admit to a sentimental interest. You do not see your forefathers build up something and hand it lightly to strangers. But my motives in urging rejection are based on sound business principles. I think shareholders will do better if they stick with a tried and tested formula rather than switch now to a firm which, though undoubtedly successful, has yet to prove itself long-term.' He sat down, trying to read the faces around the table, but not succeeding. These people were practised poker players.

Peter Hammond was, as usual, adept at marshalling facts and figures. 'My allegiance is to the tried and tested firm I have been proud to serve for nine years.' He followed this with a stream of statistics and then it was the turn of the others. Some asked questions, others merely listened, fingers poised together steeple-fashion, expressions non-committal. Carteret said nothing, but significantly his eyes did not meet those of his brother-in-law. 'He's going to rat on me,' Ben thought and rued the brief time he had thought otherwise. At last he put it to a show of hands. 'In favour.' One by one the hands went up. Only Ben, Peter and Cyril Evans sat immobile.

'Seven to three, gentlemen and lady. The ayes have it. Which leaves me with no option but to tender my resignation.' Hammond shook his head despairingly. No one else spoke. Ben gathered up his papers and quit the room. But not before Neville Carteret, with a smile meant to be winning, had whispered, 'Sorry, old chap. Had to think of the shareholders.'

So Diana had had her revenge. But even without her

brother it would have gone through, so not such a victory after all. He was halfway back to his office when he saw Pyke, perched on the corner of his old desk, one suede-clad foot swinging. 'It's over then,' he said cheerily as Ben advanced. 'Sorry and all that. Still, you'll be filthy rich.'

'And you, no doubt, will be sitting behind my desk.' As he said it Ben wondered if he should feel angry, but in fact he didn't. 'My wife and my job. Not a bad hand. I should knock you down, shouldn't I? Instead, I'm going to give you my sympathy. You'll need it in both cases, but especially the former.'

'Done?' Madge said, looking up as he approached her desk. Ben nodded.

'Done. Don't worry, though. I'll still need someone and you'll get a generous settlement.'

'I'll need it. We're off to Spain, Sparrow and I. Don't smirk. I want some sunshine and he, poor fool, thinks I'll be a loving companion.' Ben wanted to put his arms around her but if he tried, she wouldn't permit it. Instead, he said, 'I thought he had more sense. Still, there's one born every minute.' She promised to see to the packing up of his effects. 'You needn't come in unless you want to. I'll see to things here. And Pete... Peter Hammond will see you're all right. What will happen to him?'

'Money. Perhaps a job of sorts if he wants it.'

'He'd be a fool to stay on. If what I suspect happens, that is.'

'Pyke?'

'Pyke. He's so far up Headey's arse he's eyeballing their appendix.'

Ben laughed aloud. 'Well put. Not the most elegant turn of phrase but well put all the same.'

He rang Adele to tell her what had happened, then opened his briefcase. He took only two or three things from his desk. The penholder that had been his father and grandfather's, a photograph of his parents and a silver perennial calendar. It had never told the right day but he felt sentimental about it all the same. Diana's photograph he left in place. Pyke was welcome to her.

He walked out into the street, smiling at the staff clustered in groups here and there, looking crestfallen. It hadn't taken long for news to spread! 'I'm sorry, Sir,' said the doorman. 'Yes,' Ben said. 'It's a pity. I'll be in touch.' He would write to them all. Madge would arrange it. He felt afraid, but at the same time he felt elated, as though he had at last emerged from under a cloud. Out on the pavement, English was waiting, the silver Bentley at the kerb. 'Can I take you somewhere, Mr Ben?'

Ben smiled. 'As of this moment, I am no longer part of the company, Mr English, so I must gratefully decline.'

'I know that, Sir, but I'd still like to take you.' It would mean trouble for the man if someone as petty as Pyke got to know of it. Ben held out his hand. 'No thank you. But you'll be hearing from me.'

It had begun to rain as he headed down Farringdon Street. He had only gone a few yards when a car drew up alongside him. It was Barbara. 'You lost?'

He nodded ''Fraid so.'

'Well, get in. You're getting soaked.'

'You called me a chauvinist pig.'

'You are one. Now get in.'

They had turned onto the Euston Road when she spoke. 'I can guess what happened. What will you do?'

'I don't know. Lick my wounds, I suppose.'

'Maggie and Dolly are planning a cruise. They did it last night on the phone.' Her hands on the wheel were firm and there was a faint pattern of freckles on the white skin.

'I hope Dolly's not going to lead Maggie astray.'

'I hope she is,' was the fervent reply.

There was silence for a moment and then he asked, 'Where are we going?'

'Nowhere in particular.' He could sense she was getting ready to say something and he waited. 'I know something you could do, once you've got your breath back.'

'What?'

'Maggie had a child. A boy. When she was about fifteen. They made her have him adopted.'

'I know. Madge told me.'

'Your Madge doesn't waste time.'

Ben was smiling. 'They were together in that flat for a week. I shouldn't think she left a stone unturned. It's sad but what has it got to do with me?' They were turning towards Regent's Park now.

'You could find him for her. He's the one thing she really wants.'

Ben shifted in his seat. He had fulfilled his grand-mother's promise. He had found them and restitution had been made, but if they did not have their hearts' desire was that enough? 'I'd need help,' he said.

'Sparrow's off to Spain.'

She took her eyes off the road for a second and looked at him. 'Of course you'd need help.'

He watched as she turned back to face the road ahead. Her hair was the colour of leaves turning red in October. If he put out his hand and touched it, would it rustle or be soft enough to twine his fingers in? He had been a fool to think there was something sisterly about her. She was nothing like a sister at all. He turned back to look at the road ahead.

'Where would I start?'

She put her foot down and the car zoomed forward. 'We'll talk about it tomorrow.'